D0325970

DIXIE
CHURCH
INTERSTATE
BLUES

DIXIE CHURCH INTERSTATE BLUES

Ingrid Hill

VIKING

VIKING
Published by the Penguin Group
Viking Penguin, a division of Penguin Books USA Inc.,
40 West 23rd Street, New York, New York 10010, U.S.A.
Penguin Books Ltd, 27 Wrights Lane, London W8 5TZ, England
Penguin Books Australia Ltd, Ringwood, Victoria, Australia
Penguin Books Canada Ltd, 2801 John Street,
Markham, Ontario, Canada L3R 1B4
Penguin Books (N.Z.) Ltd, 182–190 Wairau Road,
Auckland 10, New Zealand

Penguin Books Ltd, Registered Offices:
Harmondsworth, Middlesex, England

First published in 1989 by Viking Penguin,
a division of Penguin Books USA Inc.

1   3   5   7   9   10   8   6   4   2

Copyright © Ingrid Hill, 1989
All rights reserved

"Whistling After Laval" first appeared in *Iowa Journal
of Literary Studies*; "Dead Man's Spoons" and "How I Got
Legendary" in *The North American Review*; "Roadie" in *Sonora Review*;
and "Baptism of Desire" and "Pyrotechnics"
in *The Southern Review*.

"The Golden" was selected for the Iowa Women's Writer Award.

LIBRARY OF CONGRESS CATALOGING IN PUBLICATION DATA
Hill, Ingrid.
Dixie church interstate blues / Ingrid Hill.
p.   cm.
ISBN 0-670-82616-2
I. Title.
PS3558.I3886D59   1989
813'.54—dc20   88-40645

Printed in the United States of America
Set in Sabon

For James Gindin

*Thanks to The Yaddo Foundation,
The Michigan Council for the Arts,
and The MacDowell Colony.*

Contents

Whistling After Laval   1

Dead Man's Spoons   23

The Golden   37

Salvaging   55

Roadie   81

Baptism of Desire   97

Snowmobile Country   123

Pain Perdu   147

Siege, with Swans and Starlight   167

Pyrotechnics   189

How I Got Legendary   211

DIXIE CHURCH INTERSTATE BLUES

Whistling After Laval

The house in Biloxi is mine now, tall chalk-white Queen Anne thing that it is, and my heart beats with odd trepidation, as if I were finally met in the dark with a lover long missed. It is dark inside with the sepia-toned shadows of lives, and the impulse in me is to paint it all white, or off-white, or in pastels of peach-white, or mint-white, and leave ghosts no corners to fold into.

One Twenty-Three Lillian Street sits imperial on its green lot facing toward the Gulf, which is six blocks away but not visible through the trees. Summers, I came here to visit. I remember the heat, the benign desperation that characterized these near, yet distant, relatives. If I bring wicker in, and central air, if I curtain the rooms in bouffant polished cotton and varnish the floors till they are wooden mirrors, I can banish that heat and that desperate longing. Perhaps some rattan—though the wicker adds lightness. Perhaps some pale tiles, some brass accents. Benign ghosts are ghosts, nonetheless, and perhaps will be charmed away by such decor.

The last summer I spent here went on with a soft, wanton vengeance, and so did the war. Gnats fat as pebbles swarmed everywhere all day, and wispy, bloodsucking mosquitoes, and green iridescent mosquito hawks, who never caught anything we could see.

The cook sweated about in the kitchen of Grandpère's house wiping her brow on the wrist-length white sleeves of the uniform Grandpère insisted she wear, mumbling under her breath about what Mr. Sheridan must be up to about now, dodging bullets as thick in the air as our gnats and bloodsuckers. I sat with my fan from the funeral home, feeling grateful I could not sweat blood like the rosy-cheeked Jesus in the garden who adorned the Technicolor front of the fan.

I watched Azarene wipe her forehead again. It amazed me that the wonderful chocolate-brown of her skin did not wipe off with the sweat, but I did not mention that. Once I had told Tante Laurette, and she had laughed in that arch, brittle way that she always had and gone off and told someone as if it were a cruel joke. I felt sucked into her marble-heart spite, tainted.

Azarene and I sweated. Laurette slept so she would be up for the evening, her beauty sleep, she said. I told Azarene I did not see that it had done any good yet, though of course everyone considered Laurette a great beauty. ("Absolutely *embalmed* with that damned Emeraude," said Laval, in our sharing of whispers. "Of *course* she stays young!") Grandpère was off in the Lincoln somewhere doing business. And Sheridan was off in Korea, in places with damn-fool names, dodging the bullets of Communists.

No one knew where Laval was, for the moment. He disappeared like morning mist when he wanted to. He was off to downtown Biloxi to buy some more shirts—that boy loved his shirts, daffodil seersucker, elegant white-on-white striped, or what have you—or just down the road to his friend Carlton Janes' to play bourrée and drink seven-and-sevens all afternoon. We would see Laval just before five, when he would come home and switch on the TV.

Laval and I would sit and watch Liberace, Laval entranced, I amused in my superior ten-year-old way, and then Laval and I would play duets on the dark, heavy upright that sat in the parlor. Laval would sing, in his wonderful falsetto, "I'm only a bird in a gilded cage." And we would talk about gildedness—pictures of clouds on a ceiling in Austria, touched with gold, Chinese furniture we had seen at a great aunt's in Pass Christian, birthday cards with gold edges and satin puffed hearts inset, smelling like essence of roses.

Laval had the secret of life sometimes. I knew that; Azarene said it; Laval made it plain. He breathed confidence, a sense of beauty and gentleness, things I could not put my finger on. The white-on-white stripes of his shirt were the staff of a music we almost could hear. Then again, Laval carried a darkness with him, or a deep pain. For someone so young—he was nineteen—he seemed to have lived lives beyond us all. Azarene said that, pouring the brown-sugar filling into the crust for pecan pie, and I had to agree. I was ten, he was nineteen, we were cousins, and that nine-year span was an abyss that only our afternoon duets could bridge.

"He is an odd one, that Mr. Laval," Azarene said. "Not like Mr. Sheridan. No ma'am. An odd one." But she smiled as she said it, with great delight. We were odd, she and I, we had decided; Laval could be odd, too.

Sheridan sent me dolls from Japan, dolls with matte-china pale faces and hair stiff and black as a horse's. Their stands held them upright on my guest-room bureau, their bright brocade dresses reflecting back from its broad glass. Sheridan sent a jacket embroidered with fire-breathing dragons. I hung it in the chifforobe and left the door slightly open so that I could catch a glimpse of the emerald satin whenever I liked. I had not worn it yet because Sheridan had sent it only this spring. I would take it back to New Orleans in the fall when I went home. I would wear it, walking to school under the row of imperial live oaks that lined the Avenue, and I would be the cynosure of all eyes, a green comet flying low. I longed for the coming of fall.

I had nothing to do in the daytime. I watched Azarene and spoke self-conscious wisdom with her in the kitchen. I walked to the little store across the green field and down Crawford Lane and came back with Archie and Veronica comics. I traced the shapes of Veronica's and Betty's breasts, and drew dresses for them on onionskin paper, with built-in bosom bulges. I drew cotillion gowns, trying to replicate the look of tarleton and taffeta and Chantilly lace, and failing utterly. My colored pencils made thready pale green or pale coral or whatever color, and that was it. Detail beyond that was all in my mind.

I was drawing one afternoon at the dining-room table. Dust motes danced in old yellow sunlight that grazed through the curtains. Azarene was out back, on the edge of the porch, with her shiny brown legs hanging over the garden. She swung her legs as if she were dreaming, as if she were twenty or thirty years younger. The kitchen was filled with the onion and garlic and smoke-sausage smells of the red beans. It had to be Monday. I sat with my Archie books, tracing Veronica's buxomness into a white wedding gown. I envisioned seed pearls and fine lace, but what I drew resembled small warts and mere scribbles.

I hated this all-too-apparent discrepancy between the dream and the penciled reality. There was a pretense that I was here to have a good time, to spend the summer happily, loved, in the lap of the relatives. But the truth was that Grandpère was off making his money, buying and selling commodities, whatever they were. And Grandmère—had my mother forgotten?—was dead for two years now, her pink silky night-things languishing in the sachet-scented drawers, her stiff-starched doilies drooping slightly on the living-room end tables. Laurette should have been dead. I could see no use for her. I wished that Laval would come home from wherever he was.

And, voilà, he was there. He breathed sweet breath of card-playing seven-and-sevens. He put his hand on my shoulder. "Eh, chère?" he said. "You marrying off Veronica now, chère?"

I was happy. I felt tears well up in my eyes. I had not thought that I was so lonely. Laval's face was smooth as a baby's. He shaved, but not much. I wondered why men needed whiskers.

"No," I said. "Only drawing."

"Papa wants to marry me off, too," he said, rueful. "Wants me to take up the business and raise up a bevy of brats."

"Brats," I said. "Hmph." It was clear that I felt he included me under that rubric.

"Not you, chère," he said. He winked. His smooth cheek wrinkled reassuringly at me. "Mais, Laval is nineteen and not at college, so Papa thinks that he ought to get married."

"Then go off to college," I said, sensibly. I was not fond of the idea of anyone's marrying Laval.

"And what would I study? Accounting and all that damn merde? That is all that there is, in Papa's mind. You think he would want me to study art? Learn about music?" He made a spitting sound. "Who would want to go away to learn book-keeping?" He made it sound like morticians' school.

"Then go off to college and play bourrée," I said. "Some people do that. I have second cousins in New Orleans who do that. Go to cotillions and play bourrée, but they say they are going to college."

"Papa has eyes like the hawk's," Laval said.

"Does he love you?" I said. Grandpère was opaque as ice. I had no real idea whether he loved anyone. He treated me civilly, but Azarene gave me more love than Grandpère, or his daughter, my mother, who wanted me here for the summer so that she could pursue and be pursued, looking for a second husband with more money than her first had had. My father had been as civil as Grandpère, but had gone away.

Grandpère was in complicity with my mother, I was certain. When she remarried, he would no longer have to send her checks for my tuition or my dance-revue costumes or for the enormous chrome bumper on our sky-blue Buick, which shattered when she hit the rear of a Holsum delivery truck.

"Papa?" Laval said. There was a vast silence, and he sighed into it. I held my pencil in midair and looked through the open door out to the porch where Azarene sat, smoking still, swinging her leg. "Papa loved Mama, and Mama loved Sheridan. Mama's gone, Sheridan's gone, for the time, and Papa can't think who is this boy in his place."

"Me, too," I said. I meant I felt the same. Mother loved Daddy and Daddy had gone to the woman in Baton Rouge. So I was here.

Laval made a sidewise smile. I made one back.

Azarene got up from the edge of the porch and sauntered inside. I thought she must have been beautiful when she was young. I thought further that Laval ought to marry her, or me, but no one else in the world.

"Marry Azarene," I said. "I will draw her a dress. Ivory lace on her beautiful beautiful brown skin. And I will be your kid, and people will ask y'all if I am adopted, and y'all will say certainly not. And Grandpère will inherit you the house, and the cream-colored convertible he has got stored in the old garage, and I will wax it myself, with my old PJs I will not have to wear anymore, and we will go riding on Sunday afternoons when everyone else is bored. I will eat Mint Bublets in the back seat, with the top down, and lick my fingers all I want, and get stuck to the funny papers if I feel like it."

Laval hugged me. My arms felt cushy inside his sinewy embrace.

"What you all talking about there, so sneaky?" said Azarene.

"Nothing," I said.

"Anything we want," Laval said. "What you think, you the FBI?"

Azarene laughed from deep down. "If I was I would put you in jail both, and throw them keys so far."

"And then?" he said.

"And then I would lock up you papa in a gypsy wagon and send him around the world. But slow. And then I would go down to the cemetery and make my apologize to you mama, but she understand. And then I would move in my people to this house, and bounce on them mattress and drink from them crystal cup in the sideboard. Is what I would do," she concluded.

"And hire Liberace to play at the takeover, hey?" said Laval.

"Liberace?" she scoffed.

"Then who?" I said. This was wonderful fantasy. I was enjoying the sight of Grandpère disappearing over the horizon in the gypsy wagon, which was as gilded as the Austrian ceilings and Chinese chairs we had invented.

"No fairies," said Azarene. "I would have the gospel choir from the Church of the Radiant Holiness, over Mobile, with they rosy-brown robes and they collars as white as wings. That is who."

In the driveway we heard Grandpère's car. Something died in us. We sighed in unison. Azarene turned to go into the kitchen.

"He wants me to marry Miss Caroline," Laval said.

"She has an excellent bustline," I said. I was conscious of these things, being ten years old and immersed in the world of my buxom comic heroines.

"An excellent bustline," Laval echoed. He seemed amazed.

"Yes," I said, somewhat defensive. Perhaps I should not have pointed it out to him. Perhaps he would wait till I grew, and would marry me instead.

"An excellent bustline," he said again. "I have to tell Carlton Janes." He always said Carlton Janes, as if there were more than one Carlton. "Carlton Janes will love that."

"Mr. Carlton do love the womens," said Azarene.

"That is not what I mean," Laval said. "He would take some delight in the phrase."

"In the phrase. In the phrase," Azarene mumbled, wandering

toward the kitchen, her head weaving side to side slowly, like seaweed.

Midnights I sat up reading so that I could sleep through the morning. I loved the cool nights, with the moths beating against the screens and the dark liquid light from the guest-room lamp spilling across my late pages. My room was at the back of the house, upstairs, looking out onto the grass of the yard and the pea-vines that climbed the strung twine and the dirt-covered side street, Saville Way, its name elegant as the contents of Grandmère's deep closet.

In the dusty book I read, a girl crossed the ocean to France and wore jewels in gaslit salons. A horse so black it was blue ran through a lightning-lit storm, throwing the puddles that mirrored the dark sky every which way. I put the book aside and walked out into the hall.

The door to the back upstairs gallery was open. The night was bright, lit by a full moon. Its light shone back off the green leaves of the vines. Its light seemed to emanate from the white trumpets of flowers that climbed the chicken-wire fence along the street.

I listened to the night. There was a radio somewhere down Saville Way, old melodrama with organ chords, the sort of thing we did not listen to anymore here at the Levasseurs since we had the new Muntz console TV Laval had bought. There were crickets, in a constant hum overlapping another constant hum. There were dogs in the distance, and the sound of automobiles in the other direction, down toward the beach, then the sound of the Gulf water, distant and moaning against the shore. Nothing moved in my field of vision. I was queen of the night here on my high back balcony, empress of Saville, and of all this immobile, meshed sound. I heard, or rather felt, a screen door slam lightly.

Then, suddenly, in the corner of my eye, a white shape made whiter by moonlight moved away from the house. I squinted.

It moved slowly and my eyes focused. It was a man, wearing a sleeved undershirt and white boxer shorts with broad, ballooning legs. The man was thin and walked like a ghost, like a dream. He was sleepwalking. It was Laval. His thin legs, like the clappers of foolish bells, looked milk-white, cadaverous.

He had not taken five ghostly steps before I heard a sound behind me in the hall. It was Grandpère.

"Move, child," he said. He seemed to need to stand in the exact spot where I was standing. I stepped to the side. I could not pass him to return to my room. That did not matter. I was transfixed.

Laval continued down Saville, past the pea-vines, past the white luminous trumpets, as unwavering as a small boat on a still midnight pond.

"Hush, child," Grandpère said. I had not said anything.

Laval floated past the green leaves and the flowers of light. He was past the shed now.

Suddenly a shrill note split the air. Grandpère's lips were pursed. The first notes of "La Marseillaise" leapt from our perch and flowed on one long sweep of air to Laval. He turned as if on command and aimed his walking dream toward the back door. Past the shingled shed, silver with moonlight, past vines and past flowers. Grandpère stopped short only a few measures into the song, as if this were a long-familiar signal, but Laval kept coming. He disappeared under the ledge of the gallery, moonlight shining on his Brylcreemed hair, and we heard the door squeak open then shut.

Grandpère seemed to have forgotten my presence. "Laval, Laval," he said softly. Then he seemed to remember me. "Child," he said. "You must say nothing to Laval."

"Yes, Grandpère," I said.

"One must not wake a somnambulist," Grandpère said.

"Yes," I said.

"Talking about it is just as bad," Grandpère said. "One must not talk to Laval about it afterward. Do you understand?"

"Yes, Grandpère," I said. "I understand."

I did and I did not. I had heard that waking a sleepwalker might kill him, might stop his beating heart, might send his blood rushing in pyrotechnic paroxysms to his brain and cause a fatal quake there. But I did not understand why I must not talk about it afterward to Laval. It would be a great subject for talk.

"Or to anyone else," Grandpère said. "To the colored girl."

"Girl?" I said. Grandpère did not let me play with the black girls who walked past our house, who lived only a block away but might as well have lived on the moon. How would I tell them?

"Azarene," he said, somewhat impatient.

"Yes, Grandpère," I said. I began to understand. To discuss Laval's midnight weakness with someone was a kind of killing. If it were true, as some said, that the soul left the body at night and that to wake a sleepwalker would trap the soul in the air, then perhaps to discuss a sleepwalker's excursions would be to foredoom his next time. Or something. If I talked about what I had seen, I would give Azarene access to Laval's secret and shame him, and in the bargain bring a curse upon him.

Grandpère turned and walked down the dark of the hall to his bedroom, but not before I had seen something much like a tear in his eye. I waited until he had closed his bedroom door, slowly and heavily, then went inside myself. On the wall at the back of the hall were old family pictures in dark frames. Laurette in long blond ringlets, wearing the narcissist's face that she must have been born with, and sitting on a rug on a studio table. My mother at her wedding, with my sleek and civil father. Sheridan in knickers and showing off a shiny bicycle. Laval astride a dark pony, in a picture taken by an itinerant front-yard photographer. I imagined Grandmère looking on as the picture was taken, Grandpère as he hung the framed photo some time later, still young, this young son his pride quite as much as the bicycling

Sheridan, but never showing that love and that pride to Laval. I climbed back into my bed. The sheets smelled of Azarene's ironing. The night in France was filled with intrigue, and bright conversation, and wine the color of my garnet birthstone, but I was a ten-year-old girl and slept deeply.

August came on like the breath of a giant dog, hot, damp, and indisputably natural. Grandpère ignored nature and wore his suits every day, dark stripes with shiny dark ties. Laval dressed in Bermuda shorts and his pastel nylon seersucker shirts. I wore nothing but my swimsuit from the moment Grandpère left in the mornings until the time he might conceivably reappear. Azarene sweated in her uniform.

Liberace played "Summertiiime . . . and the living is easy. . . ."

"Boo hiss," said Laval.

I went to the refrigerator and got another ice cube to suck on. Laval and Azarene drank iced tea.

Liberace played "In the cool cool cool of the evening."

"Boo double hiss," Laval said.

"If Grandpère is so rich, why don't you all have air condition?" I said.

"Honey," said Azarene. "That is why Mr. Leon is rich."

"Cause he doesn't have air condition?" I said.

"Cause he don't spend his money," said Azarene.

"Storing up treasures," said Laval, his eyes rolling mightily. "Where moth and rust consume."

"You be glad that you daddy can't hear," said Azarene.

"Never matter," said Laval. "I was never on his hit parade. There is Sheridan, Mama, Laurette, and Isolde, then commodities. I am not even in the top ten."

Azarene looked at Laval with a jewelly, quizzical eye. "I would say you are probable right, Mr. Laval. But how can you just say it so cool?"

I wanted to say that he could be wrong. But to reveal even

that would be to endanger my secret, the look in Grandpère's eyes the night I first watched Laval walk.

"I am cool," Laval said. "I am seersucker-soul himself."

Azarene laughed and threw the tails of a handful of scallions at him.

We had a letter from Sheridan that week. He described some shooting he had been involved in as if it were all a stage play. He told of the odd, puffy dresses the Korean girls wore, and of how expressive their dark eyes were. Laval and I opened the mail when it came.

"Ooh," Laval said. "We had better not show this to Papa. He would not care to hear of Sheridan dating the ladies there."

"He never said he was dating the ladies," I said.

"It is understood," Laval said, as if imparting to me some sophistication for which I should be duly grateful.

"Grandpère wants *you* to go out on dates," I said. "But doesn't want Sheridan to? But he's older."

"Not Korean girls," Laval said. "Sheridan played football for Biloxi High School. You wouldn't remember that."

"So?" I said.

"Sheridan does not have to prove himself," Laval said. "I do. All Sheridan has to do is provide heirs. And not slanty-eyed little Chop Chop Levasseur Juniors. Papa would be oh-la-la! incredulous at the thought. We won't show him the letter."

And so we did not. As it turned out, we never did.

The following week we heard Sheridan had been killed. The best we could calculate, he had been killed just before Liberace's show, Thursday afternoon, when Laval was just coming back up Saville Way from Carlton Janes', and I was stuffing big purple-black eggplants with breadcrumbs and shrimp to help Azarene out. We had had no idea.

We sang along with Liberace: "I want to ride to the ridge where the West commences, gaze at the moon until I lose my senses."

"Not Mr. Sheridan," Azarene said. "So much life in him."

"What a thing to say," Laval said. There was something between them, a stillness, a humor, not anger. "How much life does anybody have? So much life, my foot. No life, anymore." He was almost incoherent.

"You right. That stupid. What you going to say when somebody die," Azarene said.

He had been blown to bits. It was not a stage play. There was nothing left of him to come home.

"What was that song?" Laval said. " 'Don't Fence Me In'?" We sang it again.

Grandpère sat in the living room until it was quite dark drinking port wine. He talked to none of us.

Laval tiptoed past him in the half-lit hall, ostentatiously, farcically, bringing broad wedges of Azarene's custard pie upstairs for us to share. Azarene had been sent home early. Dinnertime had passed unnoticed. I laughed at Laval from the top of the stairs. I wondered if I were blaspheming.

"Oh. Sheridan won't mind," Laval said. "He surely has gone to heaven. He was a good boy. I am certain that heaven has custard pie." He sank his teeth into the point of his pie and then, chewing, leaned back and admired his teeth-marks. His eyes were wet.

"Did you and Sheridan fight?" I said.

"Hell yes," said Laval. "What are brothers for?"

"I don't know," I said.

He bit again and mused on the scallops his front teeth had cut in the custard. "Papa loved him," he said. He was talking through his pie. "Excuse me," he said, and he turned and went up to his room.

I read late. I had finished the France book and found one about a charming invalid girl at a spa in the Virginia mountains. I was sure she would be cured by the end of the book. I had read *Heidi* long ago, and expected the righting of Nature's inequities. Laurette had not yet come in. She had gone to Mobile with some lawyer from Jackson the afternoon before and was not back yet. Sheridan was not dead yet, for her. I wondered if she would care.

I sat up reading under my bed lamp. The air was quite still and the moths pushed against the screen. Someone's cat yowled. There was no other sound. Down the hall, I heard a door open. Grandpère had gone to bed two hours earlier, staggering under the burden of his port wine. I went to my door and peered out.

It was not Grandpère. It was Laval. He was sleepwalking. In the moonlight in the hall his face frightened me. It was white, stiff with repose and suffused with the stuff of dream and nightmare.

I started to speak out his name: Laval. But I remembered. His soul was at large, or the blood would rush somewhere it ought not to be and kill him on the spot. So I stood watching as he turned and headed for the stairs. Grandpère would wake when he heard the screen door, and Laval would be called back. I had best stay out of the way.

I sat lightly on the edge of my bed and tried to read. Instead, I sat staring at an idealized watercolor of the velvet-green hills that surrounded the spa where this miracle cure would take place. I heard Laval's step on the stairs. Soft creak, soft creak. Thirteen creaks. He was downstairs, and rounding the banister. Grandpère would catch him.

And then I heard Grandpère's snore. Grandpère did not snore. It was the port wine, and he would not hear Laval go out the screen door. Laval could keep going forever, and Grandpère would never know. Laval would keep going, inland and inland, and be woken by someone he did not know. In the next state, perhaps. I was trying to think what was north of us.

Then I ran. Down the stairs, through the dining-room door.

The dining-room table was broad as an ice rink, night-dark waxed mahogany. Sonja Henie might have skated there, deep nights while we all slept. There were fourteen chairs.

Laval navigated it all with ease. His back was straight, his thin shoulders like hangers in his short-sleeved undershirt. I wanted to call him. I watched him go through the kitchen, past the table where he had cut custard pie and left crumbs. Azarene would raise Cain in the morning.

I ran upstairs and out onto the back gallery. Laval was passing the peas and the trumpet-vines. He was passing the shed.

I licked my lips and assayed the arpeggio. All the flags of France waved in my whistling. Laval heard and turned. Four measures, and I brought him back. Small hairs stood up on my neck. Such strange power to have over someone, and him full-grown.

It was not two days after we had heard of Sheridan's death that Miss Caroline called and asked Laval over for dinner. Laval made his face hard, as if he were a prisoner being offered his last meal, and said certainly he would come. I heard him announcing it to Grandpère that evening.

"Well." Grandpère said. "I am glad you have finally come to your senses."

I could not see Laval's face. I was sure it was the telephone face, the last-meal face. I asked him later why he would bother with Miss Caroline.

"Bother," he echoed. He did not answer me.

I went out to the kitchen.

"Laval is going to go to that horrible girl's house for dinner," I said.

"Pass me that bell pepper," Azarene said. "By you elbow."

"To Miss Caroline's," I said. "I hate her nail polish."

"I said pass that bell pepper," Azarene said. She was sliding diamond-chip-sized pieces of onion around on the chopping board with the sharp edge of the cleaver.

I looked around for the bell pepper. "And I cannot see why she would ask Laval, anyway."

"Lord," Azarene said. She reached across the table and pulled the contorted green pepper toward her. She sliced into it. "Miss

Caroline don't have the brains of a fish. She just got dollar sign in her eyeballs."

"But Laval's smart," I said. It sounded defensive.

"Yes ma'am," Azarene said. "You don't worry 'bout him. He mought go visit just to please old Mr. Leon, but she ain't gone catch him, no sir and no ma'am. Get that chair, child, and climb up and get the cayenne."

Laval went to Korea the week after I left for home. I was glad I did not have to watch him go, packing up his bag with razor blades and Aqua Velva.

I wore my dragon-backed jacket that Sheridan had sent as I walked to school, even before it was cool enough. Girls were snide and mocked me to hide their yellow envy. Boys threw acorns. I was the belle of the ball.

Laval did not even write. He did not have to. Anything we could say could wait till he came home. I did not want polite trivialities. Letters were useless.

My mother was dating a man who she told me was heir to the Murphy's Oil Soap fortune. He wore an onyx ring set with three diamonds. He went to a manicurist and wore flawless clear nail polish. He had thick lips I would recognize in Elvis Presley's, when he came to prominence. I detested him.

At Christmas we went to Grandpère's. Tante Laurette was everywhere. She was engaged again, to a friend of the lawyer from Jackson.

Azarene grumbled. "Mr. Leon expect me to turn everything into Christmas. It seventy-eight outside and he be wanting me to make it snow, jingle bell, everything. I don't know what he be thinking."

"How many times has Tante Laurette been engaged?" I said.

Azarene looked at the ceiling and ticked silent names or epithets off her fingers. "I believe they be four."

"Dashing through the snow," I sang, unthinking.

"You want do that stuff, you go outside." She pointed with

a spoon. "You go way past the shed and you keep on. Where Azarene can't hear you."

I thought of Laval. "If I could have, I would have sent Laval a white coat for Christmas. White wool. I bet he would wear it. Korea is cold, you know."

"Jingle bell," Azarene said disgustedly. "Eighteen-pound turkey and who gone to eat it. Miz Laurette and you mama they eat like a parakeet do. That fine Jackson man with them spectator shoes come, I will leave for sure. That man the worst yet. Got a face like a heart like the root of some tree. Knotted up. You and Mr. Leon and that fiancé got to eat the whole turkey?"

"Why did Laval go to the war?" I said.

"Honey, you have to ask that?" Azarene said. "My boy done gone, too, and I don't like to think about that."

"Do you know? Why he went?" I persisted.

"It Miss Caroline, Mr. Leon, and that Mr. Sheridan dead in the grave—oh Lord, did I say that, and him scatter—put together made Mr. Laval go."

I waited for her to say more.

"You know Miss Caroline. Why. He went to get far, far away. Mr. Leon be pressing on him to go marry her. Then Mr. Leon be wanting him to go be in Mr. Sheridan's place, or what. I hear them arguing. Mr. Leon say, 'You don't want marry Caroline, you rather play cards with Carlton Janes, what be the matter with you, kissy-kissy with Carlton Janes, you got no balls at all?' "

I remembered how Grandpère had cried watching Laval at his sleepwalking. Dear baby boy, said his eyes. Sheridan, then Laurette, then Isolde, then Laval, baby boy.

"This some Christmas," Azarene said. "Mr. Sheridan die, then Mr. Laval go, then Miz Laurette bring home this warthog from Jackson, and you mama all depress because the Oil Soap man find somebody else. This some Christmas."

In February I left my emerald-green jacket with dragons in a seat on the Saint Charles streetcar. I realized it as soon as I stepped to the sidewalk and shouted, but the streetcar just pulled away, clanging. We phoned the car barn but no one turned it in.

The next week we heard about Laval. He had gotten the flu in Korea, and then meningitis, and died. The body was shipped home. My mother said Grandpère did not want a funeral, but I found out afterward there was a funeral and we had simply not gone. My mother had a date with her new beau, a perfume wholesaler.

April first Grandpère dropped dead of a stroke, sixty-one years old. He was buried between Grandmère and Laval. We went to that funeral. I watched my mother making eyes at the perfumer as they lowered Grandpère's coffin.

Back at the house, she and Laurette wrangled over the furniture.

"Don't want to wait for the will," Azarene said, watching covertly through the archway from the dining room. She shook her head and continued ironing curtains. I wondered why she was doing that, why we would need fresh-ironed curtains now. Who would she work for now, with Grandpère gone?

Laurette insisted that the furniture from Grandmère and Grandpère's bedroom was hers. My mother wanted it. The china cabinet in the front foyer with all the St. Louis World Exposition souvenirs had been Grandmère's. My mother wanted that. "You'll get the house," she said. "You know that. Must you have everything?" Laurette shrieked and wrestled the cabinet key into its lock, insisting that seven or eight things in there were hers, no matter what my mother said. The claw-footed thing wobbled side to side.

Azarene shook her head. "They break that curve glass on the front of that thing, they gone to stop then, maybe. You just go down to the beach, honey child. Put you sweater, it chilly. Go watch them wave hit for a while, then come back. These two gone to get tired of it."

My mother's perfumer and Laurette's warthog had gone off

for some whiskey, ostensibly so Azarene could make sauce for the bread pudding. They would come back with two fifths, and the four of them would drink it all. Or my mother and Tante Laurette would rip the legs off Grandmère's walnut dressing table, fighting over it. I could not see a good end to the day. So I went for my sweater.

Upstairs in the hall Laval's picture hung in its accustomed place. I went to the end of the hall, looked out the door down Saville Way, and whistled the opening phrase from the French anthem. Laval did not come back. I took down his picture from the wall to look into the little-boy eyes. I walked into the bedroom where my sweater lay on the bed. I opened my little suitcase and laid Laval's picture there, between the two extra dresses my mother insisted I bring. I went out to the hall again and, one by one, I took all the pictures down, stacking them on the hall table. By the time anyone noticed they were down, there would be too much going on to worry about rehanging them for a while. It would be weeks or months before they knew that Laval was gone, riding the front-yard photographer's pony.

Laurette married the warthog, who proceeded to become mayor of some little town outside Jackson. We saw her occasionally, far too often for my tastes, but my mother said that we had to keep in contact. We were all that each other had, she and Laurette, she and I.

Time telescopes easily from this distance. Laurette died when I was a freshman sorority pledge at Sophie Newcomb. She had breast cancer. I decided that I had no heart, or that it pumped ice water, because all I felt was a numb concern for myself. I crossed my hands over my bosom and resolved to borrow someone's genetics textbook. I would see if the gene could jump sidewise. I heard the relief in my own breath as I realized we would not have to take those trips north anymore. I was still all my mother had, and she insisted I come along.

But then she married. The perfumer became a bore and she

took a new, more outgoing approach to the game. She did not have to put up with bores. She took up with a widower who owned a boat dealership. It worked out. One Twenty-Three Lillian became her house now, and she and the boat dealer lived here for ten years, till he died, and then twenty-one more, till she died, just last Thursday.

The house needs some work. I will call in the college-boy carpenters I got to work on our house on the Parkway. The three of them have degrees in useless pursuits like English literature and geography, and they do wonderful detailing. They made the oak of our back parlor mantel just come alive: dentils, lion's mouth, all of it.

But once I have got the house done, when will I get away to come over here? Weekends, my husband has this and that. Tulane games, business trips, forays across the lake to see his old mother, who lives outside Mandeville and makes me happy. They are a family fraught with felicity. My sons swim on their high-school teams and bring home medals. I do watercolors and have had a number of shows. We are fine.

I will see Azarene this evening. My rough calculation tells me she is seventy-four or so, having been far younger than I imagined when she and Laval and I lived among scallions and peppers and made mouths behind Laurette's back. She still lives, I hear, out where she used to, with her son who survived Korea. I will ask her if she would like to come here and be my permanent housesitter. Bounce on them mattress. We can decide whether we will come over when summer comes.

Underneath my feet now, the old wood of the gallery floor creaks and groans. Down Saville Way, it looks much the same. It is too early in the year for the vines to be quite full, but they still climb the rusted wire fence. Looking around me to be sure my husband and sons are not within earshot, I whistle the eight bars of deathless French pride. Laval's ghost does not heed me, but marches on, past the shed, past all the houses, across mountains, over the ocean floor. He will not turn back.

Dead Man's Spoons

There goes Jillaine again whining she won't eat with dead man's spoons. Make Regis wash up the stuff in the dishwasher, she will say next. All the breakfast and lunch stuff is in there, the cereal dishes, the sandwich plates, all the good spoons are used up. I am not about to get into that again. She's perfectly capable.

I have this picture I took. It's me on the back of my dad's truck, perched up on the tailgate. You can see the bumper sticker that says No Mo Bo, which means that my dad hates the guts out of Michigan's football team. Bo is Bo Schembechler, who's their coach. On the other side there's one that says I ♡ Ohio State. (Which is a twin to the one on my mother's Gremlin that says I ♡ Couponing.) Jillaine gave those bumper stickers to him for Father's Day last year and what can you do. She stuck them on there herself and only partly covered up his old I'll Give Up My Gun When You Pry My Cold Dead Fingers et cetera. She hates anything to do with the word Dead. Oh Dad, she says, I get the willies. He tells her to shut up.

I took the picture of me on the truck with a tripod and a self-timer, posing to look real serious and self-important. But just before the whir of the timer went off, something odd struck my mind. So I have this face on that is puzzled and pensive and slightly amused and as sad as I guess I have ever seen anyone be. The truck is filled up with the stuff that we got from the dead man. You can see it behind me, like a mountain range.

It was the first picture in a bunch that I took, three whole rolls of Tri-X shot up. My language-arts teacher, Ms. Frame, gave us a choice on this project we had to do. We could write this big essay or make an art thing, any kind. I said could I take pictures and she said sure, but when I showed her my camera she said no way. It was this hand-me-down thing. Not with that, she said. She got the newspaper teacher to lend me a camera that takes real clear pictures, as sharp as your eyes, and she said to use black-and-white film. Which is cheaper and also makes neat pictures. I was surprised.

See, the dead man was no one we knew. It's like this. My mother works at this car dealership, Kazel's Buick-Datsun, just over off I-75. Kaz Kazel used to be a baseball player, third base, Nashville Vols, about sixty-eight hundred years ago. Never got over it. Still has his pictures up in the hall, right outside my mother's office. She does their bookkeeping and I don't know what all else. And there is this parts clerk, a guy, that she knows. About twenty years old or like that. And his roommate died, and that is who all the stuff in the truck, which included the spoons, belonged to.

My mother comes home this particular day and she says to my dad, You know Al, the parts clerk that moved here from Tipp City?

And my dad says, kind of mocky and snarly, No, I don't know Al-the-parts-clerk-that-moved-here-from-Tipp-City.

And my mom ignores all that, like because she's used to it so it sounds normal, but you know it doesn't. So she says, Well, his roommate died.

Good, says my dad, like he didn't hear her, but he did.

So she ignores that, too. He was a colored fellow, she says.

Black, I butt in.

All right, Regis, she tells me. It was this black fellow that Al had been rooming with, do you see, she says. And I can't tell you why he was forty-eight years old and rooming with Al, you would think a young boy like that would have a roommate his age.

And my father says, Regis, go tell Jillaine to turn her damn radio down and get me a Buckeye.

And I want to hear this so I haul ass. When I come back my mother is saying, And so I guess he was a health nut or something. Anyway, he played tennis. And there he was, playing, and wham-o.

Wham-o, my dad echoes, and there is this odd look on his face, as if he has actually heard her. Which is an event. My dad is forty-six himself, so I guess that accounts for it. Then he says, I hope you got the roast ready. I'm going to Jamison's right after dinner.

I just walked in, my mother says. Which she did.

Four hundred and sixty-nine bucks I spent on that damn microwave oven for you and here they are in the paper a couple years later for less than half, he says. He kind of punches the opened-up newspaper with the backs of his knuckles.

Anyway, we were having corn dogs, she says. Corn dogs and nachos. She waves the little white Colonel Sanders bag that she's carrying, like it's a bell. I got the coleslaw here, she says.

Corn dogs, shit, he says, and goes and gets in his truck and roars off to his friend Jamison's, or at least he would like us to think that's where he's going.

So she turns to me, without missing a step, as if it had been us that was talking. So Al came to work today kind of shook up, she says. You can understand that. There was stuff to be done, but Al's nothing to him, not a relative. Him being colored and all, she adds, because she had forgotten.

I make this superior blink at her and she says, Black, okay, black, Regis.

So Al had his brother's number, she says. This fellow's brother's number. Lives on the West Coast somewhere. He is the personal manager for some rock star, I guess somebody you would know. Enos Bright, do you know that name?

Holy shit, I say. Enos Bright?

That's what he said, I believe, she says.

Enos Bright's only the hottest, I say. We are talking multiple platinum albums. I went on telling her about his keyboard style, which is only the finest, and about his albums, "Dark N Bright" and "The Man with the Fingers."

She plops the coleslaw into a glass dish, like it was homemade. She shakes the corn dogs out of their box and pokes them in the microwave. This brother of his, she says, is supposedly coming to town to take care of the funeral arrangements and like that. She yells for Jillaine to come eat.

Holy shit, I say. Enos Bright.

Well, it was maybe three months later, she comes in again from work in the evening, and by this time it's winter and dark out, and there is my dad with the paper. The usual.

You know that Al the parts clerk with the roommate that died, she says. He is getting a new roommate.

My dad looks up at her like: You better not keep going on.

And he has to get all of the stuff from the other guy out, she says. When the brother came to get the fellow cremated and like that, he told Al that he could have anything that the guy left and get rid of the rest. I don't know if he took anything at all, she says.

My dad just looks back at the paper. Egyptians, Iranians, Lebanese, he says. They ought to blow each other up and leave all of us in peace.

Us civilized people, I say, and he looks at me funny.

When the brother came, my mother says, turning to me, Al says he rented a Mercedes to get around town. And how big is town anyway? You could practically walk, she says, and she is right. He must be rich.

Well, Enos Bright, I start to say, but she's going on.

Al says he had cowboy boots that were red, made of snake-skin, and this watch that was thin as money, and this look like he owned the world, she says. Would somebody's personal manager be that rich?

Well, Enos Bright, I say, is only a genius, but I've got to say that I guess that his personal manager must have some brains, too. I pulled out a pair of his albums and showed her.

Oh, my, she says. Dark glasses? Is he blind?

I was amazed that she could live in this world and not know.

I guess he IS, I say. Only as blind as he possibly could be, and never has seen a thing, born blind and lived blind but oh that man's fingers. Can he play.

I guess lots of those black-type musicians, she says, looking at me to make sure I notice, are blind, aren't they?

My dad says, Can this crap, would you.

So we go in the family room.

Anyway, she says, Al said he didn't know what to do with all this stuff the guy left so I volunteered our truck.

Dad's? I say. I can't believe she has volunteered him.

You can drive it, can't you? she says. Because I said you would.

So I perk up, because I haven't gotten to drive it yet. Dad always has some reason. But I know that she'll tell him that if he wants to drive it, that's fine, too. And he won't say just take the offer back, because Mom got a bill last week for some silk nightgown that was charged on their MasterCard and it was not hers and she made a stink about it and he halfway confessed, being he is so bad at excuses, and so she's got something to hold over him.

So I got to drive it, and load all this stuff in the truck with the tarp over it and bring it here, which was a surprise, because I figured she wanted me to bring it to the Goodwill or out to the dump or something.

No, she says, we'll sort through it, and that will be our payback. There is sure to be something good there. She is a pack rat, my mom. The neat kind, not one of these old crazies that hoards like newspapers and hairy shit.

And I bring it home, and it's dark and the snow is this nasty Thanksgiving-week slosh, so I pull into the garage and my mom turns on the light, which is this bug-yellow color and makes everything look all drained and you know what I mean. And she's standing in the door out of the kitchen with her coupon box in her hand beaming like she has struck gold, and she says to me, with this grand sweep of her hand: Unload.

Jesus, I think. And I'm not much on homework, if you get my drift, but I do have this big assignment to do. But I'm working, unloading, and my nose is all red and my fingers like white with the cold, and my mother keeps coming out saying to put my gloves on and I'm sixteen and ought to have more sense.

So this is when I think about taking pictures, and I don't know where the thought comes from. But when I come in I've decided that this would make a project I could do because Ms. Frame has said we've got to portray the life of a person by describing objects that make up that person's life, and the dead man's stuff has got me hooked.

So my mother has got her stuff spread out on the kitchen table. My dad is off somewhere in her car and I think I know where because the nightgown, I figure, was for this girl that works the cash register at the Sunoco and lives in the mobile-home village in back of the IGA. I look at my mom. She is bent over her clipping stuff.

She has these scissors with kind of padded rubberish bright yellow handles, and envelope files, and tape, and a roll of these boring postage stamps instead of commemoratives (which I got once when she sent me for them and she says Regis, so what if they've got pictures of bighorn sheep and wildflowers and antique trains, I want the ones on a roll). This stuff is her special stuff, and we knew since we were little: don't mess with it. Hell to pay, you get my meaning.

Kind of pathetic, I think, how she throws herself into this stuff, and especially evenings when my dad goes chasing tail, mostly these jailbait types that are barely older than me. Sometimes I'd like to see her go off with old Kaz, maybe just like to Dayton, go dancing, eat steak, whatever, just get the old man good and pissed, good and jealous.

But here she sits, cutting her coupons. She's got these lines like a plowed field all across her forehead, and lines like a barn roof beside her mouth. Lately I can picture what she will look like when she is old. I'll move out of this godforsaken burg, who knows where, and not see her much probably, but Jillaine will stay here, marry some half-wit when she is like my age, and she and my mom will spend the rest of both their lives bitching at each other, happy.

So I make conversation. What's up, I say.

I've got the four proofs-of-purchase, she says. She has little scraps of traffic-light-green plastic that she has cut from her panty-hose bags. She waves the coupons like they were winning lottery tickets. I'm going to get a wallet with a Velcro tab and my initials in gold, she says. Script.

Script, I say, then I hear how I sound and be careful.

She's got Bisquick box tops, and these thousands of UPC barcodes, and the words CHOCOLATE MOUSSE cut out from the package of this gross stuff she puts in her hair. I just watch.

It's an art, she says.

I just listen.

You have to watch all the sales, she says. Save labels and register receipts. Switch brands sometimes. She sorts through a stack of bright-colored coupons. Do you know I saved sixty-eight dollars last month and got fourteen dollars and something in free gifts, plus eight ninety-eight in refunds? It's an art.

That dead guy had a hell of a lot of weird stuff, I say.

Did you fold up the tarp? she says. You know your father.

I nod my head yes. I am going to take pictures of it, I say.

What for, she says.

This project for school, I say.

Pictures of junk, she says.

It's art, I say, testing.

That would be that young teacher from the East. Am I right? she says.

Right, I say. Allison Frame. All that newfangled East Coast shit. Art for art's sake, I say. Testing.

She shrugs and counts four labels she has soaked off laundry-soap bottles into a big envelope. Oh, well, she says, the world goes on.

I am not in the mood for an argument, anyway. There's this picture of her and my dad on the wall right in back of her when they were newlyweds and I am thinking, I wish she would put it away. It makes me sad to see them young, looking like they had life by the balls. Maybe it could get knocked off, the broom handle, something.

So it took me a couple of weeks to get this stuff together and do all the pictures. It got kind of interesting. Jillaine came in and out of the garage going Oh God, Oh God in her Valley-girl voice, which is not like anything you've ever heard, while I was setting up lights and arranging the stuff. You, Regis, she said, and she made my name sound like a thing she found in the back of the refrigerator growing a beard. You, Regis, are the most weirdest asshole I never couldn't even think of.

This guy had a whole drawer of earrings, junk earrings, with rhinestones and plastic pearls the size of like vanilla wafers, and dangling things like Christmas bells and señoritas dancing like a banana ad. He had salt and pepper shakers up to here, some shaped like windmills, some like just plain eggs, one brown, one white, some like old cars, some like stars and moons. There were two that were like liquor bottles, and one said Scotch and held pepper and the other one said Bourbon and held salt. There was a pair that were bookend type things to squish your napkins in between, and I wondered what you did with the napkins when you had to like *use* the things. There was a cow with these big china udders that matched with a bull with a pizzle. You wouldn't believe.

This guy had books. He had books up his ass. He had books of all weird kinds of things, like abnormal psychology books like for college. It looked like he might have been some kind of psychologist himself. Nobody has all this stuff if they are just a person. He had this box of Rorschach blots, inkblots shaped like wild dancing and goats and the end of the world and a clown making faces into a cracked mirror. I saw about these in a movie one time, but I never imagined I'd have a whole box of them in my garage.

He had records. I hoped when I opened the box I would find stuff like Enos Bright's, but no. By this point I guess I was not amazed. He had Barbra Streisand. He had stuff like Scheherazade. He had a record of Danny Kaye telling old animal fables like from Germany.

He had fancy bottles, men's cologne bottles shaped like other things. A red paddle-wheel steamer. A brown glass convertible with its top down. A rooster that had Cock-o-the-Walk painted in silver on its side, where it seemed like the glass feathers had been shaved.

He had three huge old boxes of lamp oil. No shit. I have got no idea what you do with lamp oil, or what he did.

He had a Ouija board.

He had silverware, none of it like any of the rest. Plain stuff, and stuff that was actually silver, with several different initials. Big, heavy stuff that came from some hotel, you couldn't tell where, except the hotel's whole picture was engraved on the back-ends of the forks, knives, and spoons.

He must have had two thousand mirror tiles packed in boxes.

He had bunches and bunches of sheet sets, like flowered and checkered and striped, with the price tags from some place called Discount Den still stuck on.

He had a baby scale, with a picture of a stork on it.

He had seventeen lipsticks, and pots of rouge, and hair wax.

He had a blond wig, and a red one, and two black ones, all medium-length and curly.

He had a kilt. And he had a dashiki. He had women's clothes, pretty expensive-looking stuff, and hats with veils, kind of velourish. He had a dark red velvet cape, with these fancy Chinese-looking hooks. Frogs, my mother called them. She did not comment on this stuff. I never saw her face look that way.

What do you think? I said. I was setting up the tripod and the camera and the lights to be just right. I was getting into this. I was taking a kind of a sweeping shot of all the salt- and pepper shakers, arranged on the velvet cape. What do you think? Have you found anything you want? I said to my mother.

She was looking at a couple of pictures we had found. These were the only pictures in all of this. Nothing was labeled. There was a black family in the forties or something, I guessed from the clothes. They looked happy. My mother did not answer me. She just moved aside so I could shoot.

Don't trip on the cord, I said. I felt tender.

I got the stuff developed. There were only like two or three blurred.

Allison Frame was in some kind of ecstasy. Oh, Regis, she said, this is wonderful. Regis, you have so much talent. She said that to my mother when she came for her conference at the half. My mother told my dad.

Bullcrap, he said.

I still have the pictures. I got them back. I got an *A*-plus. I never got one in my life before that or since. They are just pictures. Of saltshakers, Ouija board, hair wax, Scheherazade. Some things by themselves, some in bunches or piles or arrangements.

Ms. Frame gets all hot on the subject of art. She showed my pictures to all her classes. She talks about how art does not just mirror life, but enlarges it. Makes it cohere, she says. Makes it fucking shimmer.

Sounds good, but I can tell that those pictures are just pictures, nothing more. I have one more, but it's just in my head. It is of that guy, whose name I never did find out, returning a serve, with his right arm raised up in the sunshine, stopped dead. That's a fake-out, too. Art can't do anything to make life do anything but be life, and a thing you cannot understand.

Jillaine's still whining. Oh God, she says, why do I have to eat out of spoons dead man's lips have touched. Dead man's spit. Oh God.

The Golden

Blood. Red blood like a curtain of silk all around me. Like a shower curtain and a shower just at the same time. This is what I was dreaming, this morning, before the damn dream woke me up at four-thirty and I got up to make the coffee. I thought, might as well.

But the shower was of blood, and the color of Grandmother Jahncke's carbuncle ring—garnet—which I never wear. What farm woman would? She was a town lady. I grew up in town myself so I never was brought up to this, but I tell you I have been through hell this past two weeks. This hell is called hunting season.

My husband and twelve of his friends are holed up out in the barn. He has built me this wonderful house, and I have got a window—a quadruple window—twelve foot wide across the top of my sink. I cannot tell you how many times in the past two weeks I have stood there at that window wishing that I did not have a straight-on view of that barn, or that some force would come whipping down out of the sky and just swoop the whole bunch off to Oz.

Jesper—this is my husband—is partners with one of the other

fools out there with him, Wendell Rife, in a lumber and building-supplies business, biggest in town, and he made sure that everything in this house was just the finest. Would you believe that the framing around this twelve-foot window is cherry wood, and as smooth as a sauce? Still, I have to look out at the barn, and right now I don't like that.

Jesper is quite a hunter. I'll tell you. The day we got married he had his hound bred. We got married at six in the evening at First Congregational, and he didn't get back till four-thirty to even get washed up and get in his suit. It was something that just couldn't wait. When a hound is in heat, she's in heat, is what Jesper said that day. I told you that I was a city girl, and I guess I thought that that kind of talk was real juicy and quaint back then. What I think now is, I should have known.

Well, what Jesper himself did not know, because he was not very much older than me and it was his first hound, was that that dog should have been bred repeatedly, not just once. They get pregnant again and again, and carry all these puppies, with however many fathers you want, all at the same time. So because Jesper just bred her once, we had some trouble.

Came time to deliver, and by that time I myself was pregnant with Mary Elizabeth. The dog was moaning in labor for hours, and I'll tell you I was thinking twice about this whole enterprise I had embarked on. The vet came out, and of course it was just one huge puppy, near as big as the dog herself in my memory. He had to do a cesarean. What do you know but the puppy died, and the mother soon after. I said, Jesper, I'm not looking forward to birthing this child if that's what it's like. Jesper said back, When the time comes, you'll do it fine, Marguerite. Jesper said, You are a farm woman now.

I don't know if I am or I'm not. I don't wear garnet rings, but I do use a cookbook. Jesper has got six sisters, and between them they don't own I'll bet five cookbooks. They buy big cans of lard. They laugh at me sometimes. Once, when Jesper went duck hunting, I fixed that duck like the cookbook said, all stuffed with orange slices. They just laughed, and it tasted like shoe soles. But Jesper ate most of it. He doesn't care.

I don't know what I think about all of this hunting either. You take those fools out in the barn. This is how they go hunting. They're all within sight of the house, within sight of my cherry-wood framed kitchen window. If one of the wives calls up I can just look out and give a report. But they think they're out hunting. They bring over their sleeping bags and they sleep out there. Two weeks of this! Like one long, messy slumber party.

They cook for themselves, thank God, though how they can eat what they cook I don't know. Greasy, oily stuff, usually something lumpy in red gravy. They have brought in a portion of something sometimes for me and Mother, and I say thank you but then I dump it down the Dispoz-All. I wouldn't give it to the cats, and they pretty much don't remember to ask whether I liked it, because they are drunk as skunks all the two weeks and don't even remember what they had the night before, much less that they brought it in to us.

And they've all got their licenses, so they have each got a deer coming. But they hole up out there, and they have got somebody's teenage kid's radio out there with them—don't ask me how they pried the kid's fingers off—and they play country music that they never listen to other times, loud as you please.

And Jesper's cousin's son, Norm, who is studying to be an accountant downstate at the University, somehow he gets off these two weeks and comes home, and he really hunts. He's not much of a drinker. He takes his gun and while the fools are holed up in there with their red gravy and their country music, he goes off on our land, moving out in these widening circles, until he gets his deer. We have got lots of land, so there is no need to go beyond.

Well, when he gets his deer, he comes back and then a gang of them goes out in the Cherokee and they bring the deer back. And then they have to celebrate. Which means more drinking.

If it is still light, Norm goes off again with his gun to get some-body else's deer. They joke that he is the designated hunter. Then they slap their legs and laugh and somebody always says, Yep, and I'll drink to that. Norm makes this face I could only call grim, a grim smile, and goes off. He says he just likes to shoot the deer, and he thinks they're all nuts giving up the thrill but he is perfectly glad to take what they are giving up. Hand-me-down deer, he says, they're fine with me.

As I say, I don't know what I think about hunting. The DNR people, they say hunting maintains a balance in nature. I didn't believe that, but do you know eight or nine years ago there was a snow that I still can remember real vividly. Folks who did not have equipment were snowed in for days. We were out on the snowmobiles right the next morning. We went down to the road—it's about a half-mile—and right there at the gate, where those blue flowers whose names I can never remember bloom in those thick patches in summer, there were I swear over a hundred deer, all come out looking for something to eat in the snow. That's the way that they do it, they follow one deer who has found something. Jesper put out six bales of hay every morning last winter to keep them fed, and it would disappear. I think that's downright kind, but then I don't know how he can kill them. He keeps saying that it's the natural order of things.

Natural or not, I just cannot stand the blood part. And that's what they're in now. It's like a big butcher-shop factory out there. At least they don't drink for this part. Except that Jesper's brother Al did one year, and I will never forget it. They set up their plywood on sawhorses. The sacred plywood, I say to myself when I see it standing against the wall in the barn all summer, unused. It's not used for anything else. No one would think of it. When they set up, they've got two that will work on skinning, and maybe four at the butchering, then two more working the grinder and trimmings. I swear it is like Santa's workshop, with blood, blood, blood, all of them jolly as elves, and the radio going. I guess I thought of that Santa's elves thing because last time I went out there they had some station on that was playing Christmas music already. They are moving it further and further back, almost to Halloween. I guess the way it looks out in the barn now, it's halfway between Halloween and the elves at the North Pole.

The year Al was drinking it was a mess. It was last year, come to think of it, because we already were in this new house. They had come in the house, a few of them, and they were sitting around smelling like they smell, watching some football game on television, and I went in the bathroom and there was blood on the toilet seat. Well, I knew Al had just been in there, and my first thought was, my God, did he get his thing caught in the saw? But then I saw it was on the light switch, too, and on the hall carpet, so I went after him. Turned out he had cut his finger and not even known it, he was so numbed up. I was pretty mad about the carpet, but I cleaned it myself. I wanted it done and done right. Mother said she had never seen anything like it—the trail of blood everywhere, into the bowl of potato chips, even—and she's eighty-four.

When they're doing the butchering, they slit the throat right away, so as to let the blood drain off right, then they gut the deer, which I cannot watch at all, because it still looks just like a deer. Which it is. Then they send in the heart and the tongue and the liver and kidneys and pancreas to me for me to deal with. I do it because that is my job, but I don't like it much. This year they even sent in the testicles. Down in Kentucky where Darden Bell comes from—he's one of the fools out there right now, he owns a feed store—they serve them in restaurants, he says. On the menu, as plain as that, though he says they call them lamb fries. Why, I do not know. So this year they saved up all these deer testicles and made themselves a grand Sunday breakfast. It was like some damn-fool cave ritual. I told Jesper, what did he think, that they would give him their power? That he would be all over me every night now instead of just snoring off? That he would sire a son now, at the ripe age of fifty-nine? We just had daughters, and that always got to him.

Well. It was just last night that this thing happened. I was looking out the side window, the hall window, not the twelve-footer. The moonlight was something. I had had too much coffee. I can't drink that decaf. They say they make it with formaldehyde, which I understand is what they pickle the frogs in that we cut up so many years ago in high-school biology. So I thought, what the hell, might as well be hung for a sheep as a lamb, and I was having one more cup, standing and staring out into the moonlight.

Well, don't you know but that these two silhouettes, like black-paper cutouts, crisp as that against the night, which was silver, and mist coming out of the trees for a backdrop, these two silhouettes come out of the side door of the barn. And between them they're struggling something along. And I see it is a light-colored dog. And I think, Oh my good God, it's the Golden. My neighbor, Rosaleen Poikonen, has this sweet Golden she's had for oh seven, eight years, just the color of her children's hair, it is. All of them grown and gone. She is an Irish girl. Her husband—they call him Finn, and he has that child-white hair like they have up in reindeer land—hates that dog.

So I think, Holy Jesus, what are those two up to? They've dragged the thing back to the fence by the chickens. And before I have half a chance to think what to do, there I see, in silhouette, sharp as anything, Finn lifts up something that looks like the Louisville slugger that Jesper keeps out on the hook in the toolshed, and CRACK! it comes down on the Golden's head.

Here I was, in the hall, shaking, and thinking about the caffeine that I shouldn't have had, knowing that wasn't why I was shaking. And all I could think was: I'll never be able to play euchre with the Poikonens, ever again. I could sure not tell Rosaleen what I had witnessed. Nor could I look Finn in the eyes straight on.

So in the morning I go to the barn. As if it were all business-as-usual. But I had not slept a wink. I see Finn, and he looks like the aftermath of a tornado, which is why Rosaleen has these dark circles most of the time, and I say to him, casual as that, "Did you kill something last night?"

He says, "What?"

So I say it again.

And he says, "Oh, shit, Marguerite, we thought that you couldn't see us out of the big window."

"There's more windows than one," I say.

So he points to the wall back of him, and I near faint. They've got the skin pinned to the wall.

"You women," says Finn. "You got eyes in the back of your heads."

Then I see there is a spot, diamond shaped, in the heart of the skin, pretty dead center. I can see that even in the barn's shadows. I know that the Golden has not got a spot like that.

"Goat," says Finn. "Damned goat was making a pest of itself on our place. Ate the moss roses all summer. Rosie bitched about that. Then the goat starts in on the Steel-Saks, eats right through 'em. On garbage day, holy shit, you should have seen. Every week. So we're barbecuing the damned thing for dinner." He makes this gloat-face, like this was some great triumph.

I look in his eyes. They are pale, like the northern lights. "Goat," I say.

"Goat," says Finn.

I am thinking about all our euchre nights coming up. I am relieved that I'm going to be able to face Rosie and not have to hide Finn's crime. "Goat," I say, and I turn, and the light outside through the barn door is so bright that I squint, and I can't tell who's coming toward me.

Well, it's Norm. There is something about this boy I cannot figure. I guess that you have to have this kind of person on earth. You have got to have people who don't think too deep about things, so that work gets done. Norman will make a dandy accountant, I'll grant you.

The thing is, he will marry some girl from the University who thinks she is going to save him, who thinks there are deep places in him that the rest of the world hasn't seen. Poor girl, if she's not careful she'll drown in his shallows. About two and a half inches deep, but the bottom is dark as hell, dark, dark and I have to say kind of scary.

I have spoken to Rosaleen Poikonen about this. And, on a different occasion, to Enid Rife, that's Wendell's missus. I don't want to say, Enid Rife, Wendell's wife, because that will sound silly, and this was about the most serious talk I have had in my life. It is not the kind of thing you can talk about to everyone, and when you do talk about it you have to be careful to say it real casual, so they are not fearful they will be caught in a trap talking over forbidden things.

In this neck of the woods, people don't talk about things. They do things or don't do things, but they don't talk about thinking about things, and I always have gotten in trouble for that. Ever since I was small.

My mother would say, Uh-oh, Marguerite's thinking the Emperor's naked again. She would see that look in my eye, that I had got things figured out and was about to say something, and she'd warn me off. I would listen sometimes. Mostly not. I'm surprised I survived.

Papa'd hit me when I would say something too really outrageous and Mama would not back me up, because she'd warned me off. But I figured I would rather have a black eye than have truth fester down in the heart of me. She meant the Emperor in that kids' story, the one who was naked and went out parading bare-assed, but the whole country lined up along the streets watching him just would pretend things were normal.

So I said things like, Mama, why'd Papa go in to the court yesterday? And she'd glower and knot up her forehead and I would get hit later, by either one of them, over some other thing, maybe a dustball beneath my bed. Papa would go to court for his drinking, or one time I am pretty sure it was over a servant girl from one of the houses down the road who had got pregnant and Papa had probably done it. I didn't say anything that time. I valued my life.

So when I married Jesper I thought that I had it made. Out of that craziness. But it's like they say, out of the frying pan, into the fire. Which is what we were talking about, Rosaleen and me, Enid and me. We could not have talked about the thing between all of the three of us sitting together.

It was last December. And December is when they are finished with all of this two-weeks-of-camping-and-butchering foolishness, but there is still hunting going on. December is when they are baiting.

And what that means is this. You have your snow on the ground and of course all your deer are out looking for something to eat, and whatever is down in the grass is hid good, for the winter. So Finn and Jesper had gone to town in the pickup to load up on bait. They came back with the bed of the pickup piled way high with sugar beets, carrots, and corn.

I don't know how they can get so tender about something they are about to kill, but when I say to them, why do you go to the trouble of setting the deer up a salad bar, why don't you just get a whole load of corn or of carrots or beets, they just look at me like I am nuts.

I say, well, you are going to kill them. They look at me odd again. There is no talking to them. When I see the deer out in the field, they are so really beautiful. Just the way they arch their necks, the way the sun hits their backs and lights up their spots, the way you can see them listening, smelling. You think nature is something.

I say that to Jesper and he will agree with me. Yep, he says, they are beautiful animals. Then he will go straight from that to talking about how good Judd Orley is with a knife.

Judd is the person they bring their deer to when they're not in their bloody barn-orgy time. Judd does six hundred deer every season. His wife Lacey works with him—he made her quit her job at Thrifty Acres to do it—and they've got this son Jerry George who would be playing football, that's how he is built, and the coach at the high school is furious but Judd won't hear of it, and Jerry George does it, too. They are up to their elbows at least in deer blood. Jerry George skins and quarters and Lacey does wrapping and freezing and then Lacey's sister Ruth Ella comes in in the afternoons to do the bookkeeping.

Judd's got contempt for the amateurs. "Waste," he says. "Waste, waste, waste. I could take what they throw away and make enough venison sausage to feed the whole Lower Peninsula." I pity Lacey, but then we are all in the same boat, the wives.

What I said to Enid—we were making Christmas balls, Styrofoam globes that you stick kind of shish kebabs of beads and sequins into and it looks real peculiar until you have enough of them to be nearly covering the thing and then it gets to looking real pretty. Though I've got to say I get truly bored doing it every December, damned shish kebab, shish kebab, and our tree's more cram-packed every year. We seem to be cutting them smaller and smaller since our girls are grown. But I guess it's a ritual we've got to go through or it wouldn't somehow be Christmas.

What I said to Enid was this: I said, Enid, did you ever think it would come to this, shiny and perky as we were in high school? Remember? How we used to listen to songs like "Begin the Beguine," and they sounded so good, though we never did know what the hell a beguine was. We thought we would like to begin one. Remember the sky, how it hung just as blue as that over the high-school football field, and we had crushes on boys who already are dead of two heart attacks? Remember the way we would roll down the cuffs of our socks thick as bakery rolls, and those socks so white-bleached they would glow in the twilight, the same socks the kids today are picking up again? Did you ever think it would come to us sitting here sticking these pins in these Styrofoam balls, making breakfasts of deer testicles? Did you?

Enid got this scared look in her eyes. It was funny. She looked around, there in my kitchen, like Wendell and Jesper had bugged the place, or maybe the FBI. She looked at the toaster. She looked at the Tupperware tray full of all-colored sequins that we two were threading on pins, doing shish kebab, shish kebab. She looked at the buttons lined up on my new Osterizer—blend, whip, puree. She just wiggled one eyebrow as if to say Lord, Marguerite, you are tempting the gods. But it was like she was saying yes, that she understood.

Then when she did start to talk it was like a dam burst. She said, Marguerite, do you know when I was in Holy Innocents Hospital three years ago? You remember, you brought me the Russell Stover French Chocolate Mints and I swore I would not eat a single one and then within two days I'd had the whole box, sixteen ounces, loving it all the way?

Well, that was not just a D & C. Wendell had brought a disease home from some prostitute up in Aubuchon, you know, up near the Soo, where his brothers have got their hunting cabin. That whole town is just filled up with prostitutes who come in just for the deer season.

Well, I was shocked for a minute, but I thought, why should I be? This whole thing is something I never will understand.

And then I recalled when I got crab lice from Jesper and that must have been the same thing, and me never suspecting. That was hunting season, too.

So Enid said she had this inflammation, that it wasn't some natural thing, which is what we had thought at the time. This is one of those things you don't talk about.

And I already had talked to Rosaleen, saying the same kind of thing. It was just a week earlier, and we were making the Jell-O molds for the Lodge supper, seven of them, blackberry, two kinds of red, lemon, orange, and Rosaleen's cola-flavored mold, which is the hit every time so we made two. I said Rosaleen, I said, would you do it all again if you knew then what you know now?

And there was that look in her eye, that kind of yellow flicker that looked like it feels when you're trying to dig out a splinter with alcohol and the bare tip of a needle and you hit a nerve. And the look said no.

Rosaleen made her lips into a funny shape, though, like a rosebud, and I'll swear for just half a second she looked like those pouty photographs of Marilyn Monroe if you'll remember, and I thought how Marilyn Monroe had died before she had to get middle-aged like the rest of us, though I guess that she had lots of her own kind of pain. Rosaleen's lips said, I might, Marguerite. You can never say what you would do. I could see that she wouldn't go far with this, but I'd heard what I needed to. That was so much more than we'd ever said before, knowing each other for all these years, too.

But then Rosaleen didn't stop. She said: You know, I have seen things I could not have made up. Not then and not now. You remember when we had that foster girl living with us? The one you used to say would be pretty if she had a couple of her bottom teeth pulled because she had too many teeth for her jaw, like a jostling crowd at the state fairgrounds? You remember she didn't stay long. I was real fond of that girl. But I had to say to the state, take her back.

I found these stains in her bed. From Finn. Not all the way, understand me. I talked to the girl. It was so hard, the hardest thing, talking to her. He would just rub against her back, singing her that little song about bears on a picnic, and she would lie still and she didn't tell me because it wasn't half as bad as what had happened to her at the last place she was and she wanted to stay with us. She loved our cats: Maxie, the calico; Flabber, the one with the broken tail. And she wanted to learn to make pies from me. She'd just go wild when I made the crust. We'd squinch the border all scallopy in between thumb and forefingers, and she'd say, Oh, Miss Rosaleen, this is so beautiful, this is so fun. She was just ten, near eleven, but I had to send her away.

And that all was when he was drunk, too. They have all been drunk all of these years, on their liquor or in that state that they get in all the rest of the time when they are on some planet a million years off in the universe. Why did we marry them?

Neither of us said a thing after that. You could feel that damned question, like breath, hanging thick in the air. We just laid out the Jell-O molds neat as you please on these bright, bright green beds of leaf lettuce, and I know that I thought about that question long and hard. I was looking I guess like I was kind of dreaming, just standing there half kind of jiggling the Jell-O, just shaking the plate, staring hard at the pieces of walnut and cherry suspended there, caught. Rosaleen laughed at me. And her question just shuddered and quivered between us, like Jell-O.

I do know why I married Jesper. I married the man for these cherry-wood windowsills, which I have got, and now that I've got them I'm too old to want what I should have been wanting or saying I wanted the whole time, long years ago.

Now this thing that they do in the barn, with the blood and the damned country music and all of the whiskey and Norm and his beady, small, terrible eyes, they don't do this the first of the season. They wait till the second week. Don't ask me why. To build frenzy or something, which they for sure do.

But the very first day of the season I went for an overnight trip with Jesper to this town where he deals with a lumber mill. We had a room that cost seventy dollars a night and a carpet as thick as you please in a color like batter with cinnamon. There was soap in the bath with the hotel's initial, not Dial or Ivory but something that smelled like I would imagine it smells in Carolina in spring. Jesper just went to sleep on me. What else is new.

In the morning it rained, and it poured and it rained, and he said that we had to get home before lunchtime, regardless. So we started out, driving in that rain, sheeting down, pouring down, you could hardly see, bumper to bumper out on the damned Interstate, all the cars traveling sixty in spite of the weather and nobody able to think about slowing down.

All of a sudden, just flash out of nowhere, there was a truck right in front of us, big white tractor-trailer with signs on the back that said just how much taxes it pays every year, so that us cars should be properly humble, and that truck hit a deer.

Crazed, it was, that's how those deer get the first of the season. The hunters come into the woods in their orange fluorescent gear. Not for the deer because they are all color-blind, but for each other because they are all drunk and will shoot at anything moving. Unless it is orange.

So here comes this deer, flying into the highway in terror, and here comes this truck, and it hits this crazed deer and I saw it all in a split second, the deer coming flying around the truck, tossed from the front in one sweep, flung, and here it is smack in our path and the rain's sheeting down and there's cars tight in both lanes on either side of us and no place to swerve and I did have to give it to Jesper, he did the right thing. I think I would have panicked and tried not to hit the thing, which would have probably killed us, and there was the deer, in the middle of dying and would've died anyway. Jesper aimed straight for it.

Here were the legs flailing high in the air, like a milkweed pod or one of those ceiling fans everyone's starting to put in their houses like it was the old days, and he aimed dead straight at the deer.

I heard a gasp—it was me—and then a clunk and we were over the deer and past it, like it was a thing made of paper. It dented the grille and the five-point hood ornament—Jesper drives Plymouths—and I guess the legs hit the door on Jesper's side because there was a crumpling-in afterward, when we got out and looked.

And I imagine the cars behind us just went over it one by one, gasp and clunk, and the poor deer thinking what had its life in the green forest come to, if it could still think, and I think that it probably could. The rain sheeted and poured and I stared at the door on the back of the white truck in front of us, not saying anything at all to Jesper.

Its sign was square-lettered, stark black, and said Rudde Egg Distributors, and I was thinking really peculiar things, life-and-death weirdness. I thought: there's more ways than one you can distribute an egg, and this deer was a deer-egg once. Deer-egg! I really did think that. And then I was doing this figuring in my head: how many dozens of eggs there could be in that truck, maybe hundreds of dozens, and not a one broke, and the deer in the highway still dying behind us. We didn't talk. Jesper just clicked on the radio and he kept driving.

There is noise in the barn now. I guess Norm has come back with one more deer, and the commotion and blood will start up again. They've been quiet all morning.

I think, when I really consider, that I cannot stand this mess one more damned year. Next November I think I'll take Mother down South to Orlando where we have a friend who's halfway between the ages of her and me. She has got a big condo she rattles around in since her husband died, but she's happier. He was in lumber, too. I don't know what they all do down in Florida except to wear gold-leather house slippers set with jewels out to the grocery, and wait to die. But we could spend the whole two weeks there.

Then again, I would be worrying myself nauseous about my house. What would these assholes do? Tear the whole place apart? Trail blood across the ceramic tile, into the grout, on the carpets and wiped, like that Manson thing, like it was towels, all over the living-room drapes? Smuggle whores in from Aubuchon? Fill my whole house with crab lice and God knows what all? It is dreadful to think of. But the peace and the quiet, they just might be worth the price.

I cannot think any more about that single question that keeps coming back to my mind, which is, if this is for these fools like some pagan sacrifice, spilling this blood to their dumb gods, what is it all saving us from, and could it be worse than this?

I think I will go over to Rosaleen's to see her Golden, real casual, pet the thing—back of the neck, where those two fragile, wonderful bones are, and on its sweet ears, hanging down like good corn silk—just to reassure myself that everything is okay. As far as anything can be okay. And I might or might not tell her what I thought I saw. We have talked once, really talked, and I think she could take it.

Salvaging

Maddy sat in the spot in her office where she could see everything. She rolled her silver-wheeled, green-seated ancient chair
back from the desk, back from the window. She set up her TV
tray with the view of Notre-Dame Cathedral—in her mind she
called it a "vue," as if to discount her dreams as touristy. It was
surrounded by mini-"vues": bookseller, Left Bank of Seine; châ-
teau country; Mont-St.-Michel. Maddy had not been to France.
Whit did not want to go anywhere, though he did not say this:
there was always a problem at Midwestern Verities, or somewhere else, that prevented them. Three times she had put de-
posits on bargain fares—first class, at that—and three times she
had had to cancel. Her vacation time was not re-schedulable.
He shrugged and kissed her and said next year.

She took out her perfectly boiled eggs and cracked them with
some delight. She had packets of salt and pepper and ketchup
she had saved from odd meals at Wendy's. She laid them out.
She unwrapped the foil from her fat, moist piece of corn bread.
Kernels of actual corn and fat pieces of walnut protruded. She
peeled the foil cap from her pout-lipped glass bottle of papaya
juice. She felt whole and substantial.

She looked out her old, dark-varnished windows, out of the third floor of Nygren Humanities Building, and saw and heard that it was a normal day on the campus. Students sauntered and scurried, with huge silky packs like strange peddlers. A couple of mangy dogs romped, their last fling before winter. A dark young man with several braids or odd locks of hair, but wearing a scrubbed look and a three-piece suit, was out by the fountain's perimeter, shouting at passersby.

Something about the harangue, which had volume enough to carry to her third-floor windows, closed, sounded vaguely religious. Or, rather, millennialist. Maddy thought the two impulses probably were opposite. Millennialists had a self-destruct impulse, the thrill at the sound of the hooves of the horsemen, that she could not stomach. She wanted the world to go on and on. On the other hand, she had had two Jehovah's Witnesses on her porch for over an hour one day putting forth their views of what would happen after the end of the world, and she was fascinated. It had been summertime, and Maddy had brought out lemonade.

"The good stuff? With the pieces of lemon?" Whit had complained. "Why do you put up with them? It's our house. We don't have to be victimized."

"Everybody has got some shred of the truth," Maddy said. "They believe heaven will be on earth. I'll buy that."

"Holy shit, Maddy," Whit grumbled. "The *fresh* lemonade?"

"They think heaven is just earth perfected," she said. "Of course, they're real selective about who gets in, and that's all prearranged, and I'll bet heathens like us are not on the guest list, but I think it's interesting."

Down at the fountain, the young man seemed not to be tiring. The students passed by unconcerned, none engaging in banter. This man was too serious, would tie you up for hours. Maddy cracked an egg happily on the roof of Notre-Dame, rolled it, peeled it. She dipped it in salt. She picked up the morning's newspaper.

On the front page there was a wide-angle view of the Keziah Piers Beeton Young Ladies' Gymnasium. The headline said BEETON GYM TO FALL TO WRECKING BALL. Maddy stopped with her egg in midair. It was a perfect egg, with its white silken sheen curved like love in the noon light: the salt crystals clung wonderfully. Maddy said it aloud: "Beeton Gym!" She set down her egg, which began rolling around the cathedral tray as if with a life of its own. She went to the phone and she dialed.

"Renovators' Delight," came the brisk answer.

"Well," she said. She did not know where to begin. "This is Madeleine Vreeland. Your man at the front desk—the one with the beard—okay, they all have beards, I didn't know that. Anyway. Your man at the front desk promised me you would give me a call when you were getting ready to tear down the Beeton Gym. Now here I see in the paper it's coming down today. I had been promised a bunch of oak flooring."

She listened. "You don't have the contract? I have to do what?" She watched her egg lurch around her tray as if it were in the labyrinth of a pinball machine. She wondered if the room leaned. She picked up the egg and bit into it, to stop the lurching. "Okay," she said, spraying pale powdery yolk as she talked.

She put down the phone and stood scowling out onto the campus. The angry millennialist was still calling down doom; the dogs pulled at the baby coatsleeves of teasing freshman boys; someone walked by with an enormous silver radio whose music sounded like a giant slush pump, a-chook-a-chook, drowning the fountain fanatic out.

Renovators' Delight had lost out on the gym demolition contract! She cracked her other egg and peeled it in a quick, slap-dash, frustrated motion, gouging the perfect white. Renovators' Delight was the only place she knew to get good old used architectural salvage, and, damn it, she needed a floor. For her ceiling. She ate her egg in two large bites and felt herself rocking with impatience. She had to get down there and dicker with these folks who were tearing down the gym.

Maddy was not a scrounger, she was not street-smart, but she had learned, in restoring the old house that she and Whit had bought two years ago, that a quick eye and a feel for the creative make-do were what that fool enterprise called for. Their kitchen ceiling had been opened up now for months with its new insulation, like candy-pink whale flesh, exposed. She wanted wood there, but new wood, besides being too expensive, would have looked out of place, raw. So she had been counting on buying up worn-out gym-floor planks, and sanding them gorgeous.

She bolted the juice and rewrapped the corn bread and threw on her jacket. She did not need to leave a note for anyone. Her next class (the freshmen, her wonderful, wearying freshmen) did not start until four. So she closed her door and headed off across campus.

The new science complex, looking Spacelab-like with its expanses of mirrored glass, astonished her as she passed it. These things went up so fast. She could not remember what had been on that spot of ground before, just last year. There was a burnished brass plate by the wide front door. Glazer Memorial Natural Science Complex, it read.

She considered the notion of having a building named after oneself: Beeton, Nygren, and Glazer had all been real people, connected in some way with the college, no doubt: grateful alumni/alumnae, or professors who had won some long-ago lottery. She constructed a fantasy building named after herself— a twenty-first century humanities center, looking rather appropriately like the Tower of Babel—then stopped dead as she put up its plaque: she did not like having Whit's name anymore and felt sheepish about that. Her old surname, her father's name, did not work either. She decided to call it the Maddy-Was-Here, and to leave it at that.

Up ahead was the Beeton Gym. It was an old building, brick browned with age, sitting on a grassy trapezoid of land. Old trees surrounded it and shed their leaves copiously. Despite her civilized teaching shoes, she scuffed happily across the lawn through the orange and brown piles. There was something about this building that was the essence of everyone's quintessential/ archetypal grade school: the old, sweet smell of urine and chalk and the feel of worn wood and air damp with the breath of long-dead generations of students. In front of the gym was a white construction trailer with a makeshift sign that said Rocco Bracci and Sons. There seemed little activity, otherwise.

Maddy entered the open front door. The old building was all shadows. "Hello?" she called. "Hello?" There was a soft clunk somewhere in the darkness. A teenaged girl wearing a white hard hat stepped out into the doorway's bright sunlight. Black letters across her hat spelled out Lee Anne.

"Hmph?" said Lee Anne. "You looking to buy up a piece?"

"Beg your pardon?" said Maddy. She was not quite into the idiom.

"We're selling off parts of this here gym," Lee Anne said. "Me and my pop. You want to buy something?"

"I had made arrangements with Renovators' Delight. . . ."

"Them," Lee Anne sniffed. She was a delicate-looking girl, blond of a shade that looked slightly helped-along. Her hard hat intensified the delicate effect of her features. "Number one, they did not get the contract. We did."

"They had said they would call me about a gym floor," Maddy said.

"Too late, hon," Lee Anne said. She said "hon" as if she were trying this gruff manner on. Maddy briefly wondered if she had wandered into an audition for a movie called *Demolition Dames*.

"Beg your pardon?" said Maddy again. She was feeling disconnected from the conversation. A dark bird flew through the hall not two feet over her head. "The floor's sold?! Already? The whole thing?"

"Bet your sweet," said Lee Anne. Maddy decided to give her the part in the movie.

Maddy wanted to cry. Her kitchen ceiling gaped whale blubber. Where would she find wood to close it up?

"Lots of stuff not gone," Lee Anne said. "Not too many folks here yet. You look around," she said. "Hon."

Maddy wanted to ask her to can the audition, to tell her she had the part, but it looked as if Lee Anne was controlling the operation, and that this was where her bread would be buttered, if it would be buttered anywhere. "You have extra flashlights?" Maddy asked. "I did not come equipped."

"I got this one and that is it," Lee Anne said. "Give you five minutes, no more. I got work to do." She handed Maddy the flashlight.

Maddy took it and went off down the hall. She could not resist muttering under her breath, to finish Lee Anne's sentence, "Hon." She turned on the flashlight and sent its beam scraping out silently through the dark.

The building had not been in use for several years. There were cobwebs on a grand scale. The first floor of the gym had a hall lined with classrooms and meeting rooms. Maddy looked into these quickly with her borrowed flashlight. The beam stroked oak panels, all around the room. Maddy's heart leapt as she thought of the possible uses. She hurried on to the next room. The beam of the flashlight lit vertical beveled oak planks. Maddy caught her breath, switched off the flashlight, and turned to run back after Lee Anne.

She passed a staircase leading up to the balcony of the gym. Two lions of oak guarded the curved lower end of the banister. Each had a paw raised, the paw that was nearest the stairs. Their carved blind eyes were wild; their manes blew in invisible breezes; their mouths were opened in identical roars, their oak canines exposed in mute majesty. "Lions!" she said aloud.

Lee Anne was showing someone into the large open gymnasium, where there was light streaming in through the old white translucent sky-windows. She turned. "Got the flashlight," she said. It was more an order than a question. The girl was enjoying her job: this was clear.

"Got the flashlight," said Maddy. She felt like a raw army private. She did not want to cross Lee Anne: Lee Anne held the power. "I know what I want," Maddy said, hoping she sounded authoritative, hoping that prices would be within reach.

"What you want," Lee Anne echoed. "Yeah, I'm taking cash," Lee Anne said. "No checks. Me and my dad are from Houston, and we don't need no checks."

Maddy named her desires: the panels, the beveled planks, and, oh dear God, were the lions sold? She had no idea what she would do with the two lions, and something in her felt as if she were participating in some vague obscenity, looting this gym. No, they all were clear, Lee Anne said. She took out a calculator.

"Damn this here thing," Lee Anne said. "It's solar." She walked to the doorway where there was sun. "Anyway, about light," she said, "we'll have light in here tomorrow. They got the electrical back on, as of tomorrow, just until we're done." In the wide, high gymnasium, footsteps knocked, hollow, across the broad floor. "Let's see. Panels are ten each; the bevels are, oh, I will give you the room for say seventy, which is like a buck a foot as you walk it around; and the lions, I'd say thirty each."

Maddy gaped in astonishment. Thirty each for the lions, magnificent as they were? She had an impulse to tell Lee Anne she certainly could get more. "Sold," she said. She was gleeful and deadpan. "But no checks, you say?"

"Nunh-unh, pardner," said Lee Anne. "We come here from Houston."

Maddy looked around. On the panels of the hall walls, in deep shadow, were pieces of scrap paper taped up with dark, shiny tape. The papers said SOLD TO this person or that; they said PAID in fat felt-pen letters that were certainly Lee Anne's, a fat, round, fifteen-year-old's scrawl. "You need cash," Maddy said. At the door, a group of students came wandering in. Scroungers, scavengers. What did they want with her lions? Maddy thought desperately. She did not have cash on her. She felt her hands suspended half-away from her sides, tapping and flicking at the air for an answer. This felt very Wild West. We are making the rules as we go along, she thought.

"Come on, come on," Lee Anne said. "I got to take these here folks around."

"Take my watch," Maddy said. "It's worth more than that. You hold it. I'll be right back. Got to run to my money machine."

"Take your watch?" Lee Anne said, for a moment incredulous. She held her hand out to cup it up as Maddy proffered it. "A watch?"

"I'll just post these things sold. Right?" said Maddy. She hoped she sounded confident.

Lee Anne shrugged and went about leading the new folks through. Her voice trailed behind. "You want chandeliers, hon, we got chandeliers. Right this way."

Maddy saw, in the gritty and swirling dirt of the hall floor, the tablet and the tape. She taped SOLD TO MADDY across the face of each oak lion. On each panel—she felt a possessiveness seeping up through her—on each single panel she taped another; in the room with the bevels she posted two SOLD TO MADDYs on each wall.

She ran to the bank across campus. She ran back. She paid Lee Anne cash. ("Since you're from Houston," she said in her head as she counted out tens.) She stood spinning with something she worked hard at naming, a hot and diffuse exultation: she named it scavenger's lust.

She taught her four o'clock with childish dust all up her forearms, streaked by water she used in washing her hands. She was fraught with joy. At five-fifteen, packing her briefcase with one hand and eating the leftover corn-walnut bread with the other, she suddenly thought: how will I do this? She said the words out loud: "How will I do this?"

Whit was gone, to Chicago. This was not the sort of project he would have been thrilled over, even if he had been here. Recently, the house had become Maddy's project. Whit was flush with success. Whit was buying new shoes every week, it seemed. Leather, with gold-stamped names inside, beneath his feet. Whit had a car phone. A cellular car phone, whatever that was. The thing sounded organic. He had, in the middle of the den—which had been the kitchen at one point in this house's history, to judge from the pipes that they found in the walls— a sleek Finnish rowing machine. He had been urging Maddy to sell, to move out to a subdivision where the houses cost three times what this one would go for, and five times what they had paid for it.

"Who wants to live in a place called Fox Meadows?" said Maddy. "For real. There are no foxes. And it is hardly a meadow."

Whit answered, she thought somewhat archly, "Well, Indian Village,"—where they lived now, a section just west of downtown, old German tradesmen's homes, turn of the century—"is hardly rife with tomahawks and tepees."

"But it's real," Maddy said. The area had been named after an Indian village there. Traces of it were preserved in the park down the block.

"Real, schmeal," Whit said. "You know what I think is real? Real drywall. None of this old plaster stuff. Real paved driveways and real air-conditioning. That's real."

Maddy sighed. There had been such zest in the start of this house: it had been their joint project, a project with all the emotional freight of childbearing without the entirely eternal implications. Practice, maybe? Maddy loved the house; Whit, it seemed, no longer did. Whit was out of this. Maddy could not get the wood and the wonderful lions by herself. Who could she hire?

* * *

At home, she stood in the shower and let her dust run down the drain. Water freed her thoughts. There was a carpenter, one they had had for the master bedroom, when Whit decided he had had enough of this hands-on stuff. She would call him.

Still dripping, she phoned. He was busy. But he had a friend. He would call him. He called. He called back. Yes, the friend was free. Here was his number. It was a toll call, some distance away, in a town named Moscow. The friend's name was Obed, stark, biblical. Yes, he could come. With his tools. He would meet her. The morning. The gym.

She called Whit. He was not at his motel. He did not call her. She wrapped her robe tightly about her and walked the house drinking Scotch, standing under the cotton candy of the kitchen ceiling insulation and staring. She walked, feeling under the soft of her slippers the smooth floors she herself had sanded—with Whit, before he lost interest—with the huge and unwieldy U-Rent-'Em sanding machine, a wild bull of a thing that could eat through soft wood in a minute. You had to be careful, keep moving. She walked and she rubbed her hands over the smooth-sanded plaster beside the fireplace: in the front hall, the tiny guest bathroom that once was a pantry.

She padded upstairs and phoned Whit again. His extension rang ten times, twelve times. He worked lots these days. Loved it. Success, he kept saying, you can't beat it. He thumped his chest as if he were on the bow of a boat cutting through Puget Sound's onyx-blue waters, as if he were breathing perfect air. Maddy emptied her glass and thought vaguely that drinking alone like this was not advisable. Her brain was thinned with the Scotch. She lay down and slept.

The phone rang, startling her awake, near midnight. It was Whit.

"Two major sales today," he said. "The Conner account and the Mac-A-Way. What do you say to that?"

"Good," she said. "I was asleep."

"I'll be gone for an extra week," he said. "The people in Indianapolis need a review. . . ." He sighed with a kind of resigned bliss.

"Guess you're indispensable," Maddy said.

"Pretty much," Whit said. She heard no regrets.

"They are tearing down Beeton Gym," Maddy said.

"What?" Whit said. "That was a switch."

"I was going to get a wood floor from there," Maddy said. "For the kitchen ceiling."

"Uh-huh," Whit said.

"There is this fifteen-year-old girl," she said, "supervising things. I have reserved a couple of rooms' worth of wood, and two oak lions. . . ."

"I'm losing the thread of this," Whit said. "You're sleep-talking, Madeleine."

"No," she said. "I've hired a carpenter to help me get the stuff out. He is coming, with crowbars and what-all. I'm canceling classes tomorrow."

"I've heard you right?" Whit said. "You're canceling classes? The gal who could not cancel classes if God Almighty came to town. . . ."

"If you're talking about that guy with the cigars that you wanted me to go out to lunch with so you could wheel him and deal him, forget it," said Maddy. "That guy was not God Almighty. If God smoked cigars, they would not smell like that."

"Hey, babe," said Whit. "That guy is where our bread is buttered."

"Anyway," Maddy said. "That is all my news."

"And that is mine."

They clicked off with good-nights like a news team. Maddy watched the leaves flutter out front around the streetlight. Maddy watched for an hour, and fell asleep propped on her elbow, and woke with a crick in her neck.

Obed Grant had a beard that looked like it had rusted. His eyes were quick. He was at the gym before Maddy got there, before even Lee Anne was there with her clipboard and fat wallet.

"What do we do?" he said. He was ready. Maddy measured herself beside him. He was less tall than Whit, but more solid. She would pay him, and he would not lose interest and go off to Chicago and Indianapolis.

Lee Anne came and unlocked the gym doors. Inside, things had changed since the evening before. Things were already being hauled away: cabinets from the old classrooms, steel lockers, light fixtures were stacked in the hall. Maddy had a sense of being in on the reversal of the first days of creation, as if this dismantling were primal.

She had new work gloves. She had the sense Obed Grant would think she was a sissy. "I've done this before," she said. "I'm a hard worker. Don't let the gloves fool you."

Obed Grant was a taciturn sort, but he made a you-show-me smile.

They worked together until lunch. Around them, the building was coming apart in small pieces. There were people on the stairs, taking the banisters down; there were people unhinging the huge oak doors to the main conference room; there were people un-plumbing the fifties- or sixties-vintage water fountains. It was plunder time.

She passed by the stairs to go out for a sandwich for herself and one for Obed Grant. Someone was fondling the nose of one of her oak lions. She felt like a child, possessive. She guarded her voice as she said it, but she said it anyway: "That's my lion."

Coming back with the sandwich, she heard in passing a conversation between kibitzers, corduroyed, briefcased, out front of the gym. It seemed this sudden demolition had been a move on the part of the college to avoid a play by local preservationists to save the gym. Tear the thing down quickly was the idea, before they can stop us. And why? Maddy asked the question in her head and the kibitzers answered.

"Whenever you see something like this," K-1 said to K-2, "you look for the economic interest. Someone wants a contract for a new major building, someone wants a building named after himself, you move fast, circumvent."

"Ho, a cynic," said K-2.

"This is the real world," said K-1. Overhead, the leaves blew in a sudden gust and came down in a bright shower of orange. Maddy shivered and strode past with three sandwiches. Obed Grant looked as if he could use two. In the front hall, someone was lifting her SOLD TO MADDY sign to see the lion's face.

"Hey, that's mine," Maddy said. "Please don't."

The kid—a pale, wild mutant sort—turned and stared. "Touch your lion? Oh, babe, touch your lion? I wouldn't. Not me." He rolled his eyes. Maddy was used to these guys wearing earrings, but this one was wearing an earring the size of a Christmas-tree ornament. Maddy mustered her tolerance. Smiled.

The boy waved a gold metal fingernail at her. He lifted the sheet from the lion's face—now the tape was detached—and caressed its nose with his gold talon. "Nice pussy," he said. He tossed back his hair.

Maddy brought Obed the sandwiches. "I saw a kid," she said. "Messing with my lion. I got paranoid. I must be getting old."

"Good sandwich," Obed said. "You point the kid out to me, Mrs. Vreeland. As we used to say in Nam, one more time and we call in the choppers, we bring in an air strike. Pure surgical."

Maddy laughed nervously. This was a chivalry new to her, but she was not sure she cared to deflect it.

They worked through the afternoon. Three-thirty brought the low shadows of fall, and Obed laid his crowbar aside—he had been working first on the beveled boards Maddy had chosen to replace the lost gym floor, a clearly superior option anyway—and began carting them to his truck. It was a neat truck, just a few years old, no rust. Obed Grant was an orderly person.

Maddy carted along with him. She had gotten her new gloves

respectably softened and dirtied, she noted with pride. She lugged and stacked for over an hour. It was nearly five now, and the truck was loaded and ready. Obed Grant ordered her to get in the truck's front seat, and she followed directions. She thought of her car in the faculty lot and it seemed an irrelevance. They had to get this wood back to her house and she had best ride here. Obed Grant was in the building now. Now he was out. He climbed into the driver's seat and started the motor up.

"I went in," he said, "and put a sign on your lions."

"And what did it say?" Maddy said.

"It said, KEEP YOUR HANDS OFF, SOLD TO MADDY, and it had enough tape to keep it there," Obed Grant said.

"Thank you," Maddy said. She thought of all her students who had been thrilled not to have class today, and she herself was thrilled, watching the long beveled boards in the truck bed behind them wave as they went over the railroad tracks halfway home. She felt rich with oak. She felt protected.

They ate dinner in her kitchen, looking up at the pink insulation and sharing a vision of what it would be like once the beveled planks were up. Maddy had thought, on the way home, that she might stop for Chinese-Hawaiian take-out, that she might ask Obed Grant to have some with her, but she argued herself down on that one. It seemed celebratory, and if it was celebratory of the project's end, it was premature: they were not yet halfway there. It seemed somehow a thing that she ought to call Whit and inform him of: Whit, I am having a carpenter in for dinner. She talked herself down on that one as well. Whit had his independence. She might carve herself some.

She made, instead, beef stew, out of a can that had a picture of beef stew on it. The beef stew on the can did not in any way resemble the mush that was inside. She made biscuits. She was shocked at the cozy, domestic air cooking beef stew from a can made. She felt at the same time wild, risqué.

She listened as Obed Grant talked of his love for wood. He went on at great length about hardwoods that he had known, and she was happy to listen. It was a whole world of qualities— grain, color, hardness—that she had not known. He said he had been here before once, been in on the party that brought the oak beam for the big bedroom's ceiling from Moscow, with his carpenter friend. Maddy remembered thinking that this was peculiar: going to Moscow for oak. She had thought the word Moscow as she lay in bed with Whit, looking up at that oak beam.

She thought she would have nothing to say to Obed Grant that would interest him. "I teach history," she said, anyway. "At the college."

Obed Grant said he had a degree in geography. He said that the college had been, a few years ago, pretty much tuned to reality when they had cut out geography. They had first absorbed it into another department, a one-celled engulfing amoeba, and then done away with it totally. He said there were no jobs in geography. He himself had not traveled to speak of. He had been to Nepal, on a trek, he said. He had been to Morocco and Hungary. Nothing more.

Maddy looked at the clock and she thought of the morning and sighed. "Lee Anne says she will open up early," said Maddy. "So we can make use of the light." It got dark early, now that the autumn time change had come. So it happened that Obed Grant stayed the night in the guest room. He showered and put his work clothes back on and was asleep early.

Maddy padded about the house in her old, baggy striped flannel pajamas. She thought of two things. First she thought that it might be the thing to do to call Whit now and say that Obed Grant was spending the night in the guest room, but that troubled her. So she went to her second thought, which was that she ought to get a cat. A cat could do her night prowling for her. She would require a fat cat, a lap cat, a long-haired vibrating cat that would lie next to her in bed and purr like a TV recliner her grandfather once had had, heat-filled and buzzy and comforting.

In the center of the den Whit's rowing machine sat, a shining thing under the track lights. Maddy slipped herself into the seat, Velcro-latched her feet into position, and grabbed the perfectly proportioned handles. She tried to think of what a rowing machine factory in Finland might look like. She had always thought everyone in Finland lived in saunas, beat each other to a stunning pinkness with soft-needled evergreen branches, and talked to their reindeer.

She rowed. She was a sixth of the way, now a quarter, and now a third, across the wide, cold Atlantic. She took her bearings, rowing, and thought that she ought to decide where she was headed. She thought of Whit and felt a sadness. She decided that perhaps she had best be flexible about her destination. There would be winds, after all, and who knew where she might wind up? She rowed till sweat dampened her pajamas' waistband and dripped from her forehead through her eyebrows into her eyes. She thought that perhaps she might be crying. She wiped with her flannel sleeve as she rowed. The nature of that salty moisture was neither here nor there. She kept rowing.

In the morning she told Obed Grant she had rowed to Gibraltar, and that it had looked just like an insurance company. Obed Grant laughed.

The second day of demolition took on a new, frantic air. The city inspectors had come in yesterday, in rather a huff, and declared that the whole crew—the children's crusade to whom Lee Anne had sold all the goodies—had, for safety reasons, to be out of here after tomorrow. Everyone seemed to be making the rules as they went along.

The real amateurs—students who never had wielded a crowbar, to whom the claw end of a hammer was mystical nonsense—were panicked. They went to Lee Anne making siren sounds. How would they do it? they whined. Lee Anne replied that they would just do it, tough. All of these people seemed to be either leisured or unemployed. Maddy did not have classes today, not until tomorrow afternoon. She hoped they would be finished by then. She was not such an amateur, and Obed Grant was hardworking, methodical, quick.

There was chaos. A fistfight broke out in the balcony that overlooked the old gym. Someone tumbled down over several tiers of seats and—rumor had it—was saved from the breakneck plunge onto the floor only by the old railing that lined the lip of the gallery. The fight was over a piece of wood molding that lined the juncture of the wall and the ceiling, way up where nobody could see. People said these things, dragging their booty down through the halls, and Maddy and Obed Grant, working away prying planks from the wall, overheard them.

Obed Grant thought that Lee Anne should have been there. He made a scenario in which she played Solomon. "That molding," he said, "is just egg-and-dart, your plain old egg-and-dart. I can see old Lee Anne: You take the egg, you take the dart, and you shut up, the both of you."

Maddy wondered where Rocco was. No one had seen the man, ever. Then there was a rumor that he had been seen indoors once and that now he was out on the grass apron surrounding the gym with the giant machines that were revving their engines and rearing back like dinosaurs at the ready.

"I guess he's off somewhere, running the show, like God," Maddy said.

"God isn't running the show," Obed Grant said.

His talk had the sound of an atheist's. Maddy liked atheists. They were the best kind of people, *right there,* and not needing lights at the far ends of their tunnels, content to live in the dark mole-moss of life without wanting more. She envied them their sureness.

Obed Grant read her mind. "No," he said, "I'm not an atheist. I just think mostly we're running the show. Or Lee Anne is."

There was more ruckus out in the hall. Maddy went out to see. People were dragging porcelain basins and painted bookcases and curlicued pieces of metal down the front hall toward daylight. The commotion was centered around the grand staircase that rose from the foyer up to the grand fistfighting balcony. The person who had bought the stair treads was ready to rip them out. Was, in fact, ripping them out. And the people who were going upstairs and downstairs were ready to string him up. Someone cried for Lee Anne, as for mama. Lee Anne came and said, "Y'all are on your own. You figure it out. No guarantees, hon. And no refunds."

Maddy looked at her lions, at the bottom of the grand staircase. The markered sheets of paper covering their faces seemed manhandled, as if they had been taken off and put on again a thousand times.

Two people came down the hall grunting, lugging a huge thing of metal and plaster. Maddy scooted around its front side to see what it was.

"Do you know what just passed in the hall?" she said. "The Great Seal of the College."

"Arf, arf," said Obed Grant, in between boards. He made circus-seal flippers of his wrists. He clapped.

They were finished with this room—the bevels—and loading it into the truck. "Second day," Maddy said. "It is good." And it was. They were finished with all of the hard part. The library panels were left, but they were by comparison easy. The lions would take almost no time at all.

Maddy stepped on a loose board and pitched forward. She landed hard on her forward foot, her right, and felt the pain. A nail bent up out of a board punctured her sneaker, broke the skin, went through the muscle and in between bones. She saw black light, then spirals of green. Obed Grant caught her, lifted her, set her aside on a rough wood box, and pulled the nail free. She cried out. People passed in the hall, dragging cabinet doors and huge industrial trash cans in the college's colors.

Two students labored along with a door so huge it would fit nowhere but in this gym. One called to Obed, "You got a truck, don't you? You give us a lift, just a couple of miles?"

"Ask Lee Anne," Obed said. He carried Maddy out to the truck and set her down. "I will get the last wood," he said, "or it won't be here when we come back. You'll be okay for a minute?"

The students came lumbering out with their door. "Just a couple of miles," they pleaded with Obed.

He looked disbelieving. Maddy expected a rising anger to break from his lips. He looked at the two men and said, simply, flatly, "Get lost."

They parked in the emergency-room lot. A sloppy October snow was beginning to fall. The fat, wet crystals piled on the wood in the rear of the truck.

"Got a tarp?" Maddy said.

Obed Grant looked at her oddly. "Your foot," he said. "Worry about your foot."

"But the wood . . ." Maddy said.

He was light then, and cavalier. "I'll put the tarp on while they're amputating your foot, Mrs. Vreeland."

The name sounded so stiff and formal. It did not sound like her at all.

"That's just Maddy," she said.

In the waiting room there were other pairs: one did not, it seemed, ever come to the emergency room alone. There were an elderly couple, a girl with her father, a pair of scraggly teenagers. There was no movement forward in this logjam of the injured: no one, it seemed, ever got called. There was some speculation as to what might constitute an emergency, and what one might expect if one had a truly dire injury.

"One time at these apartments where I lived," said the teen-aged boy, "there was a guy took a ax to his wife."

The elderly woman's eyebrows went up into her puffy white hair. Her lips pursed. "My," she said, "that would certainly be an emergency."

"Yeah, but she never got here," said the boy. "She died right on the walk, by the street. There is still bloodstains there."

"Well, you don't have to talk about it," said the girl.

"But she never got here," said the boy again. "So she was not a emergency."

Finally the jam broke. Obed Grant followed Maddy into the small examining room. She did not shoo him away. He sat quietly while they waited for the doctor. "I should have insisted on safety boots," Obed Grant said. "I should have said I wouldn't go in there with you if you didn't wear boots."

There was a tetanus shot and then an antibiotic prescription, and Obed helped Maddy back to the truck. The snow was wet and sloppy and Maddy worried about the wood. Obed assured her it would be fine. They stopped by Jimmy Wong's Maui Chow and got sweet-and-sour things in white paper cartons like the ones Maddy's guppies and black mollies had come in, years ago. It seemed that survival was something to celebrate.

After dinner, Obed offered to do laundry. Maddy gave him a pair of Whit's old sweats to wear. He took his clothes, thick with sawdust and the gym's sooty century's worth of dirt, and he took Maddy's, and went to the cellar and washed them. Maddy thought of their clothes sloshing around in the machine together. She thought of Whit in his hotel: his silky-backed vest, his tie loosened, the scent of the chase or the thrill of a victory fresh in his nostrils. She hobbled to the cupboard and made herself and Obed Grant each a Scotch. They toasted survival.

Obed Grant went to sleep early. Maddy went to her bookshelves and looked for something to read. She found it: a book called *The End of the World: A History*. Outside the window, the sloppy snow still fell. She sat on the sofa and read about the sack of Rome, the Black Death, the Inquisition, the Lisbon earthquake. The clock on the mantel chimed midnight. She sighed and closed her book. She passed the guest room on the way to the stairs. Her foot throbbed. The stairs looked high and formidable. She took a step back and opened the door to the guest room. Obed Grant slept. A yellow ribbon of light fell across his face. She stepped into the room and shut the door behind her. She sat on the edge of the bed in her clothes, with one slipper and one bandaged foot. She swung over and fitted herself, like a pewter spoon, into the calm curve of Obed Grant's sleep.

At the gym in the morning, it looked like the Last Judgment. There was shouting, the machines on the lawn pawed the earth as if impatient to devour something, there was word of an accident already, somewhere deep inside the gym. Maddy and Obed did not talk about the night's odd arrangement. They talked about their plan for the day. They would finish the panels quickly—that would go so much faster than the bevels had gone—and the last thing would be the lions.

Just inside the gym door there was chaos. People were dragging a giant and ancient wall clock through the hall. Its thin hands flapped against its greyed, glassless face. Maddy was sure it would never keep time again, after the move. She pictured it hanging huge and useless on some student's dorm-room wall. Such a waste, all of this.

At the bottom of the staircase, there were people arguing over some question of ownership. Suddenly, Maddy felt panic, a cool dribble upward of fear for her lions. She could see the lion on the left, its markered sheet flapping loose from its face, but the arguers blocked her view of the remaining lion. She stepped gingerly through the debris. She stepped past the crowd.

Gone. The right lion was gone. Where its oaken mane met the bottom curve of the long banister, someone had taken a chain saw to all of it and chewed out everything for two feet around the majestic animal. She closed her eyes and took a breath.

Obed Grant said, "Well, then." He got his tools. He worked. He had the remaining lion free in half an hour. "It must have taken them a minute and a half to rip out the other one," he said.

Maddy looked around for the young man with the earring. It could have been him, or it could have been anyone. Someone slipping in during the night, with a plan or on impulse. It did not matter now.

"Hold this," Obed said. Maddy settled herself on a box with the great cat propped between her legs. "This won't take the whole morning," said Obed Grant.

A city inspector came through with a clipboard shouting to everyone, anyone, no one, "Holy catfish! What do you people think you are doing!"

In the inner gym, there was a crash. Obed worked on and Maddy sat trapped by the weight of her lion. There were shouts for an ambulance, something about a back injury ("Don't touch that man!" an officious voice shouted).

Maddy's foot felt stiff and horrible. She thought of awful pictures she had seen in first-aid movies—when? in high school?—of gangrene and of massive infection and snakebite and tropic-mosquito diseases. She wondered if her foot, inside of its bandage, was still recognizable. She chided herself for that comic pity. She watched Obed's back as he worked the crowbar and she thought of the pewter-spoon curve of him. She thought of Whit, far away. She thought of their work clothes last night, snaking in a circle dance through the detergent suds.

"Downstairs!" came a cry. "You should see! And it's free! There are acres of marble! The shower stalls! All of it! Acres!" The girl ran on, a Paul Revere of the demolition.

Maddy looked over at Obed. "We're near done here," he said. "If you want to go and see. Couple of minutes." He finished the panels and stacked them and carted them out to the truck. Maddy sat with the lion. Obed returned and he picked up the lion, the size of a small child, and carried it with them down the broad stairs into the basement. Maddy hung on his elbow and hobbled.

Outside, there was a roar of machinery. The city inspector was upstairs shouting, "Good grief! Who ever okayed this?" The basement was indeed filled with huge slabs of white marble: shower stalls, toilet stalls, panels for no earthly purpose that Maddy could guess. Someone was unhinging a toilet-stall door with a kind of desperation; someone inside the stall was struggling with a wrench at the base of an old toilet shaped like a vase. These did not seem special, but they were free. Outside, the roar of machines increased.

"Acres of marble all right," Obed Grant said. "It must weigh six tons a sheet. Nobody's ever going to get this out of here."

Someone pried loose the hardware that held up a marble partition. It crashed to the ground and it lay there. Obed Grant looked at Maddy and shifted the lion on his hip.

There was a thud at the far wall. Then there was a crash, and the bricks shook. Someone ran to the barred windows that looked up to daylight.

"The wrecking ball! Jesus Maria!" the kid shouted.

And the ball came through the wall, not ten feet from the place where he stood. Brick dust flew, plaster powdered to ash in the air, windows on both sides of the impact point shattered instantly. The kid jumped back and ran.

"Clear out! Son of a—I say, clear out!" came the inspector's voice down the basement stairs.

Maddy and Obed trundled up the stairs with the foot injury, with the oak lion. Behind them, some students still struggled with slabs, with the toilet, with a long wall mirror that, wiggling free from the wall ("Hold it! Hold it!") reflected the chaos: the hole through the brick into daylight, the scavengers, Maddy and Obed's backs disappearing up the staircase.

The wrecking ball crashed again. The inspector came thundering down the stairs, shouting, "Out! Out!" Lee Anne was nowhere to be seen and Rocco, no doubt, was at the controls of the crane.

"Some people don't know when to leave," Obed said.

Maddy thought, with a sudden irrelevance, of Whit, his wheeling and dealing and wanting a house in Fox Meadows, where he could continue to leave her behind. She thought of the gaping whale flesh of her high kitchen ceiling. She would hire Obed Grant to close that up. She wondered if he had a life back in Moscow that would sleep between them tonight.

Maddy said, "And some people do."

Roadie

So the junkyard at I-96 and Michigan-696 is on fire. It's this kind of a dismal day where there is mist off the snow like the world can't decide if it wants to be winter or not. You can't figure why or how the flames leap up like they do, huge fireball whooms of pure orange, almost, with the way the air's so thick with wetness. It's tires burning, really, I guess. If we opened the windows, we'd get the petroleum-tire-skunk smell. But there's one thing this car has got and that's a good heater, so who wants to open the windows up even a little. I don't mind watching the junkyard on fire, shutting up for a minute. Ka-whoom.

So my mom is the star of this show, tonight. We are cool, you get my drift, we treat each other like adults. I have called her Rose since before I knew it was a flower, perfume-ish and delicate-petaled and, how you say, entirely incongruous on her. She calls me Silver, which is short for Jay Silverheels Riley, and if you don't know who Jay Silverheels is, he's the Indian guy on "The Lone Ranger." Tonto's real name. This is what it is like to grow up being one of the kids of the commune days. Those guys—Rose is one of them—would name you anything. There's a guy in my class, name of Stookey, named after some bell-bottom singer. I've got to ask Rose who that was, sometime.

The show is at Saquanac State College, up the Interstate some-where by several hours, this real backwater school where you go if you've got Cs and want to do tractor mechanic stuff, or learn to draw blood, or do typesetting. This is the first time she's been the big name, and of course it's all relative, this being Saquanac State. Once she opened for Willy Ray Brush, but you probably never heard of him either.

They have billed this gig just as Rose Riley. Not Rose Riley and her whatevers, but just Rose Riley, and that means the whole crew. They went through a time being Rose Riley and Her Five Thorns, which was after they were the Cement City Six. Cement City is where Fat Mariah, her bass player, came from. A real place. They play country and country-crossover rock, and they are not bad. Rose does the vocals. And she has got a voice.

I busted my hand one time—well, sprained it good—laying a guy out that started this shit that my mom was a butch, was a dyke, couldn't have had a kid unless she was the father. Well, they had to stitch up his lip. Rose is not what you call your most feminine type. She is not Dolly Parton. Not big on the makeup, not much in the bosom department, and no nonsense, any which way, but shit. I laid him out.

This car's a seventy-one. I guess you can estimate the rust. A Dodge, in that terrible green that they had. Sandy says we should junk it, but Rose says, why dig into our savings, there's little enough. Sandy is her boyfriend and she could do worse. The backseat is filled with guitars. Rose would rather spend money on them.

Sandy's got a great beard, and an eighty-six Jeep Cherokee plus a stake-side GMC, with Sandy Creek Log Homes stamped on this plastic sign on the door. He's gone partners with this buddy of his, just two or three months ago. Guy's a Creek Indian, which accounts for the name. I said that was too much. They've got three orders already, and I've got a job promised, come summer. I'll lift logs and come back in the fall looking like Stallone, but with a brain.

"Holy shit," Rose says. "Look at that junkyard on fire." We are right close up on it now, and the flames are shooting out like some grand catastrophe. Nobody hurt, you know that, just a grand sight, like fireworks. She turns on her tape machine, little cassette thing. She's got these old Patsy Cline tapes she's been studying since that movie came out and everybody's requesting those songs. Nothing like being famous when you are long dead.

"So you're off of school," she says. This is what she calls roadie hooky, when I get to go on gigs. "Still got to do your math. Hit the books now, and we'll have tonight free."

The flames make shapes like genies or giants. I wouldn't say that out loud, though. I'm sixteen. I watch till we pass, then watch out the back window. You wonder how fire keeps alive, in this dampness. I take out the Algebra II and Rose works on "Sweet Dreams." She's got this voice that fills the car. Real clear. Strong. She ought to be doing her own songs, get signed to some big record company. Stuff like that's random, I guess, partly. Rose is not real pushy for herself. That is another thing. But she is kind of tickled to do this gig, have her name up on the posters. She's thirty-six now. She ought to have something. All she's ever done is cashier at the Kroger's, and before that keep books for the chiropractor. What a waste.

I've got quadratics down pat. There is this girl sits next to me, Meggy Axelrod, real class, her father's some hotshot lawyer and probably a real asshole the way lawyers are, but she is real nice. She showed me some stuff. Tricks. I will get a good solid *B* this time. This girl has got *shiny* hair. Real. Not this mohawky, spiky stuff, garbage style, punk. I would like to make a move, but that's new territory for me. I have got to move out into it. Got to be more than Rose's kid and Rose's roadie. I keep feeling I've got to keep Rose safe. From what, I don't know.

We are into the country now. This has got to be the world's

least picturesque ride. Michigan is so flat here. God, I can't imagine these farmers. These acres and acres of wax beans or whatever the hell they grow, boring vegetables in mass quantities. White aluminum-siding houses, you can see their concrete-block foundations, the bushes all shriveled away for the winter. They've got wives that smell like Lysol, and plastic covers on their sofas. Their kids go wild.

Thank God all I've got is Rose and she's not a Michigan farmer. Sometimes she says wouldn't I like something to rebel against. I tell her she's it and that quadratics and Margaret Axelrod are my rebellion. I threaten to join Young Republicans. We get a good yuck out of that. I did have a father once, for a split second. Rose said that she never told him. Rose said she needed him like a hole in the head, and that I did, too.

Rose shuts off the machine. She is sucking some kind of a eucalyptus lozenge, but she never gets a sore throat, she just likes how they smell. We are passing a herd of Holsteins in the snow, black and white, black and white, huddled into the wind. It is real hot now, but you can't turn down the heater, so Rose opens up her window just a crack. You can smell the manure, even though it is winter. Her hair blows back, kind of crazy. She started going gray, early as I can remember, then went all the way white last year. Stark was the word. Then she put in something, I don't know what, so it almost looks blond. Not bad. I thought I'd never see that.

"Cow shit," Rose says. I agree. "Cows was country when country wasn't cool," she says, and we laugh. "I am going to do 'You Were on My Mind' tonight," she says. "Sandy's been ragging at me to do that."

"Shame he couldn't come," I say. I like Sandy along. He's had to go down to Dundee to pick up a snowblower. He took up with Rose early last year. He reads like you wouldn't believe. Anything. Book about Aztec blood sacrifice, book about cooking in Thailand. I meet him padding bare-ass down the hall sometimes in the middle of the night, and he makes this grin and calls back down the hall to Rose, "Yo, Rose." That's his Stallone imitation. "Young Republicans on patrol. Our goose is cooked."

We pass a water tower that's stenciled East Grapentine. We pass a field of cornstalks with their leaves still on. We pass a dark-frozen river. "God," Rose says. "I believe they should rename this place East Bleak."

"Damn snowblower," I say. Then I think: oops. I thought I was *thinking,* and there I was saying it out loud.

"Say what?" Rose says.

"Brain leak," I say. "Skip it."

"I heard you perfectly fine," Rose says. "What you mean is you wish Sandy was around day and night. Right? Well, he has got his life and I have got mine, son and darling."

I quick switch the subject. "He's been teaching me about R-values," I say. "About insulation. Did you know that Sandy Creek Log Homes have got the best ratings that you can get?"

"No prairie winds howling through, hey? No ghostly moans through the cracks. He paying you for doing his commercials?" Rose says. There is something about her tone of voice that sets up a distance, you know what I mean. Like she was nothing to Sandy and he was nothing to her.

I ignore that last bit. She is so rough and tough—I have got this all figured out—because she had to be. Drunk father put his fist into her face when she was seventeen, and she left. Graduated from high school by staying with some crazy friend for a couple of months. But that was it. She wants me to go on to college. I think she is secretly tickled I could get a scholarship, but she is cool about it. Like embarrassed that she doesn't have the bucks, twice as embarrassed that she never went herself. I could shake her sometimes. I could sing her the songs that she sings herself: "You got to play out the hand that life deals you, and honey, there ain't shame in that." This whole damn thing is upside down: like I'm her father, or sometimes I think I'm her mother.

"You aren't thinking of *just* working for Sandy Creek?" she says. "Because if you are you'd better get thinking another direction." You'd think she did not know me at all.

"Naw," I say. I just watch the roadside. It is sure as hell winter.

The greatest part of the gig is getting ready. *I* think. You get to the town in plenty time, you drop your shit at the motel, you go get some eats, you feel like a celebrity. Just getting ready to get ready. Then comes the sound check. One time back in grade school I went with a kid lived in the neighborhood to spend a day at his school. I thought, far out. This was a Catholic school. Now, there's not all the stuff like you read about, poker-faced nuns and like that anymore.

But they were having Mass that day, and when I think back I think that was probably the point, that this kid's mom said you take that hippie child to your school this particular day. I don't know what she expected: miracles? That I would beg Rose to send me to Holy Innocents with all the Brians and Mary Patricias in their little round-collared uniforms? Fat chance. But this kid that I went to the school with, he was an altar boy. I thought, far out. (Yeah, well this was the seventies.)

I got to go backstage with him while the priest and the altar boys got dressed up for the gig. Layers of clothes: a black layer, white layer, and then for the priest, for the cheese, a big poncho of gorgeous satin the color of—what was it?—like the color of the fire in the junkyard, because it was some kind of feast day.

I remember that he said that: feast day. Because I was pretty ticked—that, and like massively bummed—afterward thinking that we were going to get to chow down, have a feast. The whole time they were praying and singing I kept thinking of big, fat burgers from heaven and devil-mint ice cream (right, I thought that was kind of a cute joke myself, age of nine) that would be kind of lowered down into the church on a heavenly dumbwaiter.

Anyway, what was the point of this was that the getting-ready was astounding to me. The sense of something holy about to happen, and that you had to get your head humming for it, and get suited up some kind of way that made everything special. And that is what we do on gigs. There is this time before when you do the sound check, and this ritual where I get to go to each mike and say in a deep voice like I was that deejay on Pillow Talk: one, two, three, check, check, with each word like it was a word of love or magic. Check. Check. And Rose fiddles with the equipment a bit and the band kind of ritual-bitches about the setup, and someone finds a blue spotlight burned out, and we play like two different songs and I go around checking the mikes and then everything's set. It's a holy time, and by the end of it your head is humming.

So Rose and I pull into this town where Saquanac State is and I think, oh God, if I would have died to be on one of those farms I would die worse to have been born in this town. Its name is Brown. Just Brown. Would you like to say you were from Brown? There is this one-block-long stretch of business— your dry goods, your furniture store, lawyers, that stuff—and on either end of it, dribbled-out buildings and houses.

There is a McDonald's and there is a Pizza Hut. Rose does not go for that stuff when we're traveling. Her logic says if you travel you might as well experience the surroundings, so she looks for mom-and-pop joints. I have a different logic, which says you at least know what you are going to get at a franchise. And then she says, Which is exactly what makes Sandy call you Young Republican. And I say, Touché.

So Rose pulls into this place called Family Restaurant.

"If we just went a little further," I say, "we could probably find one called Generic Restaurant. How could you get more anonymous?"

"You got money," Rose says. "Take a hike if you want. I am eating at Family Restaurant."

There is a waitress who is no older than me but you know

she will be in this Family Restaurant—which is no doubt her own family's restaurant—until she marries some guy from the truck pool at Saquanac State, which her family will think is a step up, marrying into education some kind of way, and will raise three or four little kids and in between and afterward be waiting tables here, just getting thicker around the hips and kind of weary around the eyes. I look at her and I think all these things.

Rose has ordered the roast beef. "You want the aw juice on the side?" she asks.

Rose looks at me. I shrug.

"You want the aw juice on top or on the side?" she says. She points to the menu. Her finger slides under the line that says roast beef au jus.

"You just give me that aw juice all over the place," Rose says. She half winks at me.

The waitress looks at us kind of funny. We are not from this town, that is clear, and we're not from the college. I figure the kids from the college are not going to be too different from the residents of Brown or the farm kids from the stark houses we have been passing. Rose is wearing a Bruce Springsteen T-shirt underneath a plaid-flannel overshirt, which, if you want to be technical, is Sandy's, though she would get riled if I said that meant anything. I am wearing my favorite jacket. It's shiny, it's purple and yellow, it says on the back The Pope, Fall Tour '79. I bought it off a guy for twenty dollars. I swear I don't know where he got it. Rose thought it was a hoot. She says it was that one day at Holy Innocents that did me in. She laughs like crazy.

"I am going to do some of Emmylou Harris," Rose says. "Those two songs we've been practicing." She forgets names all the time. She hums what she means. I nod. "You got all your math done?"

"Almost," I say, which is not precisely true. I have watched the roadside the whole way, like it was something fascinating, and I have got a good bit of math left to do.

The roast beef comes. The girl looks at us like she is afraid we are going to do something real strange. Rose makes this crazy smile and the girl leaves us alone.

"The aw juice is everywhere," Rose says. She takes her knife and goes at it. The jukebox's clear-plastic bubble is not clear anymore: it is kind of smudged and rubbed dull with age, looking like it has been sitting here since the sixties when this place was built, when this girl's parents were proud as could be at the grand opening of the Family Restaurant. On the jukebox someone is playing Engelbert Humperdinck. "Spare me," Rose says, rolling her eyes. "Talk to me," she pleads. "Loud."

I don't have much to say. I am thinking about what life could be like if we were normal. I take that back: normal. Who wants to be normal. But maybe a little.

"I'm reading your mind, kid," Rose says. "Number one, Sandy is not old enough to be your father. He is two years younger than me and you know it."

"Off my back," I say. "I never said a thing."

"Fat Mariah has got a back problem she's whining about," Rose says. "I say she takes off a good forty pounds, she'll be okay."

"Right," I say.

"This aw juice is damned good," Rose says. "Eat hearty. Sound check's upon us."

At the college we pull up to the back door of the auditorium. This is another part that I like. You get to go to the back entrances. You get to see the workings of things, to be part of the workings of things. You learn, number one, that there is no magic, which is a real adult kind of feeling knowing that, and number two, that there is magic, but you have got to make it yourself, which is a real going-back-to-a-kid kind of feeling.

The auditorium is curved and has got this blue-painted ceiling, aqua blue, like the inside of a public swimming pool that curves. "For the acoustics, supposedly," Rose says. I set up the amps, which Fat Mariah and Deene and the others have brought in two vans, and Rose plugs in her two guitars and there is finally Sound. "The acoustics," Rose says, "are not world-class."

Mariah and Deene—who plays drums—come in together.

"You get your back replaced?" Rose says.

"Yeah, right," Mariah says.

Deene sets the drums up. I watch Rose shaking her head, almost invisibly. She can't figure how anyone can have the patience to haul along all of those drums because drums, she says, might be indispensable but they can't do what you can do on a guitar. I say, That's real intelligent, Rose. She says shut up.

They are all pretty glum tonight. I think the whole shot is a pretty glum enterprise, maybe just because of old Fat Mariah. She casts a pall. I wish that Rose would get with a mixed band. There's energy in that kind of thing. I don't want to get philosophical, but I think I get the idea of that when I am with Meggy Axelrod. I said that once to Rose and she said, "What you are getting is not philosophical, kiddo. What you are getting is hormonal. And anyway, where did you get a girl named after car parts?" These women in the band give me the creeps. I wish Rose would do something real radical, like go out on her own, do a demo for Atlantic, get a contract. Have a baby. Whatever. I'd like not to have to see Fat Mariah or hear about her damn disc cartilage ever, ever.

The sound check is over and we get to go backstage and do the priestly bit. I call it that in my head; I don't think I have ever told Rose that. I did tell Sandy one time when we were riding off in the truck to inspect some land that had just gotten perked and he was checking out for the excavators. He asked me what I liked about coming along on the gigs. Did I feel like a hanger-on, that kind of thing.

No, I said, when you are a roadie it is like being an altar boy. Do you know what that is?

Do I know what that is? Sandy said. I have told you already that I was a Boy Scout.

I know, I know, I said. I think that is truly amazing.

Life takes different forms, Sandy said. You are no more or less a Boy Scout than I was.

Barf my guts, I said. Cardozo, I am going to barf my guts.

Do it, he challenged me. The truck went over a big lump of earth and we both made amazed eyes and knocked our heads lightly on the roof of the cab.

Anyway, I said, what does being a Boy Scout have to do with being an altar boy.

I got this award, Sandy said. "Ad Altare Dei," it was called. To the altar of God. It was for Boy Scouts who were altar boys, the double whammy.

God, you are wrecking my image of you, I said, and I could feel myself grinning real wide.

You lie, Sandy said. Silver, he said, this roadie stuff is the same: You go along practicing for life, getting to see things before you are thrown into them.

Ad Altare Dei, I said.

You got it, Sandy said.

What do you think Rose would say if I asked her to marry me, Sandy said.

Fuck off, I answered.

You are probably right, Sandy said. He looked over at me. Do you know that I love that damned woman? he said. Do you know that I love you, too? Asshole.

I made sounds like barfing, and we hit a major bump. Go on, I said, bust your truck. What's it to me.

What we do when we get backstage is settle into the dressing rooms. Some places they feed you good and some places they do not. This is why Rose always insists on going to some Family

Restaurant. This place they seem to be ready to feed us decently, even though we have eaten not an hour and a half before. Rose can eat, I can eat. I've got this hollow leg that I inherited from her. Mariah gets furious when Rose says to lose forty pounds. If you had my metabolism, Rose, she says, they would roll you away. But I don't, Rose says. Honey, I don't.

I am munching on nachos and salsa and wondering how in this little burg they ever heard of anything like nachos and salsa and then I think we are in migrant land, all of these big farms are worked by the Chicano migrants. Of course there are nachos. Or maybe even Brown, Michigan, is part of the larger world.

Rose has got a dress—well, it is a skirt and shirt and vest— all done in sequins the color of pearls, with blue fringe like the color of midnight all tasselled around. I have not seen this thing before. I am wishing that Sandy could see her. Rose has told him to keep away from her jobs, that this is her life. I think she is just shy. If I said that she would laugh so loud, but what does she know.

"In Brown, Michigan, I'm afraid they are already dead, Silver," she says. "I hope I am wrong."

Deene and Mariah and the Wolley sisters—I never did know their names, and they are just the same to me, two clones of each other—are in and out of the room, fooling with this and that, checking the music. The ritual. Wolley One fingers the sequins of Rose's getup and approves. Wolley Two is getting Rose to do her hair. Rose gets kind of embarrassed when she is asked to do this kind of thing, because she is good at it and she thinks it's a tacky kind of thing to be able to do, like it's as if if you can do hair you're going to be trapped and zapped by some god or weird power into doing it for the rest of your life. She does not care that she is the star and is doing Wolley Two's hair. She does not have that kind of hangup.

Things are building toward the show. I can feel all of it getting electric. It kind of gets too much for me, so I go out front for a walk. I've got this silk sticker stuck to my chest, which says I am a part of the show, so I can wander freely. The people are starting to come in. The ushers and ticket takers look at me with a kind of a curious, mildly respectful look, like I was part of a mystery. And I am.

I stand against a wall out in the lobby and watch all the people coming in. I read the posters for the Saquanac College Glee Club and the Saquanac Seals' basketball schedule. I wonder whether the Saquanac Seals might dress up Fat Mariah in black rubber and make her their mascot. I consider contacting them. Suddenly I do a double take.

Sandy is walking in the front door, kind of trying to look invisible, skulking and squinting around like he doesn't want to get caught. So I yell across the lobby, "Cardozo! You have been spotted and I declare you under arrest."

He makes a finger across his lips. "For godsake," he says. "Don't let Rose know I am here."

I see that he is carrying flowers. This Godzilla-sized bouquet wrapped in this flimsy green tissue stuff, with roses that turn from yellow to orange to red, all in one flower.

"What the hell's that?" I say.

"Caulking for log homes," he says. "Dog shampoo. Relics of saints."

"Rose is going to be pissed," I say.

"Let her," says Sandy. "I think we have been letting that woman boss us around too long. I will not say she is not a strong woman. My God, she is strong. But I think we have got to let her know she doesn't have us fully buffaloed."

"Which means?" I say.

"Which means I am asking the woman to marry me," Sandy says. I notice he has got a tie on underneath his big coat. It is starting to snow outside, and he has brought sloppy flakes in on his shoulders and in his hair. "I am going to do this onstage. Bring the flowers, real public, but whisper the hard part."

"She'll deck you," I say.

"We are laying bets," Sandy says. "Two Willie Nelson tapes say that not only will she not deck me, she will say yes."

I make a guffaw, but I feel kind of spooky. I think: could he be right?

"Place your bets," Sandy says.

"I am no betting man," I say. "Roadies live cleaner than Boy Scouts and Ad Altare Deis."

"I have got a seat halfway back," Sandy says. "Rose won't be able to see me."

"The woman's a hound dog," I say.

"I will come up at the end," Sandy says. "After she does the Patsy Cline. You watch." He gives me a bear hug and goes in to the sloped auditorium. "Mum's the word, need I say."

"Mum," I say. I wander back to the backstage door wearing what must be a really peculiar face. Something inside me is shivering. Jesus H., I think, he really means it. I think of how Rose's pearl sequins will shine in the light, and how he will come up and surprise her, and wait for that minute, because things could happen just right.

Baptism of Desire

The ground in New Orleans had sunk beyond believing. People called it "the subsidence," dragging that word out uncharacteristically on the first syllable, as Mississippians might. Several years' drought had brought it on. Drought being relative, this had been drought in a city with umpty-doo inches per minute of precipitation, in drizzles and lashing wild afternoon downpours, and sodden week-long steam-bath weathers where one could not tell if it were raining or not.

Coming back to New Orleans on Delta Flight 292, with none of the ground travel in between to blunt the violent change, to habituate him to the mess and the excess of it, Fletcher Breen was stunned. The water table had dropped, because, fighting the drought, the trees had sucked up as through giant and limitless straws all the water they could, in a drunken, deciduous orgy. Up they shot, up up, leafing out wildly in unready greygreens and yellow-greens not helped along by the mist and the overcast skies. They were Javanese, Indian, Philippine beast-fable trees, they were beanstalks of myth.

Named by his mother in some fit of sweet upward aspiring (Fletcher was not a family name, and it certainly was not a saint's name), Fletcher had moved from the world he was born in—the world where his father sat stolidly at his desk stamping and stapling thin pink paper forms to each other, the world where his mother cooked okra and crawfish and prayed to Saint Anthony, finder of lost objects—to that upward world.

At thirteen he had won his first scholarship: Jesuit High School. He wore his khaki uniforms, chafed under the militarism, thrilled at the pale Jesuits' passion for logic and rigor of thought. His mother lit a candle of thanks to Saint Jude, patron of all things impossible, which he at first thought an insult, but then thought a marker of cultural progress. He smiled to himself.

The brilliance, the upward mobility worried his father. "Don't get a big head, son, is all I would like to advise you," the sad, Brylcreemed man said with solemnity. Blessed are they who do not overreach, blessed the humble, the worn-down-by-life, blessed the underachievers.

But then Fletcher did more. Really did it, ripped fabric of family and church right to shreds, in one rip. He had turned down a scholarship right here in town, to Loyola, the Jesuit college. Had turned down another to a Catholic college in Texas. "It's not far, son, but you could see what the rest of the world looks like," his father said, in its favor, when it was clear Fletcher would not stay in town for Loyola. He thought himself wildly adventurous.

"Mesquite trees," Fletcher said. "That's the world? Mesquite trees on a molehill? That place is a refuge for mental dwarfs. Texas?" His father did not like the tone of that, but simply gave Fletcher a short, sour look. Fletcher had gone north, to Harvard.

The relatives shook their heads sadly. Some put their heads into their hands. Some clapped the heels of their hands to their heads. Their heads and their hands agreed: Fletcher was in danger of losing his very identity, losing his soul. Some, indeed, felt that he already had done that, way back. "Going brainy," they called it. They pitied his parents, as if he had been born with his spine open, or rudimentary eyes like blue marbles that sat in his head making regular folks squirm and pitch in the chairs of their lives.

Fletcher had been gone for five full years, had gone straight through his summa cum laude baccalaureate into graduate school. He had insisted in letters, his brilliant excuse, that he could not come back, Christmases or vacations, because he had to work, had to have some money. His father understood that, and did not miss the boy dreadfully anyway: Fletcher always had been a queer bird, and a drain on his limited energies. His mother sighed over the pots of soft things she seemed always to be cooking and reread his letters. His sister, Carol Ann, his only sister, got married, and Fletcher did not come home, and everyone understood. He had exams that week. They could understand that. That was straightforward. These were people who had to punch time clocks, and they sympathized with that unliberty.

Now Carol Ann's husband Don's father, Etienne Bonicard, an old man Fletcher had only met once, who was dim as a springtime cold in Fletcher's memory, had just keeled over and died. "Keeled over," his mother said on the phone, as if there had been drama, a grand thud, a shudder that shook a wide, acres-wide rippling circle of rumbling marshland. Fletcher had been instructed to come home. His mother sent him a ticket, round-trip. She had bought it from money she saved weekly, out of the groceries. It was nonrefundable, though the return date was open. Fletcher had no excuse he could make. So he came.

The funeral over now, Fletcher desired to return: no, he itched to leave, craved exit, hungered for Cambridge's air, a quick cool early walk by the Charles. The heat of New Orleans appalled him now; he could not conceive how he had lived here for all those long years without being asphyxiated. The monstrous trees, too quickly grown, had the air of huge overnight lawn fungi: deflatable, insubstantial, returnable to a small withered state overnight by some fluke of rain or the water table.

In the streets and the driveways, the earth had cracked. Houses sat two feet above their lawns, concrete-slab foundations exposed like old yellowed teeth sitting in shrunken, pyorrheal gums. Children could not skate anymore on the sidewalks, but wild boys made the two-foot upheavals of concrete into jumps for their dirt bikes and their skateboards. Real estate agents wrung their hands, carrying plumb levels into the houses they showed, clucking their tongues in misery as they watched children's balls roll downhill from one corner of a room to another: they saw dollar signs with wings, flying away. No one loved it, this subsidence, except perhaps the wild boys.

Fletcher Breen felt the trees ready to suck him up: he was after all human and so mostly liquid, was it ninety-seven percent? He felt anxious around the fat, gnarled roots of oaks that spread over the sidewalks and claimed them. He felt the cracked earth as a wet, hidden mouth, ready to swallow him: he would disappear into a crevice where dirt bikes leaped, never be seen again, be given all Incompletes this semester. He carried his return ticket with him at all times. In his pocket he fingered it until it softened. And then he stopped fingering it. He did not want the ticket to decompose. He could be stuck here forever.

There was only one more day now, one day only. There was a baptism to be gotten through: Carol Ann's baby, a boy, born a month before old Mr. Bonicard died. The relatives thought it amazing, a miracle: the first grandchild, a boy, 'Tienne's earthly replacement. "You takin' my place, l'il man," Mr. Bonicard had said, propped up in bed on his thin pillows. "You replace dis ol' bone-bag, dis ol' dry-up fig," he had said, his soft, toothless mouth like a decaying jack-o-lantern's around the words. All of the relatives assumed that the boy would be named Etienne, for his grandfather.

Carol Ann, though she lived in this world and had not "gone brainy" like Fletcher—would never go brainy or uppity, never be proud, overreaching her destiny—was not so sure. She thought she might name him Dustin or Ryan or Christopher Reeve Bonicard.

Her mother, the upward-aspiring, encouraged her. Mr. Bonicard—this was not mentioned—was, after all, from Don's side of the family. The Bonicards lived in a shotgun house on the far side of the river, Westwego, and though the Breens valued humility, this was just a bit too humble, too redolent of canal-stench and the black sticky oil that the trucks laid down on the dirt streets in the summer.

Her mother did not mention, either, that Fletcher, with his upward-sounding name, had done well: that was a sore and debatable subject, and Carol Ann did not seem wholly to agree that Fletcher had done well. Carol Ann, moreover, could not conceive that her child would grow up and leave her as her mother's son had done, and would not like to be told this. Carol Ann's child was a doll yet, and Carol Ann set about naming him as she might name a doll, giving no thought to the future, no thought to the twenty-first century's image of such names as Dustin or Ryan or Christopher Reeve. A doll with a face like a fist, and a shock of hair like a small animal's out of its hole, a doll ready for baptism into the flock of the chosen, the Church that had brought Fletcher life, the Church Fletcher had left for the pagan dominions of learning.

Fletcher was lost, in their eyes; yet they watched him out of the corners of those eyes, hoping for signs that he was not indeed lost. Some small part of them conceded there might be more to this than they knew: some smug optimist impulse that says you can take the boy out of the Church but you can't take the Church out et cetera. What signs would they have wanted? Would they have wanted him to cross himself ostentatiously? Genuflect idly at traffic lights? Pick up the Saint Alphonsus Liguori Society Messenger from an end table and sit reading, absorbed, ads for rosaries straight from the carnival-style shrines of Europe, encapsulating in a plastic vial true Lourdes spring water, a vial in the shape of a heart, true Lourdes water to heal and regenerate? He did not know what signs they were looking for, but his eyes darted sidewise at moments and caught them watching. He wondered if they'd be relieved if he got the stigmata, if during a family meal his hands burst like blood-roses with mystical marks of the nails of the true crucifixion. They'd love it, he thought. When they watched him, he pretended he would be getting the stigmata soon, and he smiled to himself.

One more day. Then it came, the day, and they arrived at the church in the Lincoln that had been 'Tienne Auberge Bonicard's. Don drove. He was used to his Pontiac, smaller and sharper on corners, and so he drove pompously, with a majestic air, slow for the traffic. Fletcher's father sat next to Don, his long spindly legs uneasy over the hump of the drive shaft; Fletcher drew the front window seat. Carol Ann sat in back with her mother, the baby between them in its safety seat like a breakable egg, strapped in, fragile, its shock of light baby-chick hair like a bright fourteenth-century halo about its small head.

Carol Ann's hat was a mock of the hats of the mothers-in-law: Carol Ann looked to them, generally, for her lessons in womanhood. Her curled head in pink straw and pink veiling bobbed up and down over the baby, cooing a falsetto in infantese. Fletcher tried to distract himself. Carol Ann had not been his favorite person in the world when they were growing up in the same house; on this last day of his visit he felt, looking at her and listening to her, as if he were gagging on taffy.

He searched for distraction: he watched out the window the progress of progress, the franchises sprung up as monstrous and overextended as all of the neighborhood trees. Franchises for chicken and steak, frozen yogurt and video movie cassettes. Carol Ann cooed on. Fletcher watched out the window. He watched the heat bounce and dance on the steel frame of a small building going up. No one was working. It was Sunday.

"Yeah," Don said, as if in response to some query, as if there had been a continuous interest in the subject—as indeed there was, inside his head. Don had a small contracting business. "Yeah," he said, "housing starts are up, too." He made an emphatic side-to-side crescent swipe with his chin: yeah. "Looks good, looks good," he said.

Fletcher did not reply. His mother leaned over the baby and made extreme faces, as if the child were nearly blind, as she might shout at one nearly deaf. Mr. Breen, quiet till now, felt the conversational ball in his court. "Yeah," he said. "They are sure building things." He looked at the sign on a new Colonel Sanders franchise. "Lots of chicken," he said, pleased to add this detail.

"Yeah," Don said. "They gonna do pretty good anywhere. Them niggers likes chicken."

"Don," Carol Ann said. "*You* like chicken."

"You right, hon," he said. "But them blacks is who has got the money these days. If it ain't the Vietnamese buying up property, it is the niggers. You wonder where they get the money. The gov'ment, I guess."

"Who *don't* like chicken?" Mr. Breen added, garrulous.

"That Colonel Sanders, he sure had himself one hell of a idea, yessir. A idea whose time had come," Don said. He looked over Mr. Breen at Fletcher, hoping he'd noticed the turn of phrase. Something in him seemed to fear Fletcher's differentness but to reach out, all the same, for his alien approval.

"Does pretty good for a dead guy," Fletcher said.

"Oh, Fletcher," his mother said, giggling.

"I'm glad Miz Bonicard's not here to hear that," his father said.

"Don't you start up that dead-guy talk around her, Fletcher," said Carol Ann, twinkling. She responded well and with relief to Fletcher's rare simple humor: it had little room to insert itself into these airless conversations.

They walked into the church in a huddle, as if all the forces of evil and darkness might overtake them on the way from the parking lot. Such was theology: here was the child, small black soul, smeared as if with the *merde* of life's barnyard with original sin, black as caverns, implacable darkness, a heritage of sloth and envy and massive concupiscent impulse.

Today the Church would bring this child out of darkness and shame into light, plunge this child down into the water and bring him up vivified. Theologians were pumping the soft pedal on this aspect of the doctrine these days, but the Breens and the Bonicards, brought up trained to see infants as trailing original sin like the tin cans behind a lascivious-message-soaped honeymoon car, still felt anxious to have the baptism done with.

What if there were an accident? What if the baby died, slipped like a cooked onion out of its skin and went floating off into the pea-soupish murk of some limbo? The same theologians were pooh-poohing limbo, but what did they know? It had always been true, this place, limbo: so where were all those limbo babies now? That was a stickler.

Walking into the church from the heat of the parking lot, Fletcher thought that the forces of heat and humidity, taken together with gravity and the deadening effect of the car conversation, might do him in. But the church was cool, shadowy, damp.

Carol Ann looked at her watch. It was two, on the dot. They sat down in a pew and they waited. The priest would be in momentarily. In the baptistry, a small room carved like a cove in the side wall, the shapes of sea shells, scallop shells, were everywhere, white walls scooped out scallop-shaped, baptistry shaped like a shell. It left no room for the baroque pictorial busyness that filled the rest of the church. It was all painted white.

Scallop shapes, like the shell that bore Venus up out of the foam. Fletcher thought of breasts: Venus's breasts, breasts of girls back in Cambridge imagined beneath winter sweaters, the breasts of the women of Fragonard, Goya, Manet, Gauguin, Modigliani. The church here was one grand brassiere, concaves here, giant rotundas there, all of the church a place great breasts might rest, a grand repository for all of the tits of the world. The curved ceiling above the baptistry, curved like a seductive half-bra, that might hold the most exquisite breast of all.

Beside him, his father read the church bulletin. Knights of Columbus invited them all to a Pancake Prayer Breakfast. Our Father, thought Fletcher, who art in syrup. He thought of the Knights with their bottles of Mrs. Butterworth lining the table like brown-glass madonnas. He thought of her Butterworth breasts.

Carol Ann whispered to Don. Don's shoes clicked on the aisle's terrazzo as he made his way to the front of the church. They sat in the shadow, the marble walls' damp breath upon them, the eyes of the plaster saints fixed on the floor where Don walked, clicking. Mrs. Breen sighed. The baby squirmed. Carol Ann pulled out a bottle.

"Now aren't you glad you decided not to nurse?" Mrs. Breen said. "*Now* what would you do." It was not a real question.

"You're right," Carol Ann said. "You're so right."

Don returned, his face twisted. "The thing was at one o'clock," he said. "All of the others already left."

"Who?" Mrs. Breen said. "Others?"

"All the baptisms," Don said. "It wasn't just us getting baptized, you know. They do this like Communions now, Confirmations. A whole group."

"Shit," said Carol Ann under her pink hat. "We should have known. No one here when we got here, and then when we waited. We should have known."

Mr. Breen did not look up from his bulletin. He ran his finger under an item which said that the bingo would be moved to Fridays, by many requests. He ran his finger under an item about a novena.

"Well," Mrs. Breen said, "they are all at the house."

"The baptisms?" said Carol Ann.

"No, all the people," said Mrs. Breen. "All of the people we asked to the party."

"Oh, shit. I forgot about that," Carol Ann said. She willed quick-welling tears back down into her eye sockets. Blinked.

There had been a whole gaggle of relatives asked to the party. There would not be room at the church, the priest had said, for any but the immediate family. They had had a holy bunch of baptisms today, he had said, and then chuckled at his own wit. Six or seven of them. Holy bunch.

"Well," said Don. "What's to do. All the people are there. We'll just break out the booze. We can celebrate anyway. Just have the party, and dunk the kid later."

"Dunk," Carol Ann echoed. The word seemed to cheer her.

They got in the car and drove back past the franchises. Past the new housing starts, whole subdivisions sprouting, as if someone knew something about a projected incursion of buyers, as if perhaps all of the tilting and crack-bottomed houses were going to be abandoned and left to the wild tangle of vines that would certainly swallow them. They drove to the subdivision where Carol and Don and the still-heathen baby lived.

The smells of his mother's face powder, his father's and Don's cigarette breath, the baby's thick yellowish formula, Carol Ann's heavy gardenia perfume filled the car. Fletcher wished for air.

In the living room of the house Don had bought Carol Ann—this was how his mother described the transaction—an assemblage of relatives waited. Fletcher, walking in, had the sensation of entering a restaurant cooler, the walk-in kind that they had had at the place he had played part-time maître d' that year, fellowship notwithstanding. The air was a full twenty degrees cooler. He marveled. The sweat on his forehead seemed to threaten to turn to ice and crack. The air seemed synthetic.

"Here, Fletcher," his mother said. "You remember . . ." and she named five or six people he half-recognized, dream faces of forced childhood kisses. Fletcher summoned his high-school smile. His Harvard smile, which required fewer muscles, would not be sufficient, would start up the looks from the corners of eyes again.

"Well," said Don to the crowd, to no one in particular. "Wouldn't you know. The kid didn't get dunked after all."

Eyebrows lifted. The faces of women as frosted as cakes opened like cake-top roses, like time-lapse photography quickened. The men wondered about what Don meant but did not let on.

"How come, Donnie?" a child's voice piped. As if she were reciting, a ringleted girl with yellow-framed glasses stood up. Donnie's sister's child, Mary Alicia, named after Don's mother. Poor child, Fletcher thought. She seemed at an awkward age. Perhaps would always be at an awkward age. Her dress hiked up under her armpits. Her glasses frames glowed.

"*One* o'clock," Don said. "We had to be there by *one*."

"Whose fault, whose fault," chanted one of the men, a half-cousin, a three-quarters uncle, whom Fletcher did not know. His back hunched in a kind of enduring despair. His eyes flashed at a large woman two seats away in a taunt and an echo of long years' repetitive mockeries. She was too far away to bat him. "We have to know whose fault. It's important," he sang through his nose, in a voice that was not his own.

"They told me two o'clock," said Carol Ann. "At the rectory." She put the bundle of lace that was the baby into a frill-skirted bassinet.

"Carol Ann's fault," sang the man. There was laughter. "One point for the Bonicards."

The large woman glared. The three-quarters uncle had gone to his limit.

"You remember . . ." Fletcher's mother was saying now. She introduced cousins whom Fletcher remembered as infants. They had acne now. She introduced neighbors of Don and Carol Ann's, whom Fletcher did not know. The sweat on his forehead had dried like a surplus skin, salty and tight. He made smiles that allowed him to wrinkle his forehead and feel it.

"Why does he care whose fault it is?" said a boy, someone whose bones said he was not Breen and not Bonicard. Neighbor child, probably.

"Stop," hissed his mother, a woman who had the boy's nose.

"It's nobody's fault," said Fletcher's mother, too loudly. Her smile was too gay. It was threatening tears.

"It is everyone's fault," said his father. "We're all in this together." It sounded profound. Fletcher looked around. What was it that they were all in together, he and these women with frosting-rose faces, these men with humps, acne-faced teenagers, myopic children in white patent leather shoes? "Let's cut the cake," his father said. He was proud of himself. Fletcher had never heard him so directive. It showed in the lift of the skin underneath his eyes, crinkling with pride. He had not only codified what had transpired, he had stamped it and stapled it, then gone on to save the day by suggesting they cut the cake.

"Not yet," said Don's mother. "The presents. The baby has to open the presents.

Fletcher waited in wonder. They seemed to expect that the baby would rise up and unwrap the flat oblongs, bright cubes, soft bundles. Swaddled in christening lace, a small Moses behind the bassinet's white-ruffle bulrushes, the baby did nothing.

"Poor child," said a woman. "Poor little black soul." She laughed at her joke. No one else laughed. She went on as if she had not expected them to laugh. "Not baptized, you know. A little black soul. A real pagan baby. A joke!"

Someone laughed.

"Annhh," said someone else. "You don't believe that."

"The Church teaches . . ." someone said.

"Innocence," said the woman protesting. Fletcher saw a flickering alien gleam in her eyes. She launched into it, waxing rhapsodic. "A child is all innocence, all possibility. Wordsworth says . . ."

Daffodils flashed before Fletcher's eyes. Poor woman, he

thought. She had not been to one of these gatherings. A neighbor. An outsider.

"Delphine went to college. Dominican," said Carol Ann hastily, cutting her off, explaining it all to the relatives.

Delphine sat back.

"Bring out the champagne there, boy!" one of the men called to Don, who had vanished into the kitchen and was making clinking noises. "Champagne! Champagne! Celebrate."

Celebrate what has not happened, thought Fletcher: the baptism of this child, this bunch of fluffy lace, lying there silent. Fletcher had a fleeting thought that there might be no child there at all: not just a black soul, but no soul at all, and no body. He sauntered over to look in the bassinet. Casually, casually.

There was the lace, like meringue, frothed around the fist-face of the child. Fletcher felt slightly better. A door opened into a spacious white room in his mind: In this room, and not in some dank cobwebbed cellar, he kept all the doctrines he'd put to heart years ago, under the muscular, dry tutelage of the Jesuits. Fletcher's spacious white room held Aquinas on microfiche.

He scanned snatches of headings remembered from Thomas Aquinas. "On the Distinction of the Intellectual Virtues," he read, and beneath that the question, obliquely phrased, Whether the habits of the speculative intellect are virtues. (Fletcher heard an anonymous relative's voice in his head, Yeah, he's so smart, then why ain't he rich?) Yes, Fletcher thought, answering the Great Doctor's inquiry bluntly. It *is* good to think.

He proceeded. He scanned. Where was Baptism in this vast and unwieldy *Summa*? (The light in the white room was pure sunlight; he had a respect for these long-shelved texts that none of these relatives ever could know.)

Perhaps what he wanted fell under the rubric of "grace," the question being: Whether a man can merit the first grace for another? That was it: in the Baltimore Catechism, it was called simply Baptism of Desire. Every schoolchild knew the story: if by some fluke (ignorance, circumstance) one were deprived of baptism, desire for the grace of the sacrament would suffice for one's salvation. Even proxy desire. Fletcher wished that for his small, ruffled nephew. Baptism of Desire: the phrase snagged like a stitch on a thorn of his mind. Desire. Fletcher slipped to its alternate meaning, the wet longing Thomas Aquinas couched in words like "carnal," "concupiscent," "sensual."

"Hey, Fletch," called a voice from across the room. A cousin, slightly past acne, a few years behind him. "You like that? The kid? You going to settle down someday, have kids?" The voice held a challenge. He looked at the cousin. Twenty-one, he thought. Two kids already, he guessed.

Fletcher flashed him a grin from *Mad* magazine, meant to intimidate. No one followed that up, and the cousin retired to his seat.

Carol Ann brought out the cake, which seemed to be the size of a small desk. Blue frosting rippled around its top edge, and blue roses bloomed on it. The cake just said WELCOME BABY. They had decided to order it early, and Don and Carol still had not yet decided upon a name. Fletcher realized he did not know what they would have named the child, if they had managed to baptize it. Him.

Two female conversations dovetailed, and Fletcher heard the words "estrogen" and "polyester" in overlap. Polyestrogen. Mail-order pantsuits to keep you young, cream that transforms to a fabric, a birthday suit. Everyone wanting to be new, re-joicing in that yearning, straining toward grace, and at one with this child.

"Cut the cake, Carol Ann," said her mother. The subject of presents seemed to have been washed away in the champagne.

Fletcher looked past the two women into Don's den, through an archway. He knew, though he had never been here, that the name of the room had to be Don's Den. The wallpaper showed hunters crouched in the reeds shooting ducks out of the sky. A pool table filled the room, violent green. Bookshelves lined the walls. Collectors' bottles, in the shapes of antique cars, from some kind of Tennessee whiskey. A few books. *Live Tax-Free* sat next to *Erotic Art of the Great Painters*. *Financial Success through Prayer* stood beside *Minnesota Fats: Man with a Dream*. A couple of men disengaged themselves from the group in the living and dining room and picked up cues. Balls clacked.

Carol Ann sliced the cake. Mrs. Breen held the wobbling paper plates as if they had a life of their own. She delivered them gingerly, as if the cake would leap off and attack people's shirt-fronts and bosoms.

Fletcher looked out the window. The bushes were high. They had given up trimming them, perhaps? No, Fletcher knew Carol Ann. She would not let things go. Mrs. Breen called these bushes ligustrum: was that their name, or were they, like her "mono-gram" headaches, a fiction her tongue had created? Perhaps these bushes had just grown up overnight, beanstalkish. He had an urge to go outside, to look to their tops, to stand watch for the giant.

There was jasmine just outside the window, but it was tight shut to let in no nature, no moist, suffocating, unstoppable nature. It seemed to let in the strong jasmine scent anyway.

The driveway that they had driven into was cracked. The sidewalk out front buckled. Sweating neighborhood children, their noise silent through the tight window and the bright din of the crowd, soared above the crack in the sidewalk like death-derby motorcyclists on their low plastic cycles. They soared and they landed. Their heads jarred like heads on trick statues, spring-mounted heads wobbling in backs of cars, disconcerting anyone who got behind them in traffic jams. The children jumped, landed, and wobbled.

In the yard the birdbath had fallen over.

Fletcher looked at his mother, who seemed to be reading his mind but who simply was watching his eyes.

"The birdbath fell over yesterday," she said.

Fletcher nodded. He hoped that his nod was a solemn nod.

"It's the water table," Mrs. Breen said. "What with the drought, everything's sinking."

"Just sinking and sinking," said someone else, a ghostly echo.

"You'd think it'd be good for the concrete contractors," said Don. "But n-o-o-o. Nobody's contracting anything now. They're just waiting. They'll wait till it stops. Did you see the foundation? The house's foundation? A good nine, ten inches exposed. Damn the subsidence." He shook his head.

Carol Ann handed Don his cake directly, not through her mother, who had brought cake wedges to everyone else. She smiled at him, stars in her eyes. His cake was twice the size of anybody else's. She had added an extra blue rose, neatly scooped from the serving plate onto the side of his wedge.

"Yeah, my brother-in-law's in concrete," said a man, the first thing he had said. He was glad to be able to offer that. He had fulfilled some requirement for true social intercourse. Now he was off the hook.

"You see that plane that come down by the airport? That plane that crashed?" someone said.

Everyone knew someone who had. All eye-witnesses or witnesses at a single remove, ear-witnesses perhaps.

"Going to Vegas," said someone. That seemed to explain it.

"So?" someone else said, pricked, belligerent. Fletcher looked at his mother. She was sucking in her breath, slowly, readying.

"Gamblers," the woman said.

"God don't like gamblers?" the retort came back, testy, defensive.

"God didn't have nothing to do with it," Don's father said. "He's too busy." He smiled at himself.

Carol Ann had stopped cutting and stood with the knife in midair. "I was driving by," she said. "On West Esplanade. I saw it. Along the canal. I was going to Pik-Quik to pick up some of those, what do you call them, fabric-softener sheets that come on a roll, you know, for Don's shirts. He likes his shirts soft." She looked around, as if for corroboration. It seemed everyone knew that Don liked his shirts soft. "It came past us, right overhead, skimmed right not ten or twelve feet over the top of the car, thank God it didn't hit Don's Tempest, would he have been mad. But anyway, it landed, crashed, not even three blocks away."

Everyone sat mesmerized. Breathless. Carol Ann had their attention. A witness to tragedy. No one could top this.

"You saw it," a woman said.

"Yes," Carol Ann said.

"Two weeks ago," the woman said.

"Yes," Carol Ann said. "When it happened."

"My God."

"The baby was not a month old yet," said Carol Ann.

"My God. The baby was with you?" the woman said.

"Right there," said Carol Ann, pointing next to her with the knife. Fletcher looked where she'd pointed. A blob of blue frosting had fallen down onto the thick carpet. No one cared. "In his baby seat," Carol Ann said. "In his safety seat. Those things are marvelous. I never take him out without it. Those things are lifesavers. Miracles. Just what we should have had, always."

"It wouldn't have helped you one bit if the plane had come down on you," said a man's voice, intruding, entirely ignored.

"And what did you do?" said the woman, rapt, waiting. Carol Ann's role in the tragedy had escalated now. She had to *have done* something.

"I picked him up," she said. There were gasps.

"Picked up the baby?"

"Yes. Picked him up. Stopped the car right in the road—all the cars were stopped—and I just ran."

"Ran away?"

"Away?" Carol Ann echoed. She looked at the woman strangely.

The woman repeated herself, thinking that Carol Ann had not understood. "Ran away?"

"No. Ran toward it," Carol Ann said.

"With the baby!"

"My God, Carol Ann!" said her mother. "My God."

Fletcher looked at the child in the bassinet, wide awake now, frowning, looking at him with dark, blurry eyes.

"You don't think when you're in that," said Carol Ann. "You just react."

"My God," her mother said once more.

"And *then* what did you do?" someone else said, demanding and breathless. They all were just waiting to hear.

"Well, I got just as close as I could. You could hear all the screams and the moans and the voices. You couldn't see anything. Flames," Carol Ann said. Her knife described flames in the air, flicking infinitesimal flecks of blue frosting above the heads of her rapt listeners. "Hell," Carol Ann said, "it was just like hell." She stopped. The air in the room seemed to have been used up, for the moment. Mouths hung open. Carol Ann, and this nameless bundle of lace with its piercing dark eyes, had seen hell and lived to tell of it.

"God," said an adolescent boy-cousin, the thick awkward Windsor knot of his tie bobbing obscenely, a throaty erection.

"Can we turn the TV on? Huh?" said the boy whose nose said that he was just a neighbor.

"Oh, stop," said his mother.

"Marvin Clytie's 'Encyclopedia of the Wild' is on," the child whined. "Can't we see it?"

"Oh, let him," said Carol Ann. "Here," she said, handing Fletcher a piece of cake nearly as large as the piece she had handed Don. Fletcher took it and held it to see if it would, as his mother had seemed to imply, leap at him. It did not. He dug into it with his fork.

The TV switched on, from a remote control somewhere in the room. Fletcher scanned the room trying to locate it. There was a game they had played, rainy days in his grade school:

pass the chalk. Whose hands, extended as if in prayer, held the mysterious passed chalk? He always had found the game inexplicably absorbing. He examined himself. Was the game about hidden truths, maybe, a placing of fault or blame, responsibility? He was playing with some abstract notion there. No one else cared much. They just played the game. Looking around the room, he could not locate the remote control. Everyone sat, moved, talked, listened. It was no one's fault that the TV was on.

On the screen, in bright, overbright color, a wildebeeste out in the African veldt was giving birth. The baby was coming feet first. The mother was struggling.

Carol Ann's voice rose above the narration in answer to someone across the room. "Yeah. He came breech. I was knocked out. Demerol first, then Scopolamine, finally gas. Who needs to know that kind of stuff? I'm not one of those pain-loving martyr Lamaze types." She rolled her eyes, tossed her curled head.

The wildebeeste writhed. The camera crew stayed out of sight, tame and disengaged. All around the wild, struggling mother, the veldt stretched, now yellow, now purple, as someone adjusted the color. From off the screen somewhere (Don's Den? Fletcher thought) came a stalking hyena. The plain was hot. In the heat, the dirt shimmered. The hyena shimmered. The wildebeeste shimmered.

The hyena attacked, in one swift lunge. Went for the throat. The camera did not flinch. The boy with the Windsor knot watched, entranced, a mustache of blue frosting lining his upper lip. His cake hovered in air. The hyena wrenched at the neck of the delivering wildebeeste, shook, shook. The legs of the new wildebeeste which would not be born shook like, flapped like, boneless flesh. A girl cousin buried her face in her skirt and made sounds of disgust.

From somewhere in the room, someone turned off the TV.

"I'll *say* that's enough," said a voice.

The boy with the blue mustache sat transfixed, staring at the screen as the picture shrank down to a glow of a glaucous green dot.

"Hey, the presents! Let's open the presents!" said some aunt. She brought in the stack from another room. Silver-bowed, baby-blue glossy-wrapped, cherub-print presents, piled on her outstretched arms. The paper flew. The baby did not rise to open his presents. He lay in his basket, his eyes open, watching the ceiling, attuned to some other reality. Fletcher moved closer to the bassinet. It seemed he was the only one in the room who knew the baby was here.

Carol Ann exclaimed over a silver cup.

"Jesus, do you know what those things *cost!*" came a whisper behind a hand.

Carol Ann loved a hand-knitted blanket; she hugged to her breast a small woolly lamb; she admired a white album in which she could record among other things the dates on which the child got each tooth and then later the dates when he lost them.

Paper piled up. Fletcher watched out the window. He wondered how long it had taken the earth to sink like this. The yard was cracked up like the worst spring ice jam he had seen in the Charles. The birdbath, its green imitation-aging bright out in the harsh daylight, lay sprawled in the short, dry grass. A bird landed and pecked at the rim of the birdbath, then flew away. Tomorrow Don would roll it as far as he could in the grass and then cart it the rest of the way to the double garage. It could wait there till things stopped subsiding.

The trees seemed to have grown while they sat here. Fletcher picked up his plastic detachable-stem champagne glass and downed it all. Here's to earth and water. To fond intersections between them. He smelled the intense jasmine, magic strong jasmine that transpierced the window glass. Who had smelled like that? A girl he'd taken out once. A woman. In winter. The odd, hot, and tropical smell of the jasmine above her fake fur in the Cambridge night. A woman he had not loved. A woman on small spiky heels with a bright face who could talk about anything, everything, grandly. Articulate. Lips like a picture's. Red lips, with wet, indiscriminate kisses. He looked at his cousin, the one who had asked him: YOU LIKE THAT? FLETCH? YOU GONNA SETTLE DOWN?

Fletcher closed his eyes, moved them to one side, then the other. He was answering his cousin. No, he would not settle down, did not want that. No, cuz, not that, nosirree, thanks much.

"Mary Alicia!" said someone. "You been taking dancing, we hear! Huh? You been taking dancing?"

The girl squirmed. Her dress seemed to hike even higher. She tugged it back over her knees. Her petticoats fought her.

"Huh? What's the matter? Cat got your tongue?" said the voice. It was a merciless uncle. He would not let go.

The girl looked to her mother for sympathy, respite, escape. The mother said, "Go on."

"Go WHAT!" said Mary Alicia. Her voice was a siren, alarm. She was desperate.

"Go on and dance," said her mother. She turned to the others. "She takes tap and toe, both, and next year she'll be in the jazz."

"Awww," said Mary Alicia.

"Go dance," said her mother. "She wore her tap shoes. I made her. I said someone might ask her, and there you go, someone did."

"Awww," said Mary Alicia. "You made him. You told him."

"It's not my fault he asked," said her mother.

The girl tiptoed over the carpet and into the kitchen.

"We can't see you there, hon," her mother called.

"I know," the girl said, her voice ugly.

"But we want to see you," her mother said.

"I'll dance in here. Only in here," said Mary Alicia.

Her mother sighed. "Well. I guess you have got to tap on something hard. Can't tap-dance on a carpet. Right?" She appealed to the audience. Everyone sat where they were. A few could see Mary Alicia through the kitchen door. Most could not.

"Go on," coaxed her mother.

"To what," said the girl. "I need music."

"For Christ's sake," her mother said. "Turn on the radio."

"In the appliance garage," Carol Ann said. "Right there on the counter, hon. The little cabinet with the sliding door."

Sounds of the girl fumbling. Sighs of the mother.

"So what were you going to name him?" the girl's mother said, turning to Carol Ann. It seemed now as if the whole thing had been canceled forever, as if the child were going to go through life nameless, heathen.

Carol Ann looked at Don. Looked at Fletcher.

Fletcher frowned slightly and worked out a kink in his shoulders.

"We are going to name him for Don, but not Don Junior. Don Fletcher Bonicard. Donnie-Boo. How do you like it?" Carol Ann beamed at Don, then at Fletcher.

Don beamed back at Carol Ann.

Fletcher worked at unkinking his kink. He looked at the child and he hoped that the child would protest, but the child did not. He watched the curtains blow slightly as the air-conditioner put forth a burst of loud cold. "No," said Fletcher. It was a plea. He felt the dried sweat on his forehead make ripples, a frown.

"No modesty, now," Carol Ann said.

"It's not modesty," Fletcher said. "It's . . ." He trailed off. Poor child. He wanted to abduct him. Wretched life. Wretched life, growing up here where the birdbaths fall over, the earth sinks, blue frosting is everywhere.

From the kitchen the voice of Mary Alicia came mewling. "There's nothing but trash on this radio. Old Buddy Holly. Captain and Tennille and shit."

"Don't say shit," said her mother, her tone flat as ironing.

Fletcher smelled scorched cloth in his mind. The smell seemed to come from the mother. Or somewhere else. The smell of a sacristan burning the linens, some afternoon.

"Dance," said Mary Alicia's mother.

"Here. Fletcher," said Carol Ann. "Whistle. You whistle." Carol Ann was pleading with him; her tones were the tones of the mother of Jesus at Cana. "You whistle what she wants. Here, Mary Alicia. Fletcher will whistle for you. He's a whistler. First-class. Remember how you used to whistle, Fletch? He won the talent show once, in the seventh grade. He got a trophy. There, now, Mary Alicia. What do you want him to whistle?"

Silence. A moment. Mary Alicia appeared in the door, her glasses frames flashing like neon. Her bead-eyes were angry but ready to dance. She looked at Fletcher and put in her order. "Beyond the Blue Horizon," she said. It was a dare.

The mother looked at Carol Ann.

"He knows that. He knows everything," Carol Ann said. She was proud of him now. She was naming her child for him. Fletcher would be redeemed. Fletcher doubted that Carol Ann had any inkling of what the song was.

"It's the song that they dance their routine to. In class," said her mother.

"Go on," Carol Ann said to Fletcher. She did not doubt that he knew it.

Fletcher started to whistle. The taps of Mary Alicia's shoes started tapping across the terrazzo floor. From where he was, he could not see her. She tapped in a wonderful synchronous tippety-tapping, belying her waistless ungainliness.

Fletcher had not left the Church, exactly, but was not exactly in it either; he had seemed to this point an outsider to all the family, but suddenly he whistled himself inside of it. Mary Alicia tapped. One chorus. Two. She would not stop till he did.

He thought of the tippety-tap of the heels of the glistening-lipped Cambridge woman, the tippety-tap of the heels of the women who passed his apartment-house gate, passed the bars of the gate, never locked, but resembling a jail's, tippy-tap, tippy-tap. He thought of the soft boots of the women in winter, the sandals and bare feet in summer, the feet that made no sound. He longed for the soft summer silence of sandals and bare feet. Desire. He fingered his soft ticket deep in his pocket.

He whistled horizons, horizons, beyond. He would watch out his window and choose out a woman, a woman with lips their own color, a woman with silent shoes, and he would run down the street and stop her in her tracks. He would talk to her, quickly, articulately, about innocence and true salvation. Or maybe he only would whistle. He'd pick out a song when he got on the plane.

He would drive her out into the country and find some green pond, some pond lined with pond life, with tendrils and tentacles, soft reachings-out of life, and they would leave their clothes on a rock and slip into the water, the water so green it was black, and they both would tread water. He could feel her smooth feet now, teasing his legs.

Fletcher whistled, and out in the kitchen Mary Alicia tapped. He looked down at the baby who would bear his name, like a weight, like a talisman. He felt the unmet Cambridge girl's fingers under the water, the tips of her fingers soft on the small of his back. Outside, the ground was still sinking. Mary Alicia might tap on forever.

Snowmobile Country

I want to say this is not happening, but happening it is: I hear, no I feel, a clunk, right front wheel, and I've gone off the black-top into the soft shoulder. All mush, sad, experienced snow, with the mist rising off it. That kind of snow.

But when I yank myself back up onto the road it is worse. The reason I've gone off the road is I've blown out the tire, or maybe vice-versa. So here I am trying to drive through this damn twilight wet-feather snow that is coming down harder and harder, though light as your dreams, on the rim of this wheel, and it's over a half-mile to the intersection with M-12 where there's a gas station.

Shelley and Shawn, who are five and eleven, are home waiting for the McNuggets. I say shit softly once and then I don't breathe: holding my tonsils high up at the back of my throat, lifting my eyebrows, defying gravity (which is fear), I pretty much coast, with my foot dead immobile, light on the gas pedal.

The red light of the station sign comes into view: Dresden Jones' Marathon. Tumble, lurch, tumble, lurch, holding my breath, my toes in my boots flexed back in a peculiar paralysis.

Holding my breath. Through the mist I can read Dresden Jones'
name in flame-colored neon. The flakes are substantial now,
thick as soap, creamy. I almost pray for a green light, but I
don't pray otherwise much and so I figure God won't be much
interested: I just *will* the light green, and it's green, and I lumber
on through.

At the station the talk's of the storm. Dresden Jones has a
front on his station that's nothing if not surreal: a half-circle of
glass blocks set in concrete. Mostly glass. What it's like, the
effect, is the belly of some crazy World War II bomber, a belly
of glass. The light spills outside into the soapy snow falling and
breaks into pieces where it meets the mist.

There are four or five truck drivers crammed into this belly,
drinking his coffee. There's something about them all that is
like carny people: that slightly gray look to the skin, the sweat
smell, the wild readiness to drink anyone's coffee at all. By which
I mean the stuff from machines, or brown powder in warm
water straight from the spigot, or day-old killer stuff, its surface
sheened with hot grease. Dresden Jones takes in these truckers,
nights like this, first come, first served but with old-timer reg-
ulars getting first dibs.

I come in, and I'm no slouch, I'm wearing no coat, just a
sweater because it was warmer this afternoon and these snug
jeans, no, let's face it, tight jeans, not to drive carny-grey truck
drivers wild but simply because that's what was on the chair
when I ran out to the store. Though these guys sometimes you
would think they'd make these groans in their throats for a bag
lady. So of course there's this shuffling around and the waft-
ing of sweat in the too-hot space heat, and they all kind of go,
arrgh, ahh.

"Shut up. This here is a lady, y'all," Dresden Jones says. "Miz
Borello," he says. "What can we do you for tonight? This ain't
no weather for ladies to be out in. They are predicting a storm."

"I come down 75," one says. "Six rigs off the road. Four
jackknifed in the median, two on the shoulder. This cocksucking

blizzard—excuse my French, honey—is following me. It's a lulu."

"No rooms at Truck Haven down 23. I called ahead," one says.

"I blew my right front tire," I say.

Dresden Jones says, "You got you a spare?"

I feel foolish. I don't know. He sees that.

"We'll look," he says. "Don't you fret."

I'm not fretting, but it's been six months since Richard is gone, engineering in Saudi Arabia, working the oil fields, and every time something like this goes wrong I feel my weak center, like a soft chocolate in an assortment. It's not white, this center, it's off-color, pale pink; it drools. You don't know till you bite, and this bites. This mere blowout. I make resolutions toward toughness, but then I get pissed. I want someone else taking care of this. I'm not one of these ropy types, weight-lifting women, real or mental. I did not bargain for this.

Dresden Jones is outside and back in a flash.

"Miz Borello," he says. "Ain't no spare in that trunk You should not be out driving like that. Worse, that tire ain't one I got in stock. I can get it for you like tomorrow A.M. Not tonight. I'll send over to Coldwater, my brother's station, he's got it, but not tonight. Leave your car over, I'll have it done first thing tomorrow."

I think shit. I think of the McNuggets, getting colder and colder in their front-seat bag, and of Shelley and Shawn hopping up and down, pulling the living-room curtains close to their cheekbones to peer out into the dark, watching for me to come down the long driveway through the trees. I think why would anyone live in a place called Coldwater. I think of why I live where I do: sheer accident, circumstance, best-laid plans knotted and then come unraveled. I moved out here thinking this would be some damn kind of pastoral splendor. Peace, trees, farm kids wholesome as milk for my two to make friends with. Did I get fooled.

"You got no choice, honey," one of the truck drivers says. It sounds menacing. I look a question at him. I'm trying to figure just what he is saying. It's about this tire, but it seems to be something more.

So out of the crowd like Prince Charming steps this guy, I swear a head and a half taller than Got No Choice. Grizzling beard, Kenny Rogers sort. I want to say he's real different from the rest of these guys, but I can't. Smells of oil and tobacco. Big hands. Big, big hands. I notice this right off.

I follow the seam of his jeans up from where it snakes out of his boot—black boot with a strap, I don't know what you call them, boot that looks like he has not taken it off since he drove his first rig—and I find myself checking the curve of his crotch. Jesus Christ, I say, Rosellen, Richard has not been gone *that* long.

"Ma'am," he says, "I can give you a lift."

"This here is Vee Strickland," says Dresden Jones. "I will vouch for him."

"I bought enough diesel off you," says Vee Strickland. I think: he has got a good smile. Clear white teeth. The tobacco smell might be the group's.

"I've got groceries," I say.

"I probably could lift a bag or two," Vee Strickland says. He flexes a black-shirted bicep. The group makes a silly-boys laugh. I figure Vee Strickland has probably knocked someone's block off, in the mists of trucker history, and they're remembering it.

So he takes me home. There are the four bags of groceries and the McDonald's bag. Milk's sweated and is coming through a bag bottom. I take that one, he takes the other three. He's got this eighteen-wheeler, the tractor disconnected from the trailer, which sits in a parallel bunch of such giants in Dresden Jones' gravel lot back of the station.

This rig is as shiny as hell, black with red and gold flames coming off the grille over the fenders and his name, Vee Strickland, in red with gold. This truck looks like it has not been through a snowstorm: it is clean as that.

He reads my mind. "I just got her washed," Vee Strickland says. "Thursdays I get her washed irregardless."

I think: there are more careers than I could ever have thought up, for half-artists. Somebody painted these flames and this lettering, and with incredible love and care. *Vee Strickland* is written in letters that swoop back like long hair in wind, like long hair in the wind off the ocean. The gold leaf caresses each letter, encases and sanctifies. The flames are stylized and have a kind of dignity, as if Vee Strickland were some kind of turn-of-the-century tycoon, bullchested and filthy rich.

I'm a half-artist, too: I do photo oil coloring. Big whoop, you say. Well, I like it. The big studios like to push what they call "natural" color. What's "natural" about it? It's chemicals, that's all. Where I work we do this custom stuff, sepia-toned black-and-white, tinted with little cotton-tipped smooth toothpicks, oil coloring caught in the swab and smoothed into the picture like it was there all the time. Subtle.

I used to do pastels and sometimes acrylics, before I got married to Richard. I went to community college. They said I was good. Here I am now, a half-artist, tinting the faces of all the community college kids—the college gave us a big contract—and making the purple-blue of their gowns richer than life. It looks real classic, better than life. In life, these gowns are pretty bad. Garish. A color like ditto ink. Who wants to remember that?

I'm inside the cab now and it smells like pretty good things, something leathery and something with onions that Vee Strickland ate on the road for his dinner. I point the way home: half mile straight, left turn half a mile, right half a mile, then our driveway a quarter mile shooting straight into the woods. It's odd riding like this, high up; I figure we must look odd, too, with no trailer, a thing like a nose amputated, unnatural.

We have been living here for three months, Shelley and Shawn and me, since the lease lapsed and Richard had not gotten things straightened out yet for us to come. We had been living in the city, a not-bad apartment. We've got all this money socked away but never get round to buying a house. Something's holding us back, I don't know what it is.

This place I've got is a three-bedroom, two stories: one for me, one each for Shelley and Shawn. Shingles, shutters. A gingerbread house, Shelley says, clapping her hands together in perfect conjunction. In joy. We're surrounded by trees, more of them evergreens than not. I like this. I looked at the house on a day in the fall when the leaves were all harvest leaves, brilliant and ready the next week to fade to that bloodsucked yellow, that brilliance that lasts such a short time. I pictured what it would be like in the winter, with light sparkling off the snow, pure white snow we would see for an hour or less in the city before it all turned to gray slosh. And that's what it was like.

The first snows, I was staggered. I'd get up real early like I was a nun of the snow, worshiping. Something sang in my head. I'd make Ovaltine, drink it and listen, real quiet, to the radio station playing old classical music. I don't know that much about it, I just know out of what I hear I like a guy called Scarlatti the best. I'd watch the snow.

Then one night, there's this roar. I look out of the curtains, the way Shawn and Shelley do, making a frame round my eyes so that I can see out. There's this small headlight riding the yard. The headlight expands in the air in a cone till it dissipates; it lights the dark east sides of trunks and casts west shadows onto the snow. A red snowmobile, I can see that, and it's going around and around in a figure eight, revving its motor like it wants some noticing. We have got an acre point eight around us, which is one of the things that I liked about this: no one bumping against our apartment door, no one brushing or tapping the walls of our bedroom.

I go to the front door and Shelley and Shawn are behind me, right there on the stairs, in their white striped pajamas I made, looking like Norman Rockwell. Richard always said that. You want me to say he is an ogre, to make it all simple, but he would laugh, it was affectionate. He'd say: Rosellen, you're trying to make our life into a Rockwell plate. So there they are now: Sister and Brother in Flannel on Stairs.

I open the door and there is a slight hesitation in the snowmobile's forward movement: a bucking, a quick, near-invisible reining-in. This guy's been watching the door, so he's quick to react. I call out to him.

Pardon me, I say. As if I need a pardon. Hey, there, I shout to him, taking courtesy back. You're on our land and you're waking my children up, I yell. He speeds up. I can see this guy's short. I have no idea who it is. He is wearing a red helmet, I can see that. You get over here, I yell, as if that will make him come. What do I think I am doing, a thin woman in a T-shirt standing legs apart in the door with the heat leaking into the night and this demon in red on his snowmobile, what do I think I am doing, in challenging him?

But he comes. It's a kid. He's accustomed to listening sometimes. He's insolent, though. He pushes his clear helmet visor back. He's got this pug nose, the kid's not attractive, he's got these small eyes that are arrogant, testy. He's fourteen or thereabouts.

"You want something?" he says.

"I want you off my land," I say. "I want some peace here, and some quiet. I want you to let my snow be."

"You rent," he says. He says the word "rent" like an obscenity.

"I beg your pardon," I say. I mean You Little Shit, but there's nobody here to back me up and even though this kid is short he is probably my height and would not mind beating the bee-jeezus out of me, right here in front of my kids, and then disappearing forever.

"You rent," he says again, putting an effort into making the word seem pus-filled and slimy.

"And this land's what I rent, and you don't," I say. "Get off my land and go back where you came from."

"My dad's got eleven," he says. With a toss of his helmeted head—and I admit I want it to throw him off balance and into the snow on his head—he indicates where his dad has got his eleven. "My dad owns his own company. Bull Electric. He bought me this here machine." This whole conversation is making my head tight.

"Eleven?" I say.

"Acres," he says. "You ain't got two."

"Then you go ride your eleven," I say.

"Two you don't even own, and you're telling me what to do," he says.

So I say it again. "Go home." And then I shut the door, my heart pounding, and go for the phone book. He's pointed behind our land: "his" land must face Hell Creek Road. I look up Bull on Hell Creek. There it is: 19714. I still am not used to living so far out that we're into five digits. I dial. The noise of the snowmobile's gone, but I sense I will get paid back for my audacity.

"Mr. Bull," I say. "You've got a son. He is here on my land, I'm in back of you, my name is Mrs. Borello, and I want you to tell him to stay off. He won't listen." I think of how I would feel on his end; I know that he doesn't feel anything like what I would. Then I hear it.

"Look," he says. "I know who you are. You are the renter." He says it the same way his son said it. I have an idea where he learned this tone. "What did you say your name is? Miz Bordello?" I've heard this enough times it no longer bothers me. "I'll tell you something. I moved my family out here so my boys could do what they want. Them cops down in the city was on my boys' ass all the time. Boys have got to be boys. I moved us out here so my boys could ride."

"On your land," I say. "Not on mine."

"Miz Bordello," he says. "On my right I have got Neighbor Parkison. He lets my boys on his land. He is right kind, he knows what a neighbor is for. He has got his nine acres, and my Athanasius has got the free run of it. Then on my left I have got Neighbor Deems, who has got his sixteen. Even more than me, though he don't have a pot to piss in besides that. And he lets the boy on."

I add the three parcels of land in my head. I say, "Thirty-six acres should give him enough room." I say, "I want him off my land. I'll call the township police." I think of this Parkison and this Deems, who may be friends, or may simply be bullied.

"The hell you will," he says. He clicks the receiver down.

On the stairs Shawn and Shelley are leaning together like white candles melting. "That's Athy Bull," Shawn says. "He rides our bus."

"He took Ruthie's Locket Pal doll and threw it out the window and we told the bus driver," Shelley says. "All the bus driver said was You Sit Down, to us, not to him. And Athy Bull takes little kids' lunches. Only the good parts."

So I call the township police. They say they've heard of this kid, that his brother was like this before him, that they've got a sergeant who's laying for him on an old score. They say they can get him on trespassing or on a noise ordinance. They say if they catch him on the road they'll slap his dad with a fine he will not forget: the kid is not old enough to be on the road.

When I get off the phone, Shawn, who has been listening, says, "Athy Bull's in the road all the time. He turned over once, rushing the school bus. He was on his four-wheeler. His dad just got it fixed. Maxie Ludens' dad, he is a Vietnam Vet, he put punji sticks all down his driveway to stop Athy Bull in the summer and Maxie said Athy Bull busted about twenty tires before he caught on and went bothering someone else."

"You call us back if he returns," says the township policeman. "We do want to pick this kid up. Don't be shy, ma'am. It's what you pay taxes for." I don't tell him that I'm just a renter and so somewhere beneath contempt.

All of this about Athy Bull goes through my mind in a split-second flash as Vee Strickland turns his giant rig into our drive-way, which is now filling with snow. The truck plows through it easily. The new snow is crisscrossed already with snowmobile tracks, wild incredible tracks circling into and over each other a million times, like a Celtic ornament. I know that kind of thing from when I was in the community college: I thought I might do real commercial art then. A career. And here I am, working for what turns out, picture by picture, to be something like four thirty-five an hour, tinting these cap-and-gown pictures until I am blue in the face. Literally. There is not a day I don't come home lately without blue smudges—the purple-blue of the new graduates' gowns. I think: Celtic ornament indeed. I'm pretty sure Vee Strickland doesn't see that when he looks at the tracks.

"Looks like you been marauded," he says. "Like some maniac's been here."

"You got it," I say, and I shift the milk bag in my lap. The wet off the waxy cartons is soaking into my sweater and my gloves. I tell him about this Athanasius Bull.

"Hell," he says. "Nice woman like you should not have to put up with that. You got no husband, I take it?"

I tell him Richard's in Saudi Arabia. I don't say that I don't hear from him anymore, that I get checks real regularly, but no letters, which Richard said in his last letter some months ago means that there's no news and that if he didn't love us and think of us he would not be sending checks.

He pulls the rig up to the house. We have been brushing under the high trees the whole way, a problem that I had not thought of before. Trees don't have these signs like low bridges. The sound of the evergreen branches scraping on the roof is an odd, cozy sound. I wonder that Vee Strickland doesn't get bent out of shape over this, with the pride that he seems to have in his rig. He helps me down with the wet bag and the Chicken McNuggets. Shelley and Shawn are upon us like crazy things, loving the truck, grabbing for the McDonald's bag.

Shawn runs his finger over the red flames, traces the gold curves ecstatically. "That your name?" he says. "Vee Strickland?"

He nods and is in the house, and you have guessed it already. He knows all these kid things that win Shawn to him like a puppy, tales of ghost drivers on the highways, tales of wrecks he has seen, tales that are half his, half legend. Shawn sits enraptured.

He knows a trick Shelley loves. He persuades her to give him two Chicken McNuggets, he makes them come out of his eyes. Shelley squeals with delight. He can carry them both to their beds at the same time, and I am behind them and smell the truck smell on him, onion smell, Dresden Jones' Marathon smell. He says he is going back to Dresden Jones', says he's drawn lots and gotten the sofa in the back room.

I look out the window, the snow thick as comfort, and hear myself saying that he can stay here, have a shower if he wants, sleep the night on the fold-out divan, which is better than Dresden Jones' cracked plastic sofa. But I did say you guessed it: my sofa is not where he sleeps that night at all. I want to say—and I guess you want me to say—it takes some real hard debating on my part to get into that but it doesn't. I slip just as smooth as you please into that, and I walk into Dresden Jones' Marathon for my tire the next morning just as straight-faced as you please. Dresden Jones doesn't say anything, pretty spooky and quiet in fact, and just slides me the bill.

When I pay, he says, "I guess Vee got you home all right."

"He did," I say. Thirteen years married to Richard and faithful as varnish, but I dovetail into this like Bonnie into Clyde's career. Not that there's anything wrong with Vee Strickland: I'm not making him out any Clyde Barrow. There are good things about Vee Strickland: this man pretends to be nothing but what he is. Showered, he is just as clean as old Richard has ever been. Sleeping, he snores less. In between, he's got Richard beat, Jesus, no contest. I don't tell all of this to Dresden Jones.

And I go on to work, where I line up the green-eyed kids first. There are seven of these, and I've got my cotton and toothpicks and Atlantic Green tube of oil tint and tube of Canadian Timberline Green. Between them, with daubings of yellow or blue or Life Brown (and don't ask me where that name came from, except maybe misprint is all that I can figure: Lite Brown? how should I know?) I can do any green eyes to the satisfaction of even the pickiest. So here are all these green-eyed kids lined up (their purple-blue gowns are not done yet: I work from the top, first the mortarboard, then hair, then eyes) and I wrap my cotton and launch in like a surgeon.

You want me to say either that I am gaga with guilt or with thrill at what I have done, taking Vee Strickland into my bed like that. No, neither. You want me to say I can't work, that I moon out the window or check my own eyes in the mirror, but no, I proceed. One Canadian green, one Atlantic, the rest in dilutions from hazel to almost-blue.

I think this letter: Dear Richard, funny you should ask: yes, last night I slept with a trucker. Sure, Richard he's rough. Which ain't half-bad, not half-bad. The bed moved. No, I did not drug the kids. I've felt like cold shit waiting for your letters. I never considered this option till last night. Slow me, huh? Do you have a harem? A tent with these almond-eyed beauties with soft bellies, jewel-hung navels? Your wife, R. Borello.

I know he's got no harem. Richard is not that way. What do I mean, *that way?* What am I saying? How do I know how Richard is? Would I, could I have predicted this, that he'd vanish off into the desert, the only reminder of him these damn checks that keep coming?

I go home at four, when the kids get there. There's nothing unusual. No odd, embarrassing questions. They take this for granted. So easy, this dovetailing into an alien life that fits like those stretch gloves they are always showing on the TV. Iso-toner. I always did wonder who wore them. I still don't know. All I know is that this feels just like that: an easy fit, with the hand posed, perfect, fingers just so, the bend of the wrist comfortable. My life.

And this feeling of perfectness lasts just as long as it takes for Athanasius Bull to get into his house and eat something and get on his damnable red machine. He revs it up and comes roaring like the wrath of all of the underworld's demons through his father's wholly owned eleven acres of trees with the low winter sun at his back. He roars into the yard like the railroad-train sound of tornadoes, and Shelley starts crying. He pushed me against the emergency door, she says. He called me little shit. He called me rat crap. He took my Reese's Pieces. I think: Richard, if you were here maybe they wouldn't do this, maybe they would respect the fact you've got a dick like them. I think: they are basically cowards. I whip the wet towel I'm holding against the sink's edge in an impotent fury.

I'm on the phone quick to the township police. I'm saying, yes, it's the Bull kid again. They're coming. Athy Bull rides and rides. He's making braid shapes like a slalom between the high, leafless ash trees that stand in a near-row not twenty feet from the house. Roar, like a chainsaw: roar roar. I stand back from the curtains where he cannot see me; I have Shawn and Shelley stay back from the windows. He wants his attention, is what he wants. We will not give it to him. He can get it from the cop with the long grudge.

Now comes the cop, down the driveway. The snow crunches under his cop-car wheels. I see the flash of the rear end of Athy Bull's red machine disappearing over the property line. He is not two feet on the other side. Back and forth he rides, challenging. Back and forth. Here is the cop, getting out of the black-and-white township patrol car. Here is Athy Bull, riding the line. The cop yells to him. Athy Bull yells back, respectfully. Butter would not melt. The boy does not stop, though.

The cop motions him to a halt. Athy Bull stops and butter would still not melt. I hear the cop. You stay off this land, kid, says the cop. This land? Athy Bull says, all sweet buttered innocence. This land? This here is my daddy's land. My daddy owns this eleven. Your daddy's land stops, says the cop, and we're not playing games with you, twerp.

I cannot see the boy's eyes from this distance; I imagine that they darken and narrow. I would have to do them with the Ebony, leaving a mean, wet glint, which is a trick of omission.

The cop says it once more; we're not playing games. Athy Bull stands stock-still till the cop's in his car and the snow sprays behind him, then gives him the finger, with force, a pissed slap to the forearm. I see his lips shape fucking something.

It is not five minutes before the phone rings and it's Mister Bull, Mister Electric Bull, Mr. More-Acres-Than-You, saying I thought I told you, Miz Bordello, that you ought not to be raising this Cain if you know what is good for you. I say I remember exactly what you said, I hope you remember what I said. I hang up the phone. I'm one mean mother now. I laugh at myself and say this to Shawn: I'm one mean mother. He doubles over. We're in new territory. See you in the funny papers, Norman Rockwell, see you in my dreams.

Then I hear shots. Did I say shots? I don't know what shots sound like. City girls don't hear shots unless they are deep city girls, living where neighbors go shooting each other instead of conversing, where kids Shawn's and Shelley's age deal crack, play pimp, turn up dead, murdered over a jacket or silk shirt or basketball shoes. Nonetheless, these are shots.

I see my hand shaking. The shots are coming from Athy Bull's land, deep back into the trees. Shawn says, "He's got a gun. He goes practicing."

"That child?" I say.

"Jason Wiggins said Athy Bull shot up his house one time, just with a BB gun, but he busted their picture window and made holes in the what do you call that . . ." His fingers describe parallel horizontal bars, point to the walls.

"Aluminum siding?" I say.

"That stuff," Shawn says.

"Good Christ," I say. I call the township police. Yes, they're sorry, ma'am, but this is legal, as long as he's not shooting in the direction of your house from less than a hundred yards. I say, "You can't be serious." Yes, they are, and they're sorry.

Outside, the shots keep up, twice the rate you'd think that someone would be shooting, for target practice. Pop, pop, pop, pop, pop, quick and relentless. You'd think he could not pull the trigger that fast. "Just stay inside," I say to the kids. Damn this. Here we are, captive. They can't even go in the trees and throw snow at each other or roll down the bank to the twining, disused Concord orchard. Athanasius Bull's got us.

Vee Strickland has got a run back and forth, Dayton to North Bay, Ontario. I think of him in these odd interim days when he's on the road. He says he'll stop back on his return trip. I think of the thick black hair, ungreyed, that covers the back of his hand and his big knock-your-block-off broad shoulders. I think of myself running fingers through that, and I slip from that into remembering Richard, the smoothness of him, the square engineer fingernails, Richard's chin fresh-shaved, myself running fingers across that chin. Easy as that, flip flip.

Athanasius Bull calls Shelley little shit once more. He won't mess with Shawn, who is almost his height though he's only eleven, and won't mess with Shelley unless Shawn is at the far end of the bus.

I go right to the bus driver and make my complaint. The bus driver rolls his eyes and says, lady, I ain't a babysitter. I say you'll learn or I'll call the damn public schools' transportation department. Norman Rockwell, could you have painted this? Single Mom Swears, Threatens Driver on Bus Step. The bus driver's eyes are averted. I mean it, I say.

There is target practice, random times. I let Shelley and Shawn play out, but I have got my ear cocked and the second we hear popping they both come running in like it was air-raid time.

Shelley's birthday comes. Richard sends a check folded in company notepaper with a brief note. "No card stores here. Have a great birthday. I miss you all." There is enough money for a bike with bright pink tires Shelley has seen at K Mart.

I think: Dear Richard: If you do miss us why have you not sent for us? Do you know that the kids like Vee Strickland's tricks, pulling McNuggets and Oreos out of his eyes? Do you care that they know he slept here and seem pretty damned comfortable with that? Do you expect me to live like this forever, like some damned cactus without water? Your wife, Rosellen B. Then I think of the wetness between me and Vee Strickland. I don't feel guilt. I feel hunger.

That night Athanasius Bull comes back, his driving erratic and frenzied, his snowmobile engine a deafening whine, his headlight twisting crazily through the trees, zip, curve, U-turn, slalom, a devil-path. I watch him through the slightly open curtains, standing back so that he doesn't see me.

"Forget it, Mom," Shawn says. "There's nothing that we can do."

"He pulled my ear yesterday," Shelley says. "I told the bus driver and he pretended that he didn't hear me."

"The bus driver's an asshole," says Shawn.

"Shawn," I say, just a mild chide. I agree: he's an asshole.

Then, on the far side of the house from the wild ride of Athy Bull, there are more lights. The Marines! I think. Vee Strickland's rig is pulling in, rounding the curve of the driveway, the truck motor's roar masked by Athy Bull's demon machine's buzz-saw whine. Vee Strickland parks and leaps out and is across the yard in great leaps like the giant he is. He is in Athy Bull's path. The boy sprays snow, attempts to swerve, stops. I can see Vee Strickland picking him bodily off the snowmobile, by the neck of his snowsuit. The boy's a good foot off the ground, still astraddle, the handlebars dropped from his hands. The Marines!

Still, I don't want Marines. I want peace. I want to be able to handle this all by myself. On the other hand, I want to be taken care of. Oh, shit, I think, what do I want? I want everything perfect, which will not happen in this world. Richard always said that about my charcoal drawings. We went to an oil rig off the Texas coast where he worked when we first were married, and while he was inspecting I sketched the thing. Richard looked at it. It looks like some fairy-tale castle the way that you do it, he said. You want everything perfect and soft-edged and beautiful, he said. Damn right, I said. Perfect and beautiful.

The door opens and Vee Strickland strides in, the fresh, dry snow scattering into the hall from his boots. The Marines! Little motherfuck better stay gone, he says. Shawn grins and Shelley hugs a rag doll to her face, pleased and coquettish behind it, peering at Vee Strickland. Vee Strickland pulls two giant gob-stopper gumballs out of his eyes. Shelley squeals. Shawn grins.

"You go do your homework," I say.

"We don't get it in kindergarten," Shelley says.

"Come on, Shelley," says Shawn. He takes her by the hand.

I'm having a beer and some chili with Vee Strickland out in the kitchen when Shawn comes in. "We are studying this," he says. "The Missouri Compromise."

He says Come Promise. I say it right for him.

"What does that word mean?" he says.

I say it's when you've got to give up something in order to get something, a trade-off, meeting something halfway. He says, "Say it again?"

I pronounce it. He takes his book back into the living room. He has the TV on to entertain Shelley. This is against the rules, but I ignore it. He's doing it to give me time with Vee Strickland.

"I sure don't believe in that," Vee Strickland says. "I have never once compromised in my life."

"No?" I say. This is amazing to me. What is Vee Strickland saying?

"You want a thing, you just go after it," he says.

I think: that's the key, you have got to want just one thing, no more. That's the only way you can do it, live pure, without compromise.

"What's the one thing in your life that you wanted?" I say. I have slept with the man, ridden him like a wild horse, and I don't have half a clue what he thinks. But then I think of Richard: do I have a clue to him, either? I slept with him thirteen years.

He points out the window. "That rig," he says. "And I have got it." I don't know if he has a wife or a family; it seems that he doesn't; he seems to be saying that, too. It is true: he has got that rig, the one thing that he wanted. No flies on Vee Strickland, no mad gnats of compromise. His black rig gleams in the driveway, and snow falls around it like life was a crystal-ball paperweight. Here, Norman Rockwell: Mad Mom Sups with Uncompromised Trucker. In the painting, the chili steams and I am pink-cheeked with virtue.

The kids go to bed, and I shampoo my hair and walk nude in my bedroom in front of Vee Strickland while I towel my hair. He's appreciative, slaps my ass, tells me I smell like a million bucks, takes me to bed. Afterward, we share a single cold beer: this is ultimate intimacy. I think: Dear Richard: Tell me you like and remember with fondness the smell of my shampoo or chili. Say that you've got a tent set up, bought us a camel. I'm satisfied, Richard, right now, if we're talking sex, talking small peas. But I'm sad as hell. Write and tell us to come. Your wife, What's-Her-Name.

You want me to stop right here and draw myself up short and be more demanding of life. You want to say: Who needs this wimp Richard? You want to see Vee Strickland as my white knight. You think this is real rough-cut and cute. You think Vee Strickland's black truck and black shirt are just inside-out versions of purity. You want to paint everything perfect and soft-edged and beautiful. Yep, I have got your number.

At work now, I've finished the whole graduation batch from the community college. There are people backed up demanding their orders. The regular portraits. The babies posed on the fake sheepskin rug, some of them dimpled and cute as those soft-toilet-paper commercials, some homely. Old couples posing to please their grandchildren, their false teeth pearly in their forced smiles from here to here. The engagements, which make me sad: girls in the silky drape that the photographer keeps in the studio, their bodies' lower halves dressed maybe in shorts or something weird, looking from bosom up like they were Grace Kelly early on.

I come home and Vee Strickland's on the road heading for North Bay. The chili bowls sit in the sink from last night. It gets late, and the kids are in bed, and I'm watching a thing on TV about Arabs and mosques. Then, like killer bees mad-diving, there's Athanasius Bull out in the yard and he circles and circles. I just pull my eyelids down over my eyes. The liquid inside them is cool. It has been a hard day. Bzzz, bzzz, roar.

Suddenly there's a silence. A totally sudden thing. I'm spooked. I go to the window, and there is his headlight aimed at a queer, near-upright angle into a tree, there is the snowmobile, nose pointed skyward, and where's Athanasius Bull? I run to the phone, not real sure who I'm calling. I call Dresden Jones.

"Athanasius Bull," I say. "You know, that kid." Dresden Jones knows him. He's chased him away enough times. "He's crashed into a tree in my yard. Dear God." Why am I calling Dresden Jones? This is no business of his.

I call Mr. Bull. "Your son," I say. "In my yard again. Hit a tree." I expect him to threaten to sue me, but he does not. I suppose that will come later.

Dresden Jones is there in minutes; just behind him comes Emergency, flashing its blue roof light. Dresden Jones finds the boy, thrown clear. They're there with a stretcher, they're quick, they are scooping him up. Dresden Jones lopes across the snow toward the house. I expect him to warn me that it's not a pretty sight, I can just hear him saying this, but he does not.

Instead he says, "Clean as that, ma'am. Broke his neck."

They are pulling the sheet over Athy Bull's face on the gurney as Mr. Bull pulls in the driveway and runs toward them. I see the wild pantomime of grief. I look at Shelley and Shawn and think what is more fierce than a parent's love. Mr. Bull waves his long arms like a windmill gone nuts. I am sure as I watch him: he's going to sue me. My heart's aching six ways to Sunday.

It's maybe a week later. I'm at work, doing an engagement portrait, redoing it. Somebody's complained I don't know green from hazel, said why can't I just do it right, isn't that simple enough? I'm thinking why is this poor girl getting herself engaged? Ignorance, ignorance. Why can't we live long enough so that when we have finally learned something about life, we have still got some time left to use it? I picture this poor bride-to-be in the studio for her sitting, wrapped in the glittery wrap that they use for these portraits, her whole bottom half exposed.

Where I work's back of a curtain behind the receptionist's desk. While I'm lifting the green from the girl's eyes to make them more hazel, I'm listening to this voice out front talking to the receptionist. It's a kind of a country voice, nothing offensive.

"I want this picture copied and colored," the voice says. "I want an enlargement eleven by sixteen, six five by sevens, and three dozen wallets."

The receptionist hesitates. "This your son?" she says. She sounds real doubtful about this particular picture.

"It is," says the woman. She sounds sad and proud.

"This is going to cost you," the receptionist says. "What I'd recommend is that you bring your son in and get this retaken. This is not a good one to work from. Especially for all those wallets, the detail's too tiny, you see what I mean? Then again, it's not good for the big one either. When you blow the thing up it gets blurry and stuff. First off, there is this shirt. You can hardly do plaids with this oil tint, those tiny lines, see? All the, pardon me, zits, too. Boys just get them, you know they'll out-grow them, but if you'd bring him in we could do this portrait fresh and airbrush out the flaws. Start over from scratch, Mrs.—?"

"Mrs. Bull," says the voice, which of course you guessed. You know the part that comes next. "I can't bring him in," says Mrs. Bull. "He's been taken from us."

The receptionist doesn't quite get it.

"He's buried!" the woman says, shrill now and brittle. "He's cold in the ground! My boy!"

"In that case," the receptionist says, and her voice is real squeaky and queer and I know what she's thinking. She's think-ing, I'm glad I don't have to sit tinting these pictures, creep me out, the whole nine yards. "We'll just have to do what we can, won't we?" I like how she's saying *we.* "I'm sure Rosellen can do something nice for you. Here, let's just get down the infor-mation. . . ."

I'm not thinking about what I'm doing but when I look I see my hands packing up the toothpicks real neat in their little box, folding the paper liner to the cotton box, screwing the tops of the tubes on. I'm ready to clear out my workspace. I'll write my letter resigning as of right now. So they get bent out of shape, so they just find a new goddamn colorist. I'll stop en route home at the Wendy's right off the I-94 exit and celebrate.

The next thing I'm going to do you will criticize, I know that. You'll go, Compromise, Compromise, big exclamation point. You'll get all over my case about having some pride. But I say, who the hell are you to be so critical? Whoever it is you're sleeping with, that guy is either Vee Strickland or Richard. No-body's sleeping with Prince Charming, not even Princess Di. That Charles has got ears! Princess Di is supposedly sleeping with her chauffeur anyway, that kind of thing, if you read the *Enquirer*, and don't say you don't because there's not anyone who doesn't, sometimes.

I'll write to Richard, and I'll *send* this letter. I will say: Richard, I'm buying the tickets tomorrow. We're coming. You'll get used to it. You love us, remember? And us three will get used to it, too. We've been knowing for quite a while how to get on in the desert. So much sand. So very much sand.

Pain Perdu

I lost nothing, I said to myself on the morning after the night that I lost my virginity. I found something, gained something, grew, am wise, promise to blossom tomorrow into essence-of-womanhood, wisdom, something a Renaissance painter might raise from the dead to portray in his oils, a carmine blush on the pale hillocks of my half-exposed breasts. I looked into the silvered-glass triptych of my dresser mirror—a wholly non-functional thirties-bred thing I had not yet been able to part with—and wanted to see subtle lights of experience playing across my grey irises. But I saw nothing.

I tossed my white sweater across the high back of the chaise longue. I sucked in my breath once unexpectedly—a sound one might have taken for a quick, unwilled sob—and said out loud to no one at all, "Well. Now. Camilla." I spoke to myself. There was no one else there to say anything to.

Boulie, my grandmother, had been dead now for four years. The three orphan cousins, Jeannine, her brother Hollis, and myself, had grown up in the Boulanger house on the good end of Carrollton Avenue. We could see the green curve of the levee from our front porch; Saint Charles Avenue was not a block away.

Jeannine had married early, and now at twenty-three was moving through a divorce into bitter and premature middle age. Hollis still lived in the room down the hall, but we passed like two ghosts in the mist.

Hollis was uninterested in anything but his Bix Biederbecke collection and the restoration—in the cavernous damp garage under the living room, where the old unused push mower had become one with the shadowed white wall, by a membrane of cobwebs—of the sleek Jaguar he'd bought with a part of his recent substantial inheritance. The Jaguar had been owned by a minor Near-Eastern Shah, and Hollis found that fact an endless source of interest, the only thing he'd mention when we would occasionally meet in the kitchen for a breakfast of Creole cream cheese and Falkenstein's French bread.

We could never use up a whole loaf, so we were bound by some half-sense of guilt at potential waste to share the bread, whose flimsy white paper could not keep it fresh more than two or three hours. So we sat at the porcelain-topped table and made conversation about this imagined prince, what he might eat, whether he had a harem, if Moslems were circumcised, how this pewter-hued car with its fenders like legs of a primeval cat poised to spring might change Hollis' life. I would listen, but I had very little to offer back. Hollis bored easily. I did not test him.

Nonetheless, I thought Boulie and Hollis and bitchy, bright-lipsticked Jeannine would have all approved of the young man I had chosen. The whole act was not unromantic, but neither was it without something like plan.

The young man was of good family, which would have pleased Boulie: her dream for my life was that I should have my debut at the Saint Charles (though we had neither money nor social connections quite up to that grandeur) and in consequence marry someone with a name that bespoke old New

Orleans, a name with a scent of old money about it, silk-soft, unimpeachably Audubon Boulevard folk, of a law firm with monogrammed sterling letter openers, or a cotton brokerage, or even one of the steamship firms. The young man's background was wholly adequate: his family home was on State Street, his father had interests in oil, and his sister had married a Du Vernais.

Hollis cared little for anyone else's amours and had none of his own. Hollis seemed to have pledged an impassioned fidelity to his car. Nevertheless, Hollis would have approved of the young man's school connections. Hollis was himself a Tulane man. Roll on, Green Wave—Tulane's cheer—Hollis might have chanted, if I'd told him.

Jeannine, had she known about it, would have envied me. She had drooled over Phi Kappas but had never dated one. Here I had not only dated a Phi Kappa, but had him take me to bed, elegantly, with room-service champagne and Eggs Benedict and a remarkable grasp, for a green college junior, of where a young woman might like his hands roaming. Jeannine, Jeannine, I thought, semi-smugly, a point for me. She was always the winner, before. But I never would tell her. I'd bloom as she withered. My life was a bright path before me now.

But as simple as I told myself that event or transition had been, I slept badly that week. It was spring and that sort of weather which leads one to vacillate: open the windows? turn on the air-conditioning, the first flip of that switch for the year? So I tossed. But the tossing was bred more of dreams than of weather.

I dreamed the first night of the circus. The Shrine Circus, it was, and all that I could remember upon waking was watching a clown burst again and again through an enormous white circle of paper. It is all too clear now what was being burst, but at the time I did not make connections. I wince at the thought that my dreams had put zinc-oxide whiteface and giant bright lips (redder and broader than even Jeannine's!) on my Phi Kappa.

He was not only from an oil family but had some small tennis title, Mid-South Pan-Frat. Who knows what.

And I dreamed that same night some vague dream about my First Communion. It started a series. I dreamed first this snatch, then that. Dreamed of the night before my First Communion, of some small scene on the morning itself, of the face of the nun who instructed me or of our black maid or Boulie's friend Schillebeeckx. Dreamed of the smell of small, flickering candles in red glass, the smell of the ironing Dorotee always was doing, the harsh smell of squat Sister Cunegunde's teeth as she leaned in my face with a page of the blue Baltimore Catechism. Dreamed of odd Mr. Schillebeeckx bringing me gifts home from Holland. Dreamed of Boulie's voice asking me, "Now have you finally found it?"

I had not lived long with Boulie at that time. My parents had died not a month before. Marinel Boulanger Danvers and Randal Ray Danvers, both twenty-five, leapt from the world in an aqua convertible late one spring night, one grand manic leap over the seawall into mossy-bottomed Lake Pontchartrain. There they sat dead in their seats with warm water green up to their shoulders and lapping, their pretty pink partying necks snapped, their two faces clean and surprised as two angels'. The coffins were open.

In the two weeks I was kept home from school to make all the arrangements, to move my things way across town to the Boulanger house, to the room where my mother had lolled on the same chaise longue, dreaming of Randal, her prince, her forever, my class at Holy Angels had made its First Communion en masse. My own veil, with its circle tiara of tiny mock pearls, hung unused in the closet. I wondered when I would make my own Communion. I wondered if anyone realized.

Dorotee was the black maid, a high-school girl who came each afternoon, cooked, cleaned, and ironed and went home at an hour not long after supper. I knew Boulie loved me, but she was not quite there for me. Every afternoon Schillebeeckx came with his massive brown cowhide mail sack, slick with years, sometimes earlier and sometimes later. Boulie was getting ready for his visit, when I came in from school, if he was not already there. I smelled Toujours Moi, its incredibly vertical powdery smell an assault, when I walked in that door. To this day, when I catch in a bus or department store that primal, vicious, sweet smell I see Boulie and Schillebeeckx playing bourrée in the living room, at the card table that never came down, arguing and taking each other's red beans that they used for chips.

I would pass them by if it was Boulie's turn; she would call me back to kiss her rouged, doughy cheek. She would say the same ritual words, "You go out in the kitchen, Camilla, chère. Dorotee's gone to have something for you."

Dorotee sometimes did and sometimes did not. When she did not she would scowl. "That Miss Boulie, she drive me some crazy," said Dorotee. "She go and tell you I got something, but she never sent me to the store and I been starch, starch, starch since I got here. What she expect me to give you."

"I'm hungry," I said. I was seven. I only knew that I was hungry.

"Lord, Lord," Dorotee said. She never said anything once when she thought twice or three times might do.

"I can just go ask Boulie for money to run to the grocery. Plum Street. I can buy us both Musketeers."

"No, honey," Dorotee sighed. "You just name what you want that I got here. It would give me a reason that I could stop starching awhile. And Miss Boulie gone yell at me like I was starving you blind, if I don't give you something right now, with no running to Plum Street."

"Anything I want?" I said.

"That I got," said Dorotee. "Not nothing that's not in this kitchen."

"Then I want Lost Bread," I said. What everyone everywhere else calls French toast, in New Orleans we called Lost Bread. Why in a place where there was not much that wasn't French would we single out anything and call it French? I suppose it was twice French, Lost Bread being made of the Falkenstein's French bread—which we did call French bread—that was left over, stale, unused.

Dorotee laid aside her bluish milky starch and turned the iron off. The smell of her starching was deep in her rich, dark skin as she passed me to go take the eggs out and get the Steen's syrup.

"You smell like ironing," I told her.

"You smell like a tin can," she said. "I don't know how little white children do that. You smell them after they playing, they smell like a tin can."

She broke eggs. I watched spellbound. I wondered how long it would be before I could break eggs like that. I had tried once and made a mess I could not get cleaned up, sticky egg white and yolk mingled, spread all across the linoleum. What you done? Dorotee had said. Broke fifty eggs? I said it had been only two. You done it good, honey. This gone to take me a hour to clean, then I got to go wax it again.

I did not say that I was sorry. Dorotee had said I did not need to. "It don't matter," she said. "Miss Boulie pay me by the hour."

Dorotee had taught me to play Battle one day when Boulie had gone to the doctor's. We used the forbidden card table that day, with my promise not to tell, and I learned to deal cards with an insouciance I had envied in Dorotee. I had not mastered the fine art of shuffling yet, movements like bird wing and dance, the slick whir of their edges, flack flack, as they slipped back against themselves.

I watched Dorotee frying the bread in the pan. Her breasts pressed against her white school blouse; in back I could see the wide band of her bra in the sweat that stuck the fabric to her skin. The Lost Bread sizzled. "When did you get a bra, Dorotee?" I said. "When did you get boobies?"

She frowned at me, but her mouth smiled. "Something about

this kind of talk I believe your grandma would not think is right," Dorotee said. "Something you should not talk to a nigger about. You know what she say."

"Poo," I said.

"I got these last November," she said, crossing her breasts with the shiny chrome turnover handle. "I wrote off to a cereal box."

"You shut up," I said.

"You yourself, tin can," she said.

"I want to know something," I said. "And I can't ask Boulie."

"And what is that."

"I want to know when I get to make my First Communion. My class got to make it already and I have my veil and all," I said.

"You scared to ask," Dorotee said.

I said yes I was.

"I can mention that," Dorotee said. "I can say, when you gone to be wanting me starch that child's dress for her Holy Communion. One way to find out."

"I would like that," I said. She slid my plate toward me.

"You know something," Dorotee said. "This got more than two ways to be naming it. One, like the Yankees say French bread, and two, like the people say Lost Bread in this town, but I am in French class in high school and you know what we call it? Pain Perdu."

I said the words the way she said them.

"That is fine French for a tin can," she said. I thought her eyes were very bright and that having a black maid who spoke French was something I might mention to my new friends at my new school, rather chic, an edge.

"And you know what else," she said. "You got Lost Bread two ways. You lost your bread moving like that at Communion time."

"That is not bread," I said, knowing my doctrine. This was the one thing that we had to know to be allowed to receive our

Communion. "It looks like bread, but it is Jesus, the really true Jesus." I was sober in my awe of what I knew to be impenetrable mystery, mystery I would never break through.

"I would not know about that stuff," Dorotee said. "I am Babdist."

"Oh," I said. "I don't know what a Babdist is."

"Louder and wetter," said Dorotee. "We babtize down by the river. We sing, too, Lord, not like you sing. You can come with me sometime if Miss Boulie say."

"I would like to," I said.

"Eat your food," she said. "Miss Boulie gone to be yelling at me now about spoiling your dinner."

She did talk to Boulie, and I spent two weeks' worth of afternoons with Sister Cunegunde in the dark convent's front parlor going again and again over the questions I already knew: why God made me, what sin was and what kinds there were to choose from, what the flat thin white wafers that looked like bread really were. Then I was ready.

I was ushered, one Friday afternoon, into the red-velvet curtained confessional's darkness to tell my sins. I had to scrape for them. I knew that I really was innocent. I said that I had had bad thoughts. I felt the priest's ears perk up. What kind? he asked me. I told him that I had thought I was not sorry my mother and father had died because they were too crazy for me and my grandmother even said that she was kind of relieved because she had been waiting for something to happen and it was no more than a question of time. He said that was not really what bad thoughts meant and had I maybe talked back or lied or stolen something from Woolworth's.

I said no, but that I had skipped my Morning Offering. How many times? He said. I said, always. I didn't tell him I said my Prayer to the Guardian Angel instead, like a burst of light upon awakening, summoning that wild-winged creature in full robes who guarded me.

Well, he said, anything else? I said that I saw my boy-cousin naked twice and did not look away, but then I thought that was a mistake to say, because I was not sorry. So I said I was not sorry for that. The priest sighed.

He said are you sorry for skipping your morning prayers? I did not correct him and say that I only skipped the Morning Offering. I just said yes. So he said I should say the three ritual Hail Marys, Our Fathers, and Glory Bes. I had the feeling he was not pleased with me, his mumbled absolution not-withstanding.

That night I sat up in my bed propped on three pillows. Hollis was in his room and Jeannine was in hers. Neither of them would talk to me because they were jealous of all the attention. They were Presbyterian and they said this was just foolishness.

Boulie said I did not need to worry about them. Their parents—their father was my mother's brother—had died in a car wreck two years before mine. It seemed all very normal to us, what one's parents did, died in car accidents. Boulie said I was just to rest tonight and not to get into an argument with Jeannine, which Jeannine would have loved.

From my bed I could see everything in the whole house. The house was a raised shotgun double, the rooms a straight shot back, one behind the next, living room, dining room, two bedrooms, kitchen and bath, two sets of them.

But when Boulie had taken in Hollis and Jeannine, she had thrown up her unmotherly but not heartless hands and evicted the tenants on the other side. She had had carpenters connect the two sides like Siamese twins, through a Roman arch that connected my doorless room with what was now the dining room.

At the front of the house, in the light from the craning pleat-shaded lamp, I could see Boulie and Schillebeeckx playing bour-rée. The oscillating silver-caged table fan sputtered and buzzed. Boulie and Schillebeeckx bantered and muttered their bids and then argued, and Schillebeeckx got up and down for their drinks. They were drinking a lot that night, and they were louder than usual.

I pulled the heavy chenille of the spread up around me as I sat, though it was hot.

Dorotee passed in the hall. "It don't look to me like you are even trying to get to sleep," she chided.

Boulie waved a hand with its dark-polished fingernails in Dorotee's direction and shouted, "Dorotee, you leave that child alone. She has got to get her beauty sleep."

Dorotee looked at me as if to say, What can you do. She scuffed on down the hall in the soft bedroom slippers she always wore in our house.

"I got Miss Camilla's shoes polish," she said. "On the toe where she scuff it at practice."

"That's fine," Boulie said. "Could you bring us a drink, Dorotee?" Mr. Schillebeeckx seemed half asleep in his chair, though the game was in progress.

"I got her dress starch," Dorotee said. "I don't know why. This heat, that organdy gone to be steaming like rice, and just as soft, the time that she get to the church."

"You just mind your own business," said Boulie.

"I was just saying," Dorotee said. Once or twice a day it seemed the two of them were on the verge of an argument, but it did not ever happen.

"Well, you just go get us a drink," Boulie said.

Dorotee passed my room on her way back from serving them and said, "Your slip and your underpants ready and laid out right there on the iron board. I got your veil iron, too, and set up on Miss Boulie's extra wig stand. You all set, honey. And I am going home."

She did, but I still could not sleep. Jeannine poked her head into my room and made faces, Hollis tapped on my wall with his umbrella, Boulie and Schillebeeckx argued and laughed in quick cycles. My alarm clock was set.

Suddenly it was morning and I was awake. I called down my guardian angel. I set my feet on the floor. This was the day I would move from the ranks of mere children, who sat in the pews while their elders filed up for the Eucharist. I reminded myself that I could not let anything pass my lips: I could not slip into the kitchen and slice an end off a perfect banana, as I did some mornings, or dig out a handful of Kix and drop them down my throat. I would take it to the limit: I would not even drink water.

I went to the ironing board for my socks and my underwear, took down my dress from the place where it hung in the hall doorway, swaying in rhythm with the oscillating fan. That fan was normally on only when Boulie and Schillebeeckx were at bourrée, but I assumed Boulie had left it on, purposely, for the hot night. "Circulation!" she'd cry. "Circulation!"

I went to the wig stand. Boulie wore a wig tinted apricot white over her wispy hair when she went out. People would remark on her fine head of hair and she would let them. I took down my veil. The wig stand was of yellow wood, old and slick, shaped like an egg. It looked odd and obscene standing empty. I tried to anchor my veil on my hair and I could not.

I tiptoed toward Boulie's room for her box of hairpins and then I wondered why she was not up. The door was open. I peered around the frame. Boulie was not in her bed. The heavy crocheted coverlet was in place. All of the smocked satin pillows were laid in their places across the bed's head. I heard the fan moaning its rhythmic electric moan, back and forth. I went into the living room.

Boulie and Schillebeeckx sat upright in their chairs. For a hair's-breadth of a second I thought they were dead like my parents, and it seemed the whole world would die off this way, in pairs, suddenly, sitting up. But they were only asleep, having had far too much to drink and stayed up far too late. This had never happened before.

I went to Boulie and tried to wake her. I shook her arm, which rested on the arm of the big tapestry chair. Her skin was powdery and loose. I smelled Toujours Moi.

"Boulie," I said. "Wake up. It's my First Holy Communion."

She slept on. The hypnotic sleep-rhythm of her breathing broke for a minute and then resumed.

"Boulie," I said. "We have to go in twenty minutes."

But she would not waken. I went into the kitchen. I looked at the box of starch next to the sink and I wished Dorotee were here. She would come with me, Babdist or not. I listened for sounds from Jeannine's room and Hollis'. I would even prefer their noxious presence to going to my own Communion alone. But they slept on, their doors open, their covers flung peacefully this way and that.

So I did what I could with the hairpins and picked up my prayer book and freshly ironed handkerchief and rosary and tiptoed out the door, down the stairs onto Carrollton Avenue. It was four blocks to church, and I cried until half the way through the third. Then I said out loud, "Well. It does not matter."

I dreamed of the night before that Communion, and of that morning, over and over, again and again. Of the ceremony itself I did not dream, and I remember only scant details of it. It was not unlike the half-eclipse of memory and sense that I felt when I was taken by my Phi Kappa to the Fontainebleau.

Of that night at the Fontainebleau I have few but sharp juxtaposed memories. That boy's hands, with fine fingernails, white-mooned and seeming never to have worked in his life, sliding over my hipbones, across my smooth stomach again and again, soothing, slipping into the curled secret hair. The bottle of champagne sweating on the silver tray as it waited for us in the morning. My white corsage with its pin stuck through the gummy corsage ribbon sitting on a table under the window. My silver shoes, neatly placed, looking quite empty.

My Communion is built of sharp images in recollection as well. The sounds of the old organ behind a May hymn to the

Virgin: "Bring flowers of the rarest, bring flowers of the fairest, o'er mountain and river and hillside and vale. Our full hearts are swelling, our glad voices telling, the praise of the loveliest rose of the dale." It is more than remarkable that I remember the whole thing: I cannot think when I have sung it since then. I fixated upon the Stations of the Cross, fourteen bas-relief plaques that lined the walls along both sides of the church, which I did not yet understand: Veronica wiping the face of Christ and his face coming off, bright and in color, like a photograph on the cloth that she offers; the stripping, the nailing, the dying. I wondered in particular why the three falls of Jesus were commemorated, and how they knew that he had fallen three times. I looked at the first station, where Pilate was laying down his harsh sentence. We were to know he was Pilate because behind him in the bas-relief there was a banner that said SPQR and meant he was Roman.

When it came time to go up for Communion I realized I had been woolgathering. I looked up at the cross hanging over the altar. Above the pale corpus hung the furled scroll reading INRI. The nuns told us these were initials for Jesus of Nazareth, King of the Jews.

As I proceeded on slippery soles toward the altar, I tried hard to hold my head upright so that my veil would not slip free. I did not want to create a spectacle: I was the sole First Communicant, a mere leftover, an orphan and freak. I repeated to myself, syllabically, magically, SPOOKER and INRI, the signs from the station and crucifix. SPQR—SPOOKER—and INRI.

In a flash at the Fontainebleau, as my Phi Kappa slipped into me, I saw the image of that station JESUS FALLS FOR THE FIRST TIME, and as he moved in that piston-like dance I imagined I always had known, my head chanted on in-stroke and out-stroke, first SPOOKER then INRI.

That was seven years ago. I have not languished in celibacy; there have been more men than I would care to count, though I could probably number them accurately if I tried. I make my living in a profession where precision matters, and I carry it like an implant within me. Some of these men have been thoughtful, some rough and incredibly distant; some came back and some did not; three of them have proposed more than once. But I am not ready to marry, yet.

I do have an image of what it will be, that wedding, when it finally comes. Though I do not have anyone to give me away, I have set aside money just for the occasion. There will be a coach, black as onyx to set off the white of my gown, and a shiny black horse out ahead of it. This will be Mexico, on the coast, perhaps Bermuda; the ocean will be in view, either way.

There will be pillowy banks of cymbidium orchids surrounding me. As I leave the church I look up and see the local peasantry, or if it is Bermuda, the local gentry, waving from the rooftop of the chapel. Sun glints off the mica in the white stone blocks of the church. All I lack is a bridegroom: he never is there in the picture, and I have yet to meet, in my life, a man perfect enough to be there.

After my Communion, when I returned home, Boulie had gone into her room and was sleeping on top of the covers, but Schillebeeckx had disappeared. Jeannine was putting her thin hair up in curlers and Hollis was cutting the newspaper up. Dorotee was in the kitchen. I did not tell her I'd cried or been disappointed that no one had come. I did not say, Dorotee, I wish you had been there.

She said, "Honey, I hate to be you."

I just stared at her.

"You do not need to say nothing," she said. "These relations you got I would not give two cents for. I starch till my hands turning white to stay, and old Miss Boulie get drunk and sleep through."

I took off my veil and hung it on the obscene egg.

"What you want? More Lost Bread?"

I said no. I felt quite adult. "Three eggs," I said. "Not too hard. Soft."

I ate silently. Dorotee muttered at intervals.

It was not until Boulie died, four years ago, that I thought about her long affair with Mr. Schillebeeckx and realized that that is what it had been, an affair. I was amazed in retrospect that I had not known, but children are not tuned to the clues and do not ask the questions we might.

An image, unbidden, arose: Boulie and Mr. Schillebeeckx, romping, some night after we were asleep, Boulie, nude, prancing like some bareback circus rider on her high sweet white-sheeted hard-mattressed bed, her Mr. Schillebeeckx chasing her like a young swain, his pink buttocks bare, round as a boy's. I laughed and I conjured on purpose the image of Boulie and Schillebeeckx locked in gymnastic embrace on the trampoline of those white sheets, their cheeks red with exertion and happiness, the room filled with the smells of the juices the young think long locked away. Boulie had told me once, when I asked why she did not marry Schillebeeckx, Why should I? Why would I want to? She had had enough of that, thank you.

Mr. Schillebeeckx brought me a gift that same summer. He went back to Holland each year for a visit to relatives. That year, my first in the household, I looked forward to his return and knew what he would bring me. He would bring me wooden shoes.

But when he came he brought a fold-out book from his sisters' town, elegant, bound at the hinges in rusty-brown cloth varnished shiny and smooth. In the same rusty brown it said, in English *The Book of the Countryside*. On its eighteen fold-out panels in browns and in greens and in rich bloody reds, with a touch of gold ochre here, blue there, the pageant of someone's platonic conception of countryside spread in a hinged panorama. Each panel, cut out to peer through, was more wonderful than the next.

Here, a small silvery pond with a pair of white ducks floating royally—probably swans, I think now: far too royal for ducks. From the pond a small silvery stream going on for a number of

panels, with miniscule flashing blue fish in its depths. Trees and
trees, one creating the reason for each of the hinges, the countryside linked and created by trees. A panel of black and white
cows, grazing, udders distended with milk as they wait for the
milkmaid who sits looking off at a cloud as she milks one beast,
who looks off, too, at a cloud in the other direction, the pair
of them seemingly shy in this intimate milky connection.

A bridge, vaguely Japanese. A child out in a field picking
mythical flowers, the sun on its Dutch-looking hair. Horses,
reddish and sleek. Shy, chaste lovers who spread out a picnic
on spotless white damask. And up in the tree, giving the lie to
it all, blending well enough with the tree trunk and boughs that
it is easy to miss him, a satyr, his goat-legs crossed, nostrils
flared, nubs of horns lit by the sunlight, playing a musky and
lust-ridden tune on his pipes.

When Mr. Schillebeeckx brought me the book I took it from
his hands with what I suppose now was a look of dismay. I
tried to force back the look into the blacks of my eyes, but I
did not quite make it.

"You don't like the book?" he said, his extended Dutch Os
speaking keen disappointment.

"No, no, that's not it," I said. "That's not—"

"I think that Camilla was hoping for wooden shoes," Boulie
said.

"Boulie!" I said, caught and shamed.

"Then why didn't you tell me," he said. His *Th*s verged on
becoming *D*s; *W*s were almost *V*s. He had worked hard at the
language, but Dutch stuck to him hard, like a sap or epoxy.

I looked at the book. I had not actually seen what it was yet.
"It's very nice," I said.

"What is so grand about wooden shoes?" he said, puzzled.
"I am so glad to have these. American soles," he said, tapping
the bottoms of his mailman's shoes.

In the kitchen Dorotee said, "I think whatever it is you don't
have, that's the thing you want, honey."

I felt slapped.

"Oh, no, baby, I never meant. That is just how we can be. I am like that. You got to want something," she said.

I keep wanting it. At my Communion, the wafer dissolved on my tongue in a split-second and I was in mortal doubt God had ever been there. I do not remember my Phi Kappa's name or I would have used it, though his hands were the smoothest I ever have known. And the dream of my wedding still lacks a groom. If life is just a fold-out book, cows and milkmaids, and satyrs, that ought to be more than enough.

But as Dorotee said, you have got to want something.

Siege, with Swans and Starlight

The house had been a good plan to begin with: Cherry told herself that. They were sitting in darkness and watching a movie that Archer had just gone down to Pak-a-Video and brought back: the two of them and his twin brother's kids, Becca Lu and Marky. The movie was a Kathleen Turner movie, and Cherry was beginning to think Archer had a thing for this actress with the flaring nostrils and the well-defined teeth and the slink and the overly common name. He had brought home three of her movies in the past two weeks.

No, the plan for the house had not been an unreasonable one. Archer was a good lawyer. He had a good, substantial workload. His office had genuine teak-veneer paneling and, as he liked to joke, the obligatory Bigelow on the floor, in a shade tastefully between blue and slate grey. It was reasonable to assume a life-style in concord with that.

She, the tightwad of the family, as he affectionately dubbed her, had had a diminutive inner resistance at first to the plan: she had spent her twenties in single thrift, a prim TV-dinner-consuming librarian (media specialist, children's department). But her heart leapt with joy at the prospect: her thrift had been out of necessity, and now three years into marriage to Archer Claess she loved the thought of the brick home on the lake and all that it meant.

She loved the long drive out the river, the road curving serpentine hugging the banks, and the sun flashing off the rock-rippled skin of the clear water. She loved the white-painted brick of the house—something she thought she could never love. Who would paint brick? Who would love it? But love it she did.

She loved all of the house's hidden possibilities. There was a room in the ground-level basement—with light and a high ceiling—that would make Archer a wonderful study: it had a full view of the lake and the swans. There was a dishwasher that hummed smugly, a microwave oven that forced her—in sheer bliss—to learn to cook, over again. She had never cared about these sorts of things. There was a room, facing the front, facing the long grassy arm of the golf course, that they would make into a nursery, if things worked out.

The deal was a lease with the option to buy. Archer knew the intricacies of this sort of thing. He was a levelheaded man, and had more experience of life than she did. He had been married before, and had bought and sold two houses in the course of that eight-year union.

Cherry did not like to think of that marriage; she had come to her own nuptials as from a nunnery. She had met Archer's first wife a couple of times, the first time in the A&P. She was a beautiful woman, not unlike the Kathleen Turner who paraded across the screen now, with the other three there in her living room rapt at attention as Cherry's mind wandered. She was also, Cherry thought for the first time, not unlike Archer's twin brother Bart's wife, Paige. The world was full of Kathleen Turner clones, and Cherry had a momentary hope that the actress had not made too very many movies that had become videos, or they would spend their lives watching them.

Archer had introduced Cherry to his first wife, Lynette, with no signs of discomfort or anguish, which Cherry found rather remarkable. Lynette had left Archer, and Archer had pined until Cherry came into his life, and well into their relationship, and, she suspected, even now. The three of them stood in Aisle Five—Canned Vegetables/Fruit; Ketchup/Mustard/Mayonnaise; Pickles and Olives—and Archer watched them shake hands. Cherry found her eyes wandering over the beets: Harvard, sweet-and-sour, julienne, small, whole, and sliced.

Archer talked on, pain-free. Cherry did not want to look at the hipbones of this sleek woman in her soft wool dress and compare them to her own, or ask herself how Archer might be comparing them. Instead, she inventoried the bean section: three-bean salad in glass with the screw-off lid or in the four-serving cans, kidney beans, pork 'n' beans, navy beans in jars meant for a school or a camp, black beans with their exotic label in a language that by a process of elimination and extrapolation she guessed had to be Portuguese.

"We'll have to have Lynette and her friend out," Archer was saying. "Have them out and you can make that wonderful chicken dish you make, that Thai thing with cashews and red peppers."

"Friend?" said Cherry. She had not been listening.

Archer made a motion with his hand as if to indicate that the language had no word for this. Lynette had a lover and Archer had no word for her deepened betrayal. Instead, he would ask Cherry to cook her Chicken Cashew for the two of them, a kind of anesthesia-by-poultry.

"We have got evenings tied up, in general," Lynette said. Cherry was glad of this mercy. "I have my work, he has his, we have so little time." There was a subtext: we spend every moment we have gazing into each other's eyes, linked like the lovers of some John Donne poem. "But maybe when summer comes, we'll get together, yes? That would be nice."

Cherry thought she might be able to grow a callus around her heart, given that number of months to prepare. She smiled brilliantly. She nodded. She inventoried the kinds of corn: a vast panorama of corn, a pale-peacock array of corn: creamed corn and niblets and Mexicorn, baby corn stuffed into glass with gold pop-off lids, corn relish, and even plain, water-packed corn in generic cans, black-and-white labeled.

She took Archer's arm as he propelled the basket off toward the canned fruits, leaving all of her unmade decisions about beets and beans and corn still unmade. That was okay: she could always come back.

Kathleen Turner was tossing her hair and the children were laughing about something. Archer seemed distracted. Out the back window the broad picture window looked in great splendor out onto the lake, and the stars sparkled brilliantly in the dark water. A swan moved across their line of vision. Cherry ached at the perfection of it.

Here she was, in the house finally, with a sectional sofa on order that fit the dimensions of this room quite perfectly. Here she was, the mistress of this house, taking care of these two lovely children while Bart and Paige were off in Thailand. (Of all places, though! Cherry had taken a Thai cooking class, but had not been to that country, and her full joy was tempered: she had to admit that she felt mildly envious.) Here she was, married to Archer, with a choir-boy silk shock of ruddy blond hair and a racquetball-flat stomach—unlike his balding and paunchy law partners. Here she was, two months and two weeks pregnant, past the point where she had twice before miscarried. Her life was full.

"Oh, shit!" Archer said suddenly. He went stiff in his chair. He was staring out the front window.

"Our daddy says that, too," said Marky.

"Get the kids in the basement," said Archer. "Quick."

"What's going on?" Cherry asked. On the screen Kathleen Turner was flashing her teeth and looking as if she might bite off the soft parts of a man. Cherry wondered if that were attractive to men.

"Do it," Archer said.

"I want to see the movie," Marky's sister said.

"Becca Lu, Becca Lu," Archer said, in his most charming Pied Piper tones. "I will *stop* the VCR. I'll put the whole thing on hold." With the tip of the bone of the heel of his hand, he depressed the wee silver smooth oblong button that made such things happen. "See, there, I have done it," he said. His assurances were a magician's. He might have stopped, in the dark, and pulled scarlet silk scarves from his ears and pink-eared bunnies from out of the sleeves of his brand-new forest-green L.L. Bean chamois-cloth shirt, still mapped with the wrinkles of packing. "Get into the basement." He ushered them out of the room. He was pushing. This felt like a fire drill the teachers knew was not a drill. Cherry wondered and Becca and Marky protested.

"The fire was just getting ready to happen," said Becca.

"The fire will be right there when you come back," Archer said. If he could produce scarves like silk counterfeits of fire out of his flannel cuffs, why could he not suspend in animation a fire that was even a further remove from reality, only bright dots on a terminal screen? "Jesus Christ, Cherry," he said, not impatient with her but asking her collusion with something, she did not know what. He motioned toward the front window. Through the half-pulled drapes she could see a figure on the front walk, coming toward the door.

"Who?" she stage-whispered.

"Ned Ousley," Archer said.

"Archer Claess, I swear," Cherry said. They were on the stairs now, moving down through the dark to the ground-level basement. It had secret rooms they could hide in, and it was clear Archer was hiding them. "What or who is Ned Ousley? A white slaver? For goodness' sake."

"Get in the ironing room," Archer said. This was a room which would one day be turned to a darkroom, a room where, when the baby—the babies—the children—were soundly asleep, Archer and Cherry would come and work in close harmony developing and printing wonderful pictures. Archer had described the process—he had done it before—with great pleasure. He looked forward to the day when the house was theirs so that they could do the remodeling projects they planned. As of now, they were still—barely—tenants and lessees.

Marky and Becca were stiff-backed, resistant, did not understand. Cherry did not, herself. "Who—I *said!*—who is Ned Ousley?" she demanded, but softly. She did not use anger with Archer: she loved the man hopelessly. "You are frightening the children." Not to mention me, she thought.

Archer ushered them into the ironing room and shut the door. "He is a deputy," he said. "The township police. I deal with them in court all the time. This is how I know the man. Not personally."

"Ooh! A deputy!" Marky said.

"All right," said Cherry. "We'll make it a game." She frowned a slight warning to Archer, whose face seemed foreign and childlike, the face in his own seventh-grade photos, not yet adult, though the features were there. Her look warned: don't involve them, whatever this is. But affectionately.

"I've got clothespins and sheets in the cupboard," said Cherry. "You two make a tent." They had begged to make tents every day of their stay. They had made tents with sheets printed in brown bamboo, lavender blossoms, and candy stripes. Now, it was clear, they did not want to make a tent. They stood, arms folded identically, frowning in the half-dark, lit only by the night-light that hung in the wall socket, a sop to Cherry's own fear of the pitch dark. "Make a tent," Cherry ordered, but in her juvenile media specialist's sweetest, best voice. She followed Archer out of the room, shutting the children in behind her.

"What *is* the problem?" she said. "Why a deputy? Why should I know Ned Ousley? Why are we hiding in our own basement?"

Archer sighed his attorney's imperial sigh of slight impatience with lay ineptitude. Cherry did not like this facet of him, but she thought it would be bred out, finally, if it took *years* of love.

She was not threatened by this. "It is not our house, actually, yet," he said.

"I know that. . . ."

"All that this is is a small cash-flow problem. . . ."

"I . . . Archer? A deputy?"

"He has come out to serve us with a writ of eviction," he said, patient with explanation, "but if we are not here to receive it we can buy time."

"Buy time?" Cherry said. "Have we lost money somehow?" She heard herself using the phrase and it sounded odd, like a plane losing altitude or an Oriental paterfamilias losing face.

"Not lost," Archer said, shorthanding. "Cash flow. You know. My receivables."

"Deadbeats?" said Cherry. "You haven't been taking on more of those pro bonos than you can handle, have you?" Cherry remembered her mother's caution upon meeting Archer the first time. He looks like a damned bleeding-heart to me, she had said. You watch yourself, little girl, or he will save everybody else first and you'll be left home waiting, and no shoes to speak of.

"No, no," he said impatiently. "Not that kind of a cash-flow problem. . . ."

Cherry was not sure, then, what the term meant. She pictured some flow of cash like a flow of sand in some mystic desert or like lava, onyx-black, shiny as glass.

"I don't have the time right now," he said. "I am going upstairs."

"You said that you would handle the payments," she said. She hoped that she did not sound accusing.

"I did, and I would, and I am, and I will, but I don't have the time to explain at this moment. You get in that room, keep it dark, keep the kids quiet. We are not home, and tomorrow we'll go up North just for a couple of days, and we will have bought all the time we need, and—"

"Archer—" she started.

He took her, with staunch, firm, clear, infinite love, by both shoulders. "Trust me," he said.

Cherry went to the wonderfully organized cupboard where all of the sheets, like the world's plenty, were arranged. She rejected immediately all the usual tenting sheets, older sheets left by Lynette when she had left the marriage, sheets that made Cherry feel vaguely as if she were a replacement laundress. She did not say these words aloud, even in her head, because she knew, in every last fiber of her being, that Archer loved her with round, perfect love.

He never cried out Lynette's name in his passion's delirium, as she had heard other second wives complain their spouses had done. Archer never compared her unkindly with Lynette. Even in the comparisons in which Lynette came off poorly (Lynette had been less careful about the laundry—"a mess" was the phrase that Archer's mother used—never folding or stacking, and all of Archer's Gold Toe socks going mateless, bereft; Lynette had invariably burned the bottoms of pizzas and rolls; Lynette did not have the least idea of what to do about bee stings or poison ivy or lilac pollen in the eye, all the accidents Archer was prone to), Archer was kind to Lynette. She was, after all, a potter, with the standard and wholly forgivable vagaries of any artist. Yes, Archer was kind on all sides.

Cherry pulled from the linen stack, which smelled like spring flowers, (there was some kind of fruit blossom scenting the new fabric softener) a set of sheets she had brought to the marriage, a brand-new percale set luxuriant with peonies and bright vines and small Far Eastern butterflies, all on a background of rose-tinted brown.

"Ooh!" said Becca. "We get to use these? I can be the wise princess!" She began pinning the sheet to the edge of the ironing board, carefully, with a fine reverence.

"Wise princess!" scoffed Marky. "Wise princess! Who ever heard of a *wise* princess?"

"Help her, Mark," said Cherry. "You get the waxer." The waxer, a decadent implement Cherry had bought a few months ago, unashamed, was heavy and electric and made the kitchen tile shine without all the backbreaking labor that Archer's mother seemed to feel was redemptive. They used the waxer as a center pole for their tents, and it served beautifully, standing straight and tall, poking the sheet up like a minaret.

Cherry weighted the sheet's far ends atop the dryer with detergent bottles. "We'll have to be careful of these or they'll come tumbling onto our heads."

"We know that," Marky said. He seemed duly impressed by the tent, despite all his misgivings.

"Now climb in," said Becca. "Oh, oops. There is nothing to sit on."

I will stretch this out, Cherry thought. By the time this is all set up, whatever is going on upstairs will have become history. "I'll go get pillows," she said to the children. "Just pillows and pillows. We'll make a Scheherazade tent. You just keep yourselves hushed for a minute, like this"—she made the vertical-index-finger of the children's librarian over her lips—"and I'll be right back." They made their fingers the same and sat giggling quietly on the hard floor underneath the Levantine curves of the tent.

"What is Hershey Razade?" Becca Lu whispered loudly as Cherry opened the door.

"In a minute," said Cherry, and reiterated the finger. She closed the door swiftly behind her and took the stairs quickly. Archer was a shadow in the hall, standing against the wall peering around into the living room. Ned Ousley's shape walked across the front lawn and peered into the lit bedrooms.

"That's good," said Archer. "He'll see we're not hiding. It all will look okay."

"We *are* hiding, Archer, and no doubt he sees that two cars are right smack in the driveway," said Cherry.

"We could have *three* cars," said Archer. "It's not that uncommon. In fact I was thinking of maybe an old Chevy truck, one of those classic jobs with the roll sides and running boards. They are beauties, and once we have closed on the house, we'll be needing something like that. Carrying drywall and lumber and vats of what is that stuff, joint compound. Yes, we might have a Chevy truck, we might be out in it seeing a movie or something."

"Except that we don't have a Chevy truck," Cherry said. "And we are hiding." She listened to Ned Ousley's footsteps scruffing through the week's unraked leaves on the side of the house. "He thinks we're here," said Cherry. "He's right."

"You stop worrying, sweetie," said Archer. "This is one of life's small absurdities, that's all it is. A legality, a technicality. And I of all people know what a crock the law is. Just a game: if you know how to play it, you're okay. And if you do not, you're up shit creek . . ."

"With no paddle. I know," Cherry said. "Archer, this looks a lot like shit creek to me. What are you talking about, buying time? Where'd our money go? Why are our payments behind? Has our cash flow been diverted into shit creek?"

Archer laughed in a whisper. "Oh, honey, that's one of the things that I love about you," he said. "Wit in a pinch."

"Where's the money?" said Cherry.

Just then the light on the hall telephone blinked and Archer picked the receiver quickly from the hook as if plucking fruit, making eyes at Cherry that said, thank God we have got the light-option and what if Ned Ousley had heard it ring. "Yes, hello," he said quietly. "Oh, Bart! For sure! No, man, just a bit of the old laryngitis. Courtroom-induced. What can I say?" He winked at Cherry. "So how is Thailand? For sure, we will have to go, too, maybe next year, you know the old schedule, and what with the baby coming. . . . Kids? Oh, yeah, they're just fine. They're not here now. Cherry took them off somewhere. You know how good she is with them. I'll give them your love, though. You eating that Dow Hoo Tawt Nam Jim? That Yam

Bla? That what do you call it, that Monkey Ball Soup? Oh, yeah, sure I know all of those names. Cherry knows. No, not *real* monkey balls, for godsake. Sure, whatever you think, something silk, she loves pretty things. Paige can pick. Yeah. Good. Thanks for calling. Don't worry. No broken arms. Everything here's A-OK, you just enjoy yourselves. Monkey balls and all. Bye."

Archer rolled his eyes at Cherry. "Close call," he said.

"Poor pun," she said, but she smiled at him. Cherry had marveled before at the ways Archer bent the truth, never quite lying, but giving out part of the truth, a quite literal truth that folded back upon itself at a one-hundred-and-eighty degree angle. He had done it again, with Bart. Archer seemed genuinely frightened, this seventh-grade boy her husband had turned into, but she needed to know. "Where's the money?"

"It's a matter of, oh, robbing Paul to pay Peter and then getting caught in the middle, you know?" he said, seeming to hope that this answer was all that was necessary.

"I am waiting," she said.

Down the stairs, she could hear Becca telling Marky to shush, and she made silencing hisses herself, hoping that they carried to the children but not to Ned Ousley, who scrabbled at the back corner of the house, no doubt looking into that bedroom, which now served as Marky's and would be the baby's. Ned Ousley would see nothing but a lit, silent room, scattered with small robots and larger vehicles: space stations, fire engines, four-wheel-drive dune buggies painted with bright orange stripes.

Taking the break, she slipped into the front bedroom for pillows, came out loaded with their fluffy bulk and stood talking to Archer from behind them. "Go on," she said to Archer.

"You know how it is between Bart and me," Archer said.

Cherry was stunned into silence. This was not the answer to the question that she had asked. She found pinning Archer down difficult sometimes. He did have a skill that served him well in public; he had in fact been asked to run for judge, despite his youthful appearance, and he was still considering this, but on a two-years-away schedule.

"How is it?" she said. "Between Bart and you?"

"Odd," he said. "It is odd being identical twins. It always has been. You meet yourself coming and going for twenty-one years, if you go off to college together. But Bart always has had the touch."

"The touch?" she echoed, back of her pillows. Downstairs, Marky and Becca made slight pings and whacks against the dryer and the waxer and the legs of the ironing board. Out back Ned Ousley was peering into the dark living room through the glass patio doors: Cherry could hear him leaning against the glass, and the aluminum frame setting up a complaint.

"Bart has always been better at, well, at what counted," said Archer. "And I'm Baby A. I'm supposed to be dominant."

Cherry worked at retaining her slipping composure. "What counts, Archer? What are you talking about?" She had heard this before in another version, this Baby A and Baby B foolishness. In the hospital they labeled twins Baby A and Baby B. Cherry thought it rather a demonstration of a paucity of imagination that Archer and Bart's parents had named them A/Archer, B/Barton, as if this hospital convention had circumscribed something that tightly.

But Archer had countered that he knew a worse story: he knew a pair of twins who had had their birth certificates fouled up, with A (Roy) and B (Ray) listed as A. Roy and B. Ray, and had gone on through life with those stupid names, passive as plants. Archer maintained that he, Baby A, ought to have been the dominant twin, and he felt he had failed to be dominant.

Cherry could hear Ned Ousley now knocking on the back door to the garage, could hear him leaning into the glass of that door. Out behind him, though she could not see it, she knew that the lake sparkled beautifully, and that the pair of swans that the subdivision association supported, like a resident dance company, were in all likelihood gliding over the lake's cold November surface with ineffable grace.

"What counts, Archer? You are a successful attorney. They've asked you to run for judge. Really! At your age! And Bart, well, I know he's your brother, your dear twin, but honey, he doesn't have half the brains you've got." Bart had barely gotten through college, while Archer had been magna cum laude. But Bart had bought a car wash at twenty-three, and then another car wash, until he had a chain of six or eight throughout the southeastern part of the state, all situated nicely for the traffic and making clean, uncomplicated profits. Bart had sold them all last year and gone into restaurants: now he had three Mr. Rib franchises. They were simple, too, and profitable.

"Come on, Cherry. Bart's in the Far East, and here I am holed up with Ned Ousley scratching around like a damned squirrel outside. Bart is married to his high-school sweetheart, and here I have ruined one marriage."

Cherry did not ask if he wanted Lynette back. It seemed like a poor question, and it seemed as well that in Archer's present state of vulnerability he might give her a true and painful answer.

"I have got to go downstairs," said Cherry. "But first I would like to know about the money. This river of cash that has been dammed or diverted, and not, as you say, by your indigent pro-bono clients."

"We have got the two kids here," Archer said, as if that explained the drain on their finances.

"If they ate sixteen boxes of cereal every day," Cherry said, "and I doubt that even Marky could do that, that wouldn't explain it."

"I have been buying robots," Archer said. He had taken the boy to Toys 'Я' Us a number of times, and the two of them had come back loaded down in small-boy ecstasy. Archer had assured Cherry, quite solemnly, that he was fully aware that this was a vicarious joy he was buying, and insisted that "spoiling" a child was possible only if the parenting was in fact rotten at heart, that material abundance had nothing to do with such things.

"And what else?" Cherry said. "I don't mean *buying* what else. I just mean what else."

"The new tires for the Mazda," he said. "And the phone bill was backed up two months. I had just gotten . . . well, gotten backed up. I—well, I did not want to tell you this and I won't tell you the whole thing, but I laid away something for you for Christmas. A major gift, let us say."

Cherry blinked wetly and felt all of Archer's rhetorical der-ring-do brought to bear on her emotions. It angered her, but she was not sure that anger was all there was to it. She loved the man dearly. Ned Ousley was at the front door again, knocking.

"Mr. Claess, I do believe that you are in there, and you know that I have got something for you, and I am being obstructed in my duty, which I do not much like." Ned Ousley's voice came through the front door, but Ned Ousley was being ten-tative and uncertain. It was clear that he was not at all sure whether anyone were home, and that he felt like a fool shouting into an empty house. He had seen the dark, empty living room and the lit, empty bedrooms. He had rattled the windows and doors and been through all the papery piles of leaves.

"I am going to sit in the car now," said Ned Ousley, through the dark varnished oak. It seemed as if he felt clearly that he was addressing no one at all. "When you come home I will get you. But good." There was something surreal about his address to an absent Archer, an Archer who was right here, and listening. And there clearly was spite and revenge in that last, flung re-mark. Cherry wondered what Archer had ever done in court to ruffle the deputy so, mused that this was a question to which she might or might not ever have an answer, and thought how, in many ways, her life was truly un-tangent to Archer's.

"Thank God," Archer said.

"I thought you were an atheist," Cherry said.

"When it's convenient," said Archer.

"The money," Cherry prompted. She felt like a prosecuting attorney. Downstairs, a pop, a shush, a scraping across the concrete floor, a giggle, two thumps. No doubt the detergent and fabric softener had fallen off the dryer, disassembling the tent. She shouted in a whisper down the stairs. She could see Ned Ousley out in his car, sitting and waiting for these not only miscreant but personally resented tenants to come home, in their roll-sided Chevy truck, from seeing Kathleen Turner on the wide screen, at four-fifty each plus popcorn. She knew Ned Ousley could not hear her. "Hold on, Becca. Pipe down, Marky. I've got the pillows."

"The cash-flow problem, actually, is Bart's," Archer said. "With his restaurants, all of the setup costs, everything."

"You are saying that you loaned him the money so he and Paige could go to Thailand?" Cherry said.

"Not all of it," Archer said.

"Some of it," Cherry said, back of her pillows. She saw Ned Ousley, out in the driver's seat of his patrol car, light up a cigarette and pull out a dog-eared novel to read in the car's dim overhead light.

"Couple of thou," Archer said.

"Couple of months of house payments," Cherry said. She sighed. Archer looked younger and younger. She loved him immensely. She wondered if their child would be a girl or a boy, and she knew if the child were a boy what he would look like: Archer's face in front of her was that little boy's face.

"More like four thousand," Archer said. "I didn't want to look strapped, you know. He asked so easily. This is not big money to somebody with a whole chain of businesses."

"Mr. Ribs," Cherry said. She wondered why she had said it. She saw their new house washing away upon a dark river of barbecue sauce. Archer's pride was like sweet bits of onion in that river. "Holy . . ." She could not think of an expletive.

"Holy barbecue sauce, Batman!" Archer said. Sometimes he

tuned so clearly into her thoughts that he astounded her. This was not such a great leap, this thought, but it unnerved her and she felt tears, which she wiped casually on the pillowcases in her plump bundle, as if it were just an allergy suddenly come upon her. Archer grinned like a little boy.

"Archer, honey, this whole thing's—"

"Absurd, yes. I said that before. But I've got the thing under control. We'll go up North—how about Traverse City?—for just a couple of days. By that time, I'll have been able to scrape it up over the phone and we won't have had to suffer the indignity of a summons service. How 'bout that?" He was cheery and resolute.

"No indignity," Cherry said.

"You got it," Archer said.

"I'm going downstairs," she said, kissing Archer, this husband, this child, this soon-to-be-candidate-for-judge, lightly on his cheek. She was certain that he would bring them through this, and that he would win that not-too-far-off circuit court election. She knew that she loved him, and that he loved her. She was quite frankly crying now. She took each stair carefully, the pillows out front blocking her view entirely. In another month or two, she would be big-bellied. What would Archer think of that? Was he frightened of fatherhood? Was this a statement to that effect? This was not a time to be so analytical. This was no time to be thinking.

She thought of Lynette's face in the A&P as they had left her, by the pickled okra and mushrooms and watermelon rind, pondering. Lynette had given her a look as they departed with their basket, a look that she had been at the time unable to read. She thought that now in retrospect Archer's first wife had been flashing her visual Morse code: I'm glad that I'm out of it, honey; poor you, baby; he is a sweetheart, I know, you know, everyone knows; better you than me; and Good Luck.

In the ironing room—it would be a darkroom, certainly;

Archer would pull them through this—Becca and Marky had reconstructed the tent, slightly askew.

"The bottles fell down," Marky explained.

"I figured that," Cherry said.

"It wasn't my fault," said Marky, ready for an onslaught.

"It just doesn't matter," said Cherry. "Here, take the pillows, get into the tent, and we'll have story time."

"Hershey Zod," Becca said. "That is really a odd name. Tell us that one."

"Well, Scheherazade really *told* stories herself," Cherry said. "She was condemned to death . . ."

"To *death*!!" Marky said, with the invulnerability of the very young. He was loving the danger of this. It could not touch him.

"But she bought time, she postponed . . ."

"I don't know those words," Marky said.

"Like what you do at bedtime," Becca said. "She *stalled*."

"Stalled," Cherry echoed. "Each night she could spin out a grand story and hold the king's attention, she was spared one more day."

"Boy, this sounds like it will be worth waiting for," Becca said. She was a connoisseur of good stories. "Anyway, what was going on upstairs? You were up there six hours or something."

"A long time," Cherry agreed. "Just some confusion. We can make it a game. Do you want a good story now?"

Upstairs in the hall, Archer melted into a dark shadow. Out front, Deputy Edward Ousley sat waiting and reading a favorite Zane Grey. Cherry thought of the face of Lynette by the pickles; she thought of the face of Kathleen Turner, waiting upstairs in the VCR to flare her nostrils, with just a swift touch of a square silver button; she thought of Paige, Becca and Marky's mother, in the Thailand she had always wanted to see, and how much Paige looked like Kathleen Turner.

"There was a princess," said Cherry.

"A wise princess," Becca said.

Marky looked scornful.

"You stop, Marky," Cherry said firmly. "She *was* a wise princess. She lived in a castle . . ."

"Did it have a moat?" Becca said. "God, I love moats."

"It did," Cherry said.

"And were there snakes and sea serpents and alligators and crocodiles and eels and tarantulas in the moat?" Marky said. "To keep the wickeds away?"

"Nope," said Cherry. "Just swans."

"This is boring," said Marky. He threw himself back on the pillows.

"You just go to sleep, then," said Becca to Marky. "You big turd."

"The princess was wise," Cherry said. "But she was lonely. The prince was away, at grand battles, a long, long time . . ."

"Battles!" said Marky, sitting up suddenly. "Bloody, with axes, and everything."

"Nope," Cherry said. "More like big ceremonies, on grand, grassy fields, with bright banners, as if it were all a grand game . . ."

"Oh foo," Marky said, throwing himself back down.

"This is not your kind of story, jerk," Becca said. "That's just the way it is. Can it."

"The princess was under siege in the castle, with her three babies," Cherry said. "There was no one to defend her."

"But she was a wise princess," Becca reminded her.

"That she was," Cherry said. She did not know what was coming next. "The princess put her three babies in a backpack made of silk . . ."

"It was pink!" Becca said. Everything in Becca's world was pink.

". . . and she took a great spoon made of silver, and dug underneath the great walls of the castle, and under the moat . . ."

"Underneath the swans, who didn't even know that she was digging! Boy, that is cool!" Becca said.

"And she dug and she dug, and she started to dig upward." Cherry did not know what was coming next.

"Yeah, she dug upward," Becca repeated. Apparently she would be no help now.

"Upward and upward she dug," Cherry said, buying time in one-word segments.

"Smack-o, into a mountain," said Marky, with sudden and passionate interest. "Smack-o, she came right up through the ground into the inside of a big old mountain."

"Made out of glass," Becca said.

"Made of glass," Cherry said. She did not know what came next, at all.

Pyrotechnics

Tante Françoise was not indifferent to love, though her co-workers might have assumed that she was, had they ever considered the question. She was, on the contrary, quite consumed by love, and had been, her whole life.

For eighteen years now she had worked at Merle Granville Ford, third-largest dealership in the whole state of Louisiana, typing, bookkeeping, eventually running the office, and watching Merle Granville age from an aggressive, rawboned young man into a silver-haired, suave (she thought) middle-aged charmer, seemingly without hitting anything that could be called his prime. And for seventeen of those years Tante Françoise had ached with a fragrant devotion, sat saintly with patience, typing first the invoices and now the executive letters. Her patience was for she knew not what: Merle Granville had a wife, lumpy black-dye-haired Odile, and had always had.

Beside Tante Françoise on the front seat of her car as she drove to the company picnic, at a decent distance, sat one Durel Johnson, the man from the body shop. Slightly greyed gauze bandages wrapped his hands. His burns, they had said, were severe but would heal. Durel Johnson had that Cajun accent

Tante Françoise despised: why could he not subdue all that bayou nasality and learn the right way to speak, the way that all the rest of New Orleans spoke?

Odile Granville had called and asked Tante Françoise would she please drive this Durel Johnson today. Tante Françoise—at home after a day of work, starching her antimacassars, a regular seasonal ritual, though she knew no one else who had ever starched theirs more than once in their whole lives—took the call with annoyance. She pulled at the rubbery green mint masque on her face, wrinkled her forehead up under it, and scowled at her image framed by the gilt plaster oval mounting of the front hall mirror. She showed her teeth in a violent smile and said certainly, Miss Odile, why, I would be just as tickled to do that, the poor man.

She hung up the receiver and sucked at a piece of green pepper from dinner still stuck between her left incisors. Tante Françoise did not like to speak to Odile, did not (when you got down to it) even like to look at Merle Granville's wife. Tante Françoise might have been at first shocked to hear such a thing said of her, but upon one or two moments' reflection, she would have nodded her head imperceptibly in mute agreement. Yes, it was the vulgar dye she did not like: dye as black as the tar they used out on the country roads, out in Jefferson Parish or all of those clamshell hick towns on the river; black as new tires; black as workmen's shoes resoled. But of course it was not. It was simply that Odile was Merle Granville's wife.

Odile had explained her request. "What with the body shop being ours, what with his burns happening on the job and all, we felt responsible to see that Durel at least got to come to the picnic," Odile had said. So would Tante Françoise please bring him?

She sucked the green pepper back down her throat. She spoke aloud, dipping the doilies into the thick, bluish liquid starch: "I would be just as tickled, Miss Odile. Oh, yes. With the shop being *ours*." But she would bring the odious man to the picnic, for Merlie. In her mind he was Merlie, a name no one called him. Odile called him "Baby," addressing him, or "Granville," speaking about him to a third party. Tante Françoise was sure that their relationship was what she would have called nothing to brag about. *That* she was certain of.

The body shop explosion, which had left Durel Johnson gauze-wrapped and with permanent scars, had not been the first Tante Françoise could remember, but it had been the biggest. Fine prickles of paint in the air from the spray guns had gone up in flame, a huge whoosh of fire filling the shop. Someone had flipped a switch whose spark was all that was needed for conflagration.

So here sat Durel Johnson, smelling of his Cajun sweat and burn unguent, potentially spoiling Tante Françoise's day. Except that, of course, she told herself, Merle Granville himself had no doubt asked Odile to call, had once more given her the chance to prove her utter devotion. She decided that despite the pickle-and-medicine smell of the man, she was grateful. Merle Granville would see her with Durel Johnson. Perhaps she would be holding open the car door to let the small man stumble out. Perhaps she would be dishing him lumps of pale-yellow company picnic potato salad. Perhaps—but then the thought occurred to her, a horror, she would not be asked to *feed* him? She would pass that to one of the shop boys, but she would do everything else she might so that Merle Granville might have his treasury of gratitude enriched by just that much. One day its rim would be reached, and the wild gratefulness he had been containing all these years, something indistinguishable from love, would come flooding over. She thought of the gates opening at the Bonnet Carre spillway, the grand and immense rush of river that flooded the flatlands to save the good folk in the city. She heard her own breath catch: she did not look at Durel Johnson but feigned a slight and wholly genteel little cough. She thought of the near-to-bursting heart of Merle Joseph Anthony Granville: she knew that after all these years he would finally be overcome. In one flash he would know her true worth. But she took her mind from the subject. Past that point she could not go. It was simply beyond her imagining.

As she drove, her four-year-old Ford's engine purred: she was proud and punctual about dropping it off at the shop during work hours for both the regular and extra maintenance. The movement of the water beside the bridge caught her eye. The bridge across Lake Pontchartrain was five miles long: to stare at the water could mesmerize you. Puffs of warm breeze were rippling the surface today. That disturbed her. She liked it much better when the greyish-green water sat still, like opaque glass, under a more overcast sky. Today's sky was too brilliant, too blue. The water could almost be seen into. Something leaped out of the water and startled her. Just a fish, silver, small, tracing its little arc not a foot into the air, but it bothered her. Made her think of all the depths below, larger fish, eels, water moccasins, hard things with pincers and claws, sand sharks, who knew what else. No, it should be opaque and still. One could ignore all that rampant biology then.

"Do you fish?" said Durel Johnson. Tante Françoise felt her shoulders flinch up into the shoulder-pads of her pearly white fiesta-patterned linen-and-rayon blouse. Nasal, the man was so nasal. She sighed and let her eyelids droop. He would not take offense: he would not know that he could offend her.

Durel Johnson had sat in silence, nursing first one hand, then the other, since they had been on the bridge. Roo-roo-roo went the wheels of the car on the road's washboard surface. Durel Johnson had been watching the water all this way as if in awe. Tante Françoise thought such mute concentration the sign of a weak mind. She also thought fishing bespoke mental poverty.

She had been glad for Durel Johnson's merciful silence, but she was glad, too, that he had mentioned fishing now. It only gave her the chance to reconfirm in her mind the distance between them. She looked at the foot and a half of front seat between them, where her white basket purse with its fresh artificial chrysanthemums sat like a barricade. That was good: barricade. The chrysanthemums were powder blue, like the lettering that read MERLE GRANVILLE FORD up at the front of the concrete-block showroom building on the avenue.

"No, I don't fish," Tante Françoise said. She felt no need to explain. Perhaps then Durel Johnson would drop the subject.

"Boy do I," said Durel Johnson.

Tante Françoise looked across at him, a look that she hoped said, I Didn't Ask If You Did.

"Boy. I love to get out in 'at boat, me I don't care if it one hundred and two degrees, there just ain't in this whole world not anything else can compare wit' 'at fishing. If I was rich, me, I would, very first t'ing, I would buy me a boat. You know? I go out sometime now wit' my wife's uncle and brudder-in-law— 'at'sa one wit' the boat. But you know I would like one myself." He shifted his hands and looked out at the water.

Tante Françoise made a small sigh. She had felt a fear clutch at her throat when Durel Johnson had started talking, as if his words would swell to tidal-wave proportions and wash over them like the wide lake on each side of this ribbon of bridge. She pondered momentarily whether Durel Johnson's wife's brother-in-law were his own brother, then she dismissed the idea.

"You *like* fish to eat?" Durel Johnson said. He waited, eyes wide, for answer. It was plain he felt a call to keep this conversation going, to be social, in return for her kindness transporting him.

Tante Françoise looked out over the water again and a snake or an eel made an arc of itself in the rippling surface. She shuddered and chose to distract herself talking to Durel Johnson. About fish.

"Somewhat," she said.

"Oh, man, I do," he said. "Do I love dem trout, yeah, and dem catfish. You know some people can't tell the difference. Dem Yankees, they wouldn't eat catfish, no ma'am, if you paid

'em, but you call it trout and they don't know the difference."
He winked at Tante Françoise, creating them as conspirators.
They were one against the Yankees.

She looked at the ribbon of road, shimmer-heat rising from
it, and nodded, agreeing with something uncertain: the taste of
trout, old political feuds, the inferior minds of persons who
lived where it snowed and who spoke much too fast. Quickly,
she wrenched herself from the alliance thus formed. "I do not
like fish fried," she said. She was sure Durel Johnson would like
his fish fried.

"Boy, me, I love my fish fried. Wid some ketchup, is all, or
some tartar sauce like dat my wife's sister make. Oooee. You
ain't taste tartar sauce till you taste dat."

Tante Françoise felt herself smile. She read the man beautifully, she thought.

"You got a headache or something?" Durel Johnson said.
"Dis glare do it to you, every time. I got me some headache
powders in my shirt pocket here." He tapped the flapped pocket
over his heart with his gauze paw. "Right here, if you need to."

"No, thank you," said Tante Françoise. Then she thought
perhaps she did have a headache, and brought on by this bab-
bling.

"Sometimes you don't know when you got one," Durel Johnson said. "Not till somebody mention it to you." He looked out
the window at the water, and it seemed he was ready to lapse
back into his reverie. He turned to her just once more. "You
figure out that you got a headache, you just ask. I got me these
powders right here, maybe five, six of them. My wife make me
take dem cause she think my hands goin' to pain me." He paused
a second. "My wife don' like picnics so much," he said, "and
besides she has got her novena this evening to go to." He looked
at the water.

The mention of the novena startled Tante Françoise. For years
now she had spent her Tuesday nights faithfully at the novena

to Our Lady of Perpetual Help, where the smell of the stumpy white-wax candles inside their red glass cups made a magic that lifted to heaven the prayers of the thirty or forty women who came, praying with an athletic fervor for particular favors, perpetual help.

Tante Françoise's favor floated like a cloud behind a curtain in the alcoves of her heart. She had not named it. Tonight she would miss the novena, and she had not thought of it. This confused her, for she was the most punctual and schedule-perfect of women. Her favor—that fragrant cloud—rose in the stained-glass-lit shrine of her heart: though unnamed, it contained the bright image of Merle Granville, clear as a photo.

Of course, the Blessed Mother was not as rigid as all that, Tante Françoise told herself, in a rare lapse of her own discipline; the Virgin, the Queen of Perpetual Help, had in fact granted her today a snippet of that unnamed and vague favor in giving her the chance to spend the entire day in the near-company of Merle Granville. So what if the picnic grounds would be filled with all the body-shop, showroom, and clerical staff, with their girlfriends and boyfriends and wives, their old mothers, their dusty and tumbling children? All day, every moment, there would be the chance to catch just a glimpse. And, given grace of the best sort, he would glimpse her, too.

Tante Françoise unclenched her shoulder blades. They had tightened when she had first realized that she would miss the novena. She chided herself for her worry. She would say the prayers at her bedside this evening, not missing the Tuesday, the seventh Tuesday of the magical nine weeks required for the novena's magic. The Virgin would understand.

Durel Johnson continued, as if there had been no time lapse—and perhaps there had not, for Tante Françoise's mind raced—"Yeah, my wife, she got dat novena, and you know you got to go to dem t'ings regular, every time." It distressed Tante Françoise, this argument; even more, it distressed her to think that

Durel Johnson's wife, who no doubt had thick varicose veins and who cooked okra until it dissolved, had this same habit of the novena.

She told herself that heaven was open to all. This distressed her, but she made an effort to embrace the repellent thought. Anyway, she told herself, Mrs. Durel Johnson no doubt frequented some other church than her own. She guessed: Incarnate Word? Probably so. For that neighborhood, full of white-frame corner groceries and two-bedroom shotgun houses, Incarnate Word would probably be the right parish.

Tante Françoise herself prayed at the Shrine of Perpetual Help, where the altar was overcome with golden filigree, and where the ceilings sang back at the faithful lace chapel-veiled women below, echoing and transforming their reedy thin voices to songs of the seraphim.

The picnic had been held at Abita Springs every year since anyone could remember. Tante Françoise felt her heart thump as she pulled into the parking lot. Merle would be here already. Merle would be dressed in a nylon seersucker shirt—probably mint green—and his face would shine with the close shave he always had. Merle would be waiting, though he might not know it, and when Tante Françoise arrived something in him would feel closure and deep satisfaction, though he might not recognize it.

The cars in the crushed-clamshell parking lot sat in neat rows. They were mostly Fords, and mostly new or near-new. Tante Françoise scanned the panorama. She knew the excuses of those whose cars were not Fords. She was strong on the loyalty issue. She had casually questioned those who drove anything else. She had done this at the watercooler, drinking more water than she cared to in order to make this conversation seem less, well, intentional. She had done this out in the body shop, for which purpose she had to invent flimsy errands.

This one drove a Chevrolet: he had had it since before and

insisted with shocking stubbornness that his wages would not support anything else now. That one drove a Lincoln, new, black and shiny, and of course far less objectionable: his uncle the monsignor had died and left it to him. She knew all the reasons. She looked at the blue of her purse's chrysanthemums and knew that there was nothing like loyalty, and that there was no loyalty like her own.

"Boy, look," said Durel Johnson, pointing with a wrapped hand. His discolored bandage was starting to fray, and threads of the gauze waved in the hot breeze. "Look like they got the barbecue going. I do love that barbecue. Almost as good as my wife's sister-in-law's barbecue sauce, I swear, and she sure make some fine barbecue. I had dat stuff last year, is how I know. . . ."

"Here we are," said Tante Françoise, superfluously.

Durel Johnson was silent.

Tante Françoise was suddenly overcome by all the smells of the picnic. She stopped and sniffed the air: it was an assault on the senses, and she was amazed and awash. The pungent spice smells of the barbecue mingled with smells of the heat rising wavery-wild from the clamshells, the smell of the fifty-one Ford's perfect engine just freshly shut down from the drive, the smell of lake saltwater still in her nostrils, the smells of cut grass and mimosa and live oak. The wind shifted slightly, and Tante Françoise was downwind from Durel Johnson. Her nostrils flared.

If the body itself was a mixed blessing—and Tante Françoise longed for heaven and angelic states she could not precisely feature—the sense of smell was certainly one of its drawbacks. She had almost—not quite but almost—been seduced into momentary forgetfulness by all that barbecue-clam-lake-oak-and-mimosa perfume. One just had to be vigilant. Once more she was almost thankful for the presence of Durel Johnson. The stink of his salve had this saving grace: it brought her back with a start to the lead-glass clear notion of who she was: kin, in her heart, to both duchess and sweet virgin/martyr.

Tante Françoise surveyed the picnic. The children swarmed. There, as every year, sat the strange algae-clogged pond, something between a wild natural pit and a swimming pool, with its monstrous and mutating orange-pearl goldfish. The children threw hot-dog bits into the pool and the fish darted sluggishly after them. Several children shrieked in delight, something about fatty fish lips.

Not far from the pond the stage had been set up. It was festooned with crepe-paper spirals in powder blue. Glitter-edged powder-blue letters swooped like a hammock: MERLE GRANVILLE, they said. To Tante Françoise they seemed to name not the Ford dealership but the man himself. In the tight gold-cord knot of her heart, suddenly, Tante Françoise—for no reason she could discern—knew that this day would be the day she would come into her own. For the life of her, she could not say how she knew this, or how it would come about, but she crossed herself quietly, saying the names in thanksgiving: Jesus and Mary and Joseph.

Odile, with her black dye, her gypsy-curl earrings, her yellow sundress with its palm trees and violent tropical birds, made her way through a game of tag toward them. Durel Johnson stood like a monument: what could he do with no hands? "Oh, Miz Fran," Odile shouted above the blurred heads of the scurrying children, "how good of you."

Tante Françoise wanted to cut her off—almost literally, it seemed, for the silver shape of a scythe flashed on the retinas of her unspoken imaginings. How did she dare this curt "Miz Fran" business? Whoever had named her Miz Fran?

It was true that only she herself thought of her true name as Tante Françoise, outside of her twenty-year-old nephew who was the only one ever to have reason to use the name. He did not count: he was too tall to call her Tante anymore, and anyway he did not come around. He spent all his time driving around in a dreadful red convertible from someplace foreign, and squiring red-lipped girls who saddened his parents.

Tante Françoise remembered with something approaching joy the brief period when he was small, sweet, and docile and made her feel loved. She wanted that time back. She recalled it: tall, nasty nephew Gerard shrunk back down in time to three years old, calling out to Tante Françoise from his porch's twilight: Tante Françoise, sounding like Tawnh-Frawnh, as if he were calling through a powdered mouthful of doughnut. She once saw the boy in a dream, calling out to her this way again, and he called in the same voice: Hey hey Uncle Merlie. Tante Françoise remembered it clearly and blushed.

Odile's upper arms, white and fat-pocked, assaulted Tante Françoise's eyes. The adipose tissue hung there like the wings of some pale anti-angel. Tante Françoise could not imagine what ruse this repulsive thing had used to trap Merlie. Crude sex, perhaps. Though Odile had looked the same all the years Tante Françoise had known her, with her hair perhaps growing more black as the tinctures of nature deserted her, Tante Françoise could imagine her as a siren a few years before, turning into this fat-flapping harpy within moments of her entrapment of Merle Granville. How could he, how would he have known?

"Oh, Miz Fran," said Odile, reaching them through the swarm-game of tag. "You are such a good person."

Durel Johnson nodded agreement in medicine-smelling solemnity.

"We have always been able to count on you," Odile said.

Tante Françoise's heart leapt up at that: "we." Merlie had spoken of her then, to his wife, spoken to Odile of Tante Françoise's utter devotion, his heart overflowing. He had thought it best, had thought it wise (she conjectured) to allow himself this outlet, this paving-the-way for the day when he might say the words that she longed to hear. Tante Françoise, however, could not conjure what these words might be, no matter how hard she tried. "Thank you," she said to Odile. She wondered if Odile could see her blinking back a half-tear of anticipatory joy.

"Have you got a headache, Miz Fran?" said Odile.

Tante Françoise felt a puzzlement make itself plain on her face.

"No, then," Odile answered herself. "Just the glare, probably. You have sunglasses, chère? I've got two pair. The turquoise—" she said turk-wise "—and then there's the red." She held sunglasses toward Tante Françoise. "One with rhinestones, one not. Take your pick, chère."

"No, thank you," said Tante Françoise. She wiped her hand across her brow and felt furrows. She wiped it once more, to remove them. They stayed.

"We have got these door prizes," Odile said, leading them toward the buffet tables, where hired black waiters stood shooing flies. "We got a weekend at the Broadwater Beach in Biloxi . . ."

"Oh, man, would my wife love dat, a big fancy hotel," said Durel Johnson. "And I would love the fishing."

"We have got a seventeen-inch Motorola TV, a blond console. We have got a certificate for I don't know how much candy at that praline shop down by Pirates' Alley. We have got a manicure at the Maison Blanche salon and a hairdo at some other place I cannot get the name right."

Tante Françoise looked warily at Durel Johnson eyeing the buffet. "I believe we'll need to get someone to help Mr. Johnson," Tante Françoise said, bold and audacious. She did not want to betray her own fear that Odile might think her less than limitless in her devotion.

Odile did not hear, having walked through a whooping crowd of children. "You know that we are having the contest today?" she said to Tante Françoise.

"Contest?" Tante Françoise echoed.

"This is Granville's idea," Odile said. "He said, 'We have got to do this. We have got to share with our employees, Odile. We have got to give them recognition.' And I said, 'Baby, you are a generous man.' Because he is. He won't tell me who he is giving the prize to, but if it is a man he gets a gold Bulova watch with a brown alligator band, and if it is a woman she gets earrings and a necklace, matching, in culture pearls. Isn't that something? Granville is a generous man."

"What is the contest?" said Tante Françoise.

"Most Valuable Employee," said Odile.

Tante Françoise's heart leapt.

"Granville is going to judge it himself—or I guess he already did," Odile said. "He already has got in mind who is the winner."

Tante Françoise watched Durel Johnson holding his swathed hands in midair, tentative and uncertain as to how to approach the table. "Oh, let me help you, Mr. Johnson," she offered, effusive with the certainty of her own value. She felt her ears begin to burn with that certainty. Merle had of course planned this all, and had her in mind. She looked at Odile to see if she were being sly, dropping hints with her eyes. Tante Françoise could tell nothing.

At the table Merle Granville's son Merle Junior stood with his wife Loreen and little Todd Joseph and Candace. The two children scrabbled their small fists around in the large plastic pan that held the CheeTos. They shoveled them into their mouths with the heels of their hands, making tracks like bright orange-gold pollen up toward their eyes. Loreen stood in that wanton way she had, one hip swung out, Baby Odile slung in chubby abandon astraddle that hipbone.

Tante Françoise did not think that Loreen was genteel. She knew that she was a good mother and had been a competent parts inventory clerk before she married the boss' son, but she was not as refined as Tante Françoise would have liked. Tante Françoise had overheard a conversation once and kept it close to her heart: this was something she thought might be useful in some way someday. She had overheard Loreen talking to one of the clerks who was still in parts, someone who had been there since two years before Loreen herself.

Loreen had said, in a half-whisper, "Junior *made* me name

her after his mother. It is not like I wanted to. Not that I don't have a mother myself we could use for a namesake. But no. So I'm going to just call her Baby O. and maybe everybody would forget and you know how names get turned into something else, maybe she'll turn into Punkin. Or who knows what." Tante Françoise decided she liked Loreen somewhat. She mused briefly, turning back time, whether the baby might not have been named Françoise Marie, after herself, in a possible world where there had been no tar-haired Odile.

It was the longest afternoon of Tante Françoise's life. She was waiting for dusk and the ceremony and the fireworks. There would be a presentation of medals in little grey cardboard boxes to employees with ten years' service. There would be the unveiling of the Third Place in the State plaque. There would be the door prizes: the Motorola, the hairdo, the manicure, the Pirates' Alley praline shop gift certificate, the weekend at the Broadwater Beach.

And at dusk, the full bloom of the day and its sweet stunning pinnacle, there would be the fireworks and Tante Françoise's award, while the rockets and pinwheels went off in the nine-o'clock sky. Meanwhile, she stooped and made frozen-smiled small talk with all of the clericals' children; she served as a referee for the three-legged race; she even fed barbecued chicken, picked off the thighbones, to Durel Johnson, with a fork, sparing her fingers from brushing the man's Cajun lips.

It was eight. It was eight-thirty. Loreen was not far away. She was talking to Zoe Meringuez about breast-feeding. Zoe, a butterscotch blond with a corkscrew-curl handwriting Tante Françoise truly despised, was single, not even engaged, and she seemed enthralled and quite horrified at what might be in store down the trick road of life.

Tante Françoise was appalled. She thought that breast-feeding had gone out civil ages ago. Loreen leaned over whispering and Tante Françoise could see down the front of her halter. Her breasts were like pale pink dirigibles, rivered with tiny blue veins. Tante Françoise heard the word "nipples." She felt herself blanch. She looked at Zoe Meringuez. She was a single girl, not nursing, but if anything her breasts were larger than Loreen's. Tante Françoise cleared her throat and went for another iced tea.

At a distance she caught a quick glimpse of Merle Granville gesticulating in a small group of men. He was no doubt discussing the sales figures: he was expansive and happy. Odile was some distance away in a crowd of children around the balloon man: he was twisting the fragile, pale, translucent sausage-balloons into shapes of giraffes, swans, sea serpents. Odile clapped her hands with the children in clear, self-forgetful delight.

Tante Françoise felt a pang, felt a sweet, almost syrup-thick, deep and wild vindication of all of her long years of patience; Tante Françoise felt a pity for poor Odile. Not only did Odile not realize Merle's hidden, suffering love for Tante Françoise; even after Tante Françoise had received her award and was wearing the pearls Merle had chosen and would give her publicly, up on the stage, underneath the swooped powder-blue MERLE GRANVILLE lettering, Odile would not realize what they meant.

Zoe Meringuez came toward her. "Miz Fran," she said, in her small, nasal Ninth Ward voice, "the fireworks man wants to know when to start. Miss Odile said you was in charge of that."

"I?" said Tante Françoise. "In charge of the fireworks?"

"Well, not just exackly," said Zoe Meringuez. "What she said was you was in charge of most everything and if I axed you you'd proba'ly know."

Behind Zoe Meringuez came a nameless man from the body shop. He slapped Zoe lightly on the curve of her pink short shorts, familiarly, in a way that made Tante Françoise frown for the world's crumbling.

"The truth is *I'm* the guy in charge," he said. He was in his thirties, a man in his prime. He winked at Zoe Meringuez. Tante Françoise thought—no, she was sure—she had seen other men treat Zoe this way. "I am the Master of the Pyrotechnics."

Zoe giggled. "Say that again!" she commanded.

"You like that, huh, baby? The High Kabool of Pyrotechnics." He gestured theatrically. He built a cape and a crown for himself in the air. Tante Françoise wondered what made some men this way: rough and egocentric, with powers of magic far beyond, well, the balloon man's. She could see a quiver of something like lust in the eyes of Zoe Meringuez. Zoe pulled at the cuff of her shorts. She tugged upward at the low neck of her bright cerise halter.

"You must of went to school," Zoe said. "To be talking like that."

"You got to go to school," said the Master. "To do pyrotechnics." He smirked with achievement. "I got my diploma. Delgado. I got me some skills that ain't nobody got." Again he winked at Zoe, and she giggled.

"Then you'll have to announce that it's time for the fireworks, or get someone to do it," said Tante Françoise. She thought: I must ready myself for the ceremony. She looked at her purse, sitting on her folding chair with the green-and-white plaid plastic webbing, and on an impulse picked it up and began unwinding the wires that attached one of the powder-blue artificial chrysanthemums. "You go tell someone to get the door prizes ready."

"Who, me?" said the Master. "Not me. I got my job already." He sauntered away, having made some odd gesture to Zoe Meringuez that made her turn coyly away in a blush of delight.

Tante Françoise, detaching her burst-of-fabric blue flower, felt suddenly undone herself, at loose ends, frazzling off into no control. Someone had to take over: but who? She would be the star. She could not be, as well, the organizer. She took a deep breath and went to a boy messenger they had just hired this summer, a boy still in high school. Vocational.

"Go tell Miss Odile it's time to get started," she said.

He looked blankly at her. He had been involved in drinking a beer, and thinking about himself drinking the beer: he was not sixteen yet, but who cared? He could not comprehend, summoned out of his reverie, what Tante Françoise wanted.

"It is time for the ceremony," she said. "Tell her that. Time for the," she paused, considering, "time for the pyrotechnics."

"Oh, sheez," he said, complaining.

"You like your job," Tante Françoise reminded him. She could feel her nostrils curling upward and outward.

"Pyrotechnics," he said. He stomped out a Camel, not one-third smoked, in the dry, yellow-green grass.

Tante Françoise watched him go. She watched Zoe Meringuez putting on a fresh, thick coat of lipstick the color of cut cherries. She watched Merle Junior walking across the grass toward the stage. She watched Loreen changing the baby on a wobbly table where flies buzzed around the scooped-out watermelon rind.

Suddenly all of it was in order. The whole crowd was assembled around the stage. MERLE GRANVILLE waved in the slight, hot breeze. Tante Françoise touched her hair and found she had wound the light blue chrysanthemum there: she did not remember having done that. She thought that perhaps she looked different; that perhaps, even, she looked beautiful. It would be fitting: tonight she would be transformed.

On the stage, Odile went to the fishbowl and pulled out the names of the prizewinners. TV, pralines, Maison Blanche, beauty shop, in that order. Suitably distributed names emerged: one from body, one from parts, one from sales, and one from the office. It was a neat magic.

The crowd was hushed for the Broadwater. Odile pulled the name from the bowl. She unfolded it. It was Durel Johnson's name. Tante Françoise was confused. Durel Johnson? The Broadwater? This was not fitting. Durel Johnson rose from his chair and went toward the stage, waving his slightly unraveling bandages high in the air in his triumph. "Ooh, man," he was shouting. "My wife gone to love dat. Ooh, man. I will catch me *some* fish."

Merle came up now and unveiled the plaque. The employees applauded themselves. They had made the dealership what it was today. They were full to bursting with pride, with the sugary cake in the shape of a Model T, with beer and sheer camaraderie. "And now," Merle said, "we have a special award. I am going to make this a annual thing. Because y'all deserve it. I'm going to every year do this, give out a award for Most Valuable Employee. You don't get it this year, you just work hard and you might get it next."

Over at the lake's edge there was a pop-and-hiss and a pink stream of light shot up into the air. "Yes sir," said Merle Granville. "This is perfect timing." He said poi-fick. "The Employee of the Year!!" he announced. At the lake's edge there was a zoom and a roar and a rocket shot skyward. It burst into a pale-blue bloom. Tante Françoise touched her hair. This could not be accidental. She thought of her long weeks, months, years at the Tuesday novena: this is what it all was leading to.

"A person who has given her all," said Merle Granville. "Oh, yeah, I just gave away that much, right? That it's a woman, cause I went and said *she*." He laughed and reached behind him on the prize table for a small wrapped package. Tante Françoise did not realize she had risen from the plastic-webbing lawn chair where she had been sitting and was moving, as if in a dream, floating, toward the stage.

"This is somebody known and loved by all," said Merle Granville. *Loved!* He had said it. "I'd like to ask her to come up now. . . ." He paused, with broad drama, and at the lake's edge another fiery shot went off, whistling up into the sky, dispersing into tricolored wheels with their own twirling whistles. "This year's winner," he said (Tante Françoise had her foot on the first step of the stage), "is Miss Zoe Meringuez!!"

Zoe, out in the audience, squealed. The men roared their

approval. Tante Françoise was wide-eyed, astonished, entranced with surprise and then rage. Zoe ran mincing toward the stage on her ankle-strapped sandals with high, stylish wedges. They were pink as hibiscus, the color of her halter top.

Tante Françoise felt her own face grow pink, filled with the blood of her fury, her need to explain that a terrible mistake, mis-speaking had just occurred. Merle Granville stood unaware of her, holding the pearls toward Zoe, who took them with smug mock-embarrassment. No one had stopped Tante Françoise. They assumed she was part of the ceremony. After all, she did everything.

Tante Françoise climbed the stairs. On the beach, there was a grand burst of fireworks: orange, and bright metal blue, and a blinding white. Everyone turned, oohed, ran toward the beach. Suddenly, in a second, the ceremony had been moved, and Tante Françoise was alone on the stage. Merle Granville had led Zoe down the stairs and was a few steps ahead of her, moving as one with the crowd toward the beach. Tante Françoise said the single word: No.

Zoe thought she had been called. She turned. "Hunh?" she said.

"No," Tante Françoise repeated. She reached out and grabbed Zoe's hand that held the gift box with the pearls and the earrings. Zoe frowned and resisted. Tante Françoise ripped the box away from Zoe's tight grip. Zoe tried to recapture it.

Tante Françoise pushed at her, pushed her. Zoe fell backward onto the ground. One shoe's ankle strap broke and the shoe fell away. Zoe's halter burst two buttons as she clutched out at the air. Tante Françoise saw her puzzlement. How could she not know, not understand?

Merle Granville was at the beach now and did not know anything was going on at his back. Above them all, in the swift-darkening sky, a Catherine wheel in red, white, and blue burst: the crowd oohed. Zoe grabbed for the pearls and Tante Françoise tossed them aside, into the grass. She was on Zoe, and ripping her hibiscus bodice, her chippie-dyed hair. It came out in her hands. Tante Françoise pounded and gouged. Suddenly she stopped and looked at the hair in her hands. She felt the musculature of her face break into a deep, perfect smile. That hair! It was soft. It was good.

How I Got Legendary

You sit out in the audience at these things, you get an earful. I am in disguise, see, incognito (not that anybody would know me if I were not). I am wearing a T-shirt that advertises Headman headers and this baseball-type cap that I got off a guy that works at a feed store. The cap says Allagash Teat Dip. We are sitting in splintery bleachers set up in a lot between buildings. Apparently something burned down and they haven't rebuilt it yet.

But you have got to give it to the P.R. gang: they know how to turn ash to gold. They are calling this site Phoenix Alley. It is one of four sites where jazz happens at this festival. Jazz is not particularly happening now, though there is a band on stage playing the Two-Handed Blues, which has got to be *the* most lugubrious, downside, full-rotten blues you could want, and these assholes are peabodying through it like it was a seltzer commercial, like it had lyrics talking about marigolds and their bug-beating-back properties, like it was a tune about socks and positive thinking, and not a my-baby's-done-died-on-me blues.

Overhead there is green netting strung between buildings on splintery two-by-fours. It gives the whole burn-down alley, the site of the Phoenix, an underwater glow, a feeling of magic removal. I am off, this set, incognito and out in the audience rather than up on the splinter-built stage, singing, Calla Minou, all the rage of the jazz set now. I am invisible.

Next to me a jazz matron is flashing her rings at the jazz matron next to her. These rings are broad, artsy gold set with something that's got to be diamonds though I have never seen diamonds this big. These rings look like tall buildings, like corporate headquarters for some insurance conglomerate, reflecting back in their mirror faces the real world, where people buy teat dip and headers, and wish there were someone who loved them, and die uninsured. These jazz matrons are deaf. *Aren't they wonderful.* Artsy Insurance Conglomerate Fingers says to her next-seat neighbor. She is referring to these butts on stage, the New Potawotamie Stompers, these disturbers of peace, these malicious-destruction-of-blues agents. They have just finished Two-Handed Blues and the crowd is applauding like Jesus had come back.

I look up and above me, hammocked in the green netting that separates me and my neighbor's diamonds from the sky, there is a half-bottle of Heineken dark lying on its side, rocking with the breeze and ready to shower down onto me if it is jiggled sufficiently.

All around me, jazz matrons and patrons are stepping down through the crowd to the booth where the Arabel Island High School Boosters are selling bratwurst and sauerkraut sandwiches to benefit their athletic teams. Vinegar, spice, and sweet fat smells waft up to me but I am not having any for, number one, they don't pay shit on this gig and if I go spending three dollars here, three dollars there, I'm in the hole; and number two, I am the star, don't you know, and the hips on this absinthe-green twenties dress with the gold fringe that I bought for this festival—wiping out any profit, flat—will start puckering upward if I put my lips and my teeth to sweet bratwurst. But let us refrain from that whole line of thought. Calla Minou, incognito or not, is horny.

Artsy Conglomerate's husband is bringing back onion rings and fried pies. He has diet Sprite to mix with the Jack Daniels this group is toting in their jazz groupie tote bags, brand new, that say Arabel Island Jazz Fest '87. He is inching toward her, around the fat thighs of the middle-aged jazz groupies and the thin thighs of the Yuppies, uphill, balancing what he has bought.

A.C. says to her neighbor—who flashes an amethyst roughly the size of Rhode Island—*Would you look at this.* She is looking at the festival guidebook, another masterpiece of P.R. All the bands look like they can play!! All the blurbs attest to it. *Would you look at this,* she says. *The Rakehell Jazz Band: have you seen them? The girl singer with them is billed as the Legendary Calla Minou. Legendary. I ask you. She must be all of twenty-seven.*

Thirty-one, I say, not looking at her. *She is thirty-one.*

Legendary, says the matron again, looking at me out of the left corners of her aquamarine-crème shadowed eyes as if I were a fox terrier that she had just thought had talked. The Teat Dip hat and headers shirt have so far kept anybody from talking to me. I am the quintessential redneck, and these jazz folk are how you say, rubbing them bucks, you can hear them, new dollars right out of the mint, sounding like flaky pie crust. Got them stocks, got them bonds and, back-home, fat-ass Lincolns and Caddys. They cannot be bothered with me.

I hear she can sing, Amethyst says.

Artsy Conglomerate looks at me to see if the fox terrier has any information on this.

Holy shit, can she sing, I say.

A.C. does not look at me but it is clear that she is talking to me. *There never will be a Caucasian Billie Holliday,* she says, *there never will be a Bessie Smith. Not white. Those colored girls knew how to sing the blues. Suffered. A beautiful suffering.*

I leap at the chance. I have got my hair under my hat. I am not wearing makeup. I have got my She-Ra sunglasses on. *Calla Minou is black,* I say. *Albino.*

The jazz matrons' eyes widen. They stare at the glossy bright picture the P.R. folks have prepared. There I am. Polish and yellow-haired. They buy the story.

Albino black, legendary, and has she suffered. Ooh ee, I say. I stand up and stretch and sidle my way down through the crowd and past the sauerkraut stand.

Apparently, in these islands, in the Gliss Archipelago, named after immigrant entrepreneur Alfred Glissheimer, the residents do nothing all year but congratulate themselves on their good fortune in having been set down in paradise. Arabel Island, West Esperanza, Bride's Island (which used to be East Esperanza), Brimacombe, Oosterbaan, Owl Island, and the Shelves—Big Shelf and Little Shelf: these are the stuff of dreams. Retired folk, fishermen, tradespeople: all that you talk to are boosters.

You don't hear that, winters, when fishing is slow, these benign, ruddy-faced old guys drink, beat their wives, and sometimes go out on their boats and put a wee bullet through their brains. One, I heard whispered, last winter slit his own throat with the jagged edge of a broken peanut jar. Salted and dry-roasted. You come over on the plane P.R. has provided and you see green velvet islands, a dream of an aerial landscape, the footprints of some mythic green beast of giant proportions and jeweled benignity. No pain. So, summers, they bring the jazz patrons here, amethyst-fingered deaf folk who are ripe for the real-estate flyers they put out. We sell jazz to sell real estate, here, and jazz matrons talk about blackness and suffering.

On the wind from the harbor I can hear another band playing. No doubt Harry Gamel's Harborlights Jazz Band, Lawrence Welk-ish and even, I think, from Welk's own North Dakota. The jazz of the wheat fields, where harbor lights burn for nobody. No twinkle-lit cruise ships at anchor, no gleaming patent-leather hair, satin-lapeled tuxedoes, no ladies flat chested in shimmering shifts, no chandeliers and clinking crystal, no murmurs of late assignations in staterooms, jazz-age and slippery. We are selling illusions, all of us, and Harry Gamel's strong point—what the old-timers want—is the mythy perfume of his band's name and the strength of his saxophonist, who played once—or a thousand times—with Guy Lombardo.

The other bands here you may have heard of, or not. They are, I guess, supposed to be a cross section of something, of the jazz subculture, the tasteless along with the talented. The Inflight Jazz Band is here, and the Hotel Japonica Ragtime Ensemble: both canned and Muzak-y, but at two ends of the spectrum, your newest and oldest traditional jazz, your late swing to your early stuff. Both crap. You've got Lacey Gray and Her Basic Boys. Not bad. Some raunch, no pretensions. The Ax Murder Jazz Band, and what can I say, you have heard of them or you have not but they are the cream. Ask me about their trombone. There is the Dirty Rice Revue, purporting to be your original Noo Awlins style, and all of them imported from Canada. You've got your Blackstrap Molasses Jazz Band, the Original Laughingstock Jazz Band, the Castro Valley Six, the Grain Elevator Jazz Band, The Tombigbee River Jazz Band, the Indianapolis Cakewalk Ensemble, the Platinum City Claim-Jumpers. I have not heard these guys. You may have. I have not been in this business long. Though I am legendary.

I walk down the slope of Grand Avenue, which is not grand, to Riboc Harbor. Tourists and jazz fans are buying up festival sweatshirts at twenty-some bucks a throw, and Riboc Harbor ashtrays with black Japanese lacquer and swirly glued shells. I am incognito, invisible, and I am horny. I want the trombone player in the Ax Murder Jazz Band, I want him like I cannot believe, hooting hungry, and I only have heard him play once, the first set yesterday, on the pier at the harbor. I have this weakness for trombone players. The way that they slip that gold slide, gleaming out in the red lights and blue lights, or under the sun. Oh the things they can do, without buttons and valves; oh the tricks they can play, sweetly tonguing.

I once had a late-night talk with another Girl Singer (as they call us). This is rare stuff: there are oceans of envy and hang-nailish rivalry we are awash in. How much room is there in the world anyway for Girl Singers, jazz singers, albino black or otherwise. This was Noreen Halacy, this Girl Singer. You never heard of her. She was short-lived onstage. She was Noreen the Chorine: she did Betty Boop kinds of stuff, cutesy, all shaking her ass, Shirley Temple and Zelda rolled up into one. You can only go so far with that—though at these festivals, say, you get a good bit of exposure because you're the only one doing it.

After the last set at Sacramento one year, we went back to her motel room. A dive, even worse than the one they got us. We talked. We were crazy adrift on a sea of margaritas—salty rims and all, God, I can still taste that salt, like we'd been shipwrecked.

It was a slumber party, oh my, and we debated the relative merits of string players—she had had two string bassists, a banjo player, and a cellist with the Pittsburgh Symphony—and brass men. There was much talk about finger skills and calluses versus lip-and-tongue virtuosity. We came to no firm conclusions.

We woke up with twin headaches, and the other Girl Singer's cornetist—the little tin prick (he is playing with Len Fazel's Do-Right Jazz Band now, poor them, he cannot play a melody line without noodling)—started a rumor that we two were lesbians.

She married a CPA back home soon after, and sent me an invitation. Presbyterian Church, red brick, green lawn, white cake probably topped with fat doves and silver-sprinkled bells chiming eternity. All of it. I never heard from her again. No doubt she pities me—if she thinks of me—as I do her.

How I got legendary is this: the P.R. person here on the island—whoever made up the brochure for the festival—seems to have mated, in some sixth dimension of mind-intersection, with my manager.

My manager is the type of person who is in this thing for the fun of it. How could you be anything else? We get paid in mouse droppings, and she takes a small cut of that. She would have to be loving it. She does brilliant things once in a while.

One day at her office—which is actually the hind end of a hall cul-de-sac, stuck behind an enormous Xerox—she thrust at me one of her cups of quite terrible coffee (you could market it maybe, industrial bathroom-floor cleaner) and said, "Sit down, Carol Ann."

I looked for a place. There were stacks of flyers for this pair of twins that she handles, from Bulgaria or somewhere. They do comedy, serious poems, accordion duos. As I said, she is in this for love. There were stacks of the musicians' union paper and the *Times* and *Variety*. The whole sofa was papered this way. I pushed one stack aside and sat, keeping my elbows close in to my body. I could almost not lift my cup to my lips, space was at such a premium.

"Carol Ann," she said, "we've got to come up with some better name for you. Kiddo." The kiddo part is pure affection, sheer as Chinese silk, and she slips it in often because she knows she sounds like a hybrid of *Ms.* and *Business Week*, no fault of her own, she used to be an office manager somewhere generic, and prior to that a WAC.

I leaned back, balancing my industrial beverage at an odd angle, one elbow propped up on a stack of postcards advertising a gig for a group she is agenting, some acned assemblage with high-tech haircuts and fat sullen lips, Mass Perversion by name, who is going to make it big, since there's a market for that.

"Kiddo," I echoed.

"Nah," she said. "Not that. But nobody can spell Carol Ann Misczjenuwicz, much less say it, and let's face it. Kiddo. It has no jazz. And eighty-three syllables, all unpronounceable."

I made my serious face, like my funeral face. "A low blow," I said. "My poor mother"—who works at a Denny's off I-94, breakfast twenty-four hours—"is turning over in her grave. That the name, Christian name, of her darling firstborn should be panned so. . . ."

"Did your mother die?" she says, concerned.

"Nah," I said. "But this will kill her for sure. What the hell. She's an old broad, in her fifties, got boobs that hang down on her hipbones, she might as well." I wink.

She makes her You-Got-Me-Again look. "To continue," she says. "I propose this." She hands me a paper on which she has got rub-on letters spelling out CALLA MINOU, with a big calla lily sketched in beside. I look at it thoughtfully.

I shift elbows, balancing now on a pile of eight-by-ten glossies of these midgets who play harmonicas. "What the hell," I say, after maybe six or seven seconds. "I can live with that."

"Good," she says, WAC-ish and ready to move on.

"My mother, now," I say, "my old sainted mother, my Polish and probably precancerous mother, my old babushka-ed mother, breakfast twenty-four hours a day, novenas to the Black Madonna of Czestochowa, now she may die. But what the hell."

"Shut the fuck up," she says, grinning broadly, entirely happy. "And drink your damn coffee. You are on your way, Calla Minou."

Now the second part of how I got legendary is this: I don't know if the P.R. person in Riboc Harbor, Arabel Island, Gliss Archipelago had never heard of me or what, but all I can do is surmise that when he or she saw the name Calla Minou he or she thought this must be some person I ought to know and talked himself or herself into that. In spades. Putting in the brochure, "the legendary Calla Minou," as he or she had written about the "incomparable" Lacey Gray and Her Basic Boys, the "truly unique" Dirty Rice Revue (I'll say!), and the "juicy" music of the Ax Murder Jazz Band, which I second, that juicy trombone player, oh, give me juice, I thirst, juice, give me juice!

So when we arrive in the bright yellow Cessna at Arabel Island's airport, there is some young guy to meet us, real nerd, what can I say. He is standing there in this airport no bigger than my mother's recreation room in her basement in Hamtramck, Michigan, but done all tastefully in country-club colors, taupe, mauve, teal, colors that only women and gay designers know the names of, with this posterboard sign that says CALLA MINOU. This is so I'll find him and get driven to my motel.

He goes over to this kind of trollopy looking gal, red hair and backless shoes with nine-inch wedges, and says to her, CALLA MINOU? and she looks at him like he is speaking some outer-space language. He retreats and I offer myself. I am just a math teacher. And that's what I look like. This blond hair that wisps up, these no-eyes eyes, this Polish face. CALLA MINOU, I say. He blinks. I do not look legendary. My legend is fresh. I still smell of square roots, I still quiver with the tricks of seventh-graders doing Billy Crystal imitations while we are correcting tests. How can I be legendary? I am.

At the motel, which is called The Breezes, it is afternoon. As it was at the airport. My musicians are on the first floor, separate from me. I get a second-floor room overlooking the hot tub, which steams ferociously. A paunched businessman in a Hawaiian-print bathing suit stands looking dubiously at it, drink in hand, all alone. He catches me watching him and waves up. Come on down? Let's make a deal?

"Sorry, sugar," I say, a little too loud. Boil your buns, Roland, go home and tell the wife about this place with the hot tub, oh, let her eat her heart out.

In The Breezes the walls might as well be of palm thatch: the breezes could come through. I hear in the next room a couple in the throes of lovemaking. These beds are not the best. Squeega-squee-ga-squee. The guy finishes and groans. I note this with something not unlike dispassion, though I have been celibate too long.

I hang up my (as we say) Vintage Clothing, this stuff which

I have got to invest the whole profit from these gigs in. Stuff from stores like Vintage Clothing Emporium (ain't that inventive?) and Remembrance of Things Past, which everybody calls Proust's. This time I have brought the absinthe-green, which I have mentioned. I have brought a thing smothered in silver sequins, the whole top, the sleeves to the wrist, which is dazzling under night lights, oh far out, don't she look like a legend. And see that wee ass move inside that skirt when she do sing Give Me Some of That Jelly Roll. And a taffeta number that looks like it's cut out of bronze, like some suit of armor stuck in a hotel lobby for atmosphere, covered with black lace, but shit it is stunning. You would have to see it.

I wonder, while hanging up my clothes, shaking out my sequins in the small sunlight that penetrates the motel blinds, which are as thick as the walls are thin, who I will meet, this festival. I am aware of my proclivity for trombone players. I am no fool. I can read patterns. Twice is all it takes to teach me, and it has been twice. Last guy was a real loser, let's not talk about him. The first was my Grande Affaire, God, I imprinted on him like a newborn duck, I guess, I would follow a trombone player anywhere as a consequence. With some discretion, you know, selectivity. Last time was just a mistake. Course, I don't know what anyone else would call Loverboy Numero Uno. I thought it was holy shit, moon and the stars. He played with the Authentic O. Henry Jazz Band: you will know who I mean though I am not mentioning his name.

He went back to his wife, it was that simple. Me, I spent lots of time in the bathroom, inspecting my pores and the crinkles around my big baby blues in the mirror. As if it had anything to do with me. This guy would tell tales of having been high-jacked by female pirates in the Swedish Antilles. He'd tell these incredible stories about other musicians, you'd half believe him, and half of them, knowing musicians, were probably true. He had lips like some fruit they are going to bring out on Fruit-of-the-Month Club, some sweet meaty lip-fruit from Western New Zealand. He was quiet when he came. I like that in a man. The noise is for me to make. Our thing lasted a year, to the day, from one St. Louis festival to the next, several times in between. Sometimes I dream of him, knotty ambivalent dreams.

I have been writing songs for three years now. I guess it was when I started doing my own material that we started getting bigger gigs. There is this thing about jazz fans: they want you authentic. But then, they have heard Jelly Roll Jelly Roll till they puke, so there's something to be said for novelty. And whether or not Calla Minou is black, oh she has suffered and can write the blues. You slip inside the framework and your heart jes scribble it fo you.

I wrote Baker's Blues. This was the first. They went wild. That encouraged me. I do like men who can take, who are not just all over you, wham-bang, and this is what I was thinking. I had just lost my Numero Uno and was looking out, in the end of September, over a bleak winter of seventh-grade farting contests and no one but the track coach and Advanced Placement History teachers as prospects. Baker's Blues has a saxophone solo that sounds like old Alex Hill stuff, you could melt. It was memory and promise rolled into one, with the pain in between. It started:

> I roll you out nice and flat papa
> I butter you up so fine
> I put you in my oven
> I would be so glad you're mine.
>
> I got the Baker's Blues my papa
> Want that butter all the time. . . .

It was just a one-time thing, you know. I had just written that because of Number One, who was back in a town we will not name, with a wife who has got a face like an old Packard. Heart of gold, no doubt. Where was I when they were giving lifetime loves away? Graduate school. Exponentials and really significant stuff. So I just wrote this one-time blues. But it went over like crazy. And my saxophone player loved the showcase, so he nagged me to do more.

So I wrote Barn Door Blues:

> You are closing that barn door
> When your pretty horse gone
> You been too busy playing
> Leave your sweet mama alone.
>
> Now you got Ba-a-a-arn Door, baby,
> You got the Barn Door Blues. . . .

And I wrote the Night Table Blues:

> See that clock on the table
> Keeping me company
> He lights my room at night now honey
> Since you're not here with me.
>
> Got a clock on my table
> Got ninety pillows in my bed
> Got your picture turned round in my closet
> And an ache across my head. . . .

These went over like crazy. We put them on our first album, which is available from Jazzeteria Records, by mail, seven ninety-eight, if you are interested. Though I am legendary, I do have to eat.

I will sing them tonight, along with some of my others— Swallowtail Blues, Backslider's Blues, Streetcorner Blues—and the old standards. I am a red-hot blues mama, by category. Betty Boop ain't my dish of tea.

On the road to my legendariness, I met one woman, Dussie Lee Woulfe, who I am sure you never have heard of, who did have a seminal influence, if a woman can have something like that. Goddamn male language. Dussie Lee Woulfe was the great-grandmother of Jamal Woulfe and his cousin Landrum Woulfe, both of whom were in Remedial, which I am damned good at and no one else wants to teach. Jamal and Landrum passed with *B*s and they invited me to their house—they lived together, in an odd menagerie I never quite unraveled, who was whose what—for dinner because they had never felt so good about themselves.

I went, all dressed up in my properest. Nylons. The dress that I only wear to Brack Middle School functions. And here, in a double bed in the front room, which was a living room of sorts, where all the living seemed truly to go on, sat this small, round woman, looking actually in her majesty larger by far than she is, Jamal and Landrum's great-grandmother, Dussie Lee Woulfe, without her wig, scalp-naked as some plucked bird but dignified as Victoria Queen of the Empire.

Dussie Lee Woulfe interviewed me. It was good of me, she said, to help these boys. Now. Would I tell her about me. She wanted to know, I think, who I was that I would take Jamal and Landrum under my wing. What did I do when I was not teaching? she wanted to know. I was hesitant. Then I shrugged and let it out. There was not anything else I could say. I could not make up hobbies.

You sing jazz, said Dussie Lee Woulfe, at her most Queen Victorian. *White gal like you. That is something strange.* There was the longest pause.

I sat and looked around the room. There were old pictures framed in new K Mart frames everywhere: mantel, tables, bric-a-brac shelves. I could not make out in the dimness who or what they were.

I sang jazz, Dussie Lee Woulfe said. I was still and stunned, listening. *Till twenty-nine, that is. Race records they was not selling no more, I don't know, that Depression was something. So I sang Gospel for the rest of the time. Labor of Love Church, you know where I mean? They have good Gospel, honey. You sing jazz, you want to go there and learn something. That Gospel is just the same thing as jazz. You sing to Jesus, I wants you, my Lord, or you sings to a man. It is all the same. Course*—she says—winking at me and rolling her eyes at Jamal and Landrum, who stand like Beefeaters next to me—*when you talking to Jesus you ain't talking Jelly Roll. That's all the difference.*

I went back and visited her almost weekly that year. She showed me all the pictures, one by one. She told me the stories. She told me about how she got her name, how her relatives, who were coal-black, thought her skin color, which harked back to the grandfather from Oklahoma who was full-blooded Indian (hence the name Wolf, which she said her agent in the twenties had insisted she spell Woulfe to be more toney and high-class, the agents come round in a cycle like seasons, don't they) looked "dusty." She was the odd one in the family. She insisted her green eyes came from that same Indian. She told me about the time Lil Armstrong cussed her out because Louis wanted her to play piano instead of Lil, and she relived that thrill. She tried to sing me her Green-Eyed Blues but could not remember past the second line, so she had Jamal bring out the record, which was wrapped in old nightgown flannel. I listened in ecstasy. I got permission. I sang it. They *died* over it when I sang it. I sang her others, too: the Natchez Trace Blues, Doughnut Blues, Catahoula Blues. They were crazy go nuts, you know? I gave her credit, but nobody remembered old Dussie Lee Woulfe. She was not legendary.

Dussie Lee died last November, asleep sitting up. Landrum and Jamal walked on each side of me at her funeral, where they played no jazz. I wanted a black-suited funeral marshal to lead her parade to the cemetery, with an umbrella. No such. We drove, and drove on the expressway. Oh, Dussie Lee. I would say that the woman went to heaven, yes, but a part of her lives in me, like reincarnation, like a strange being from some planet in a B-movie who comes to earth. And I am, after all, legendary.

I have got to get back to the festival now. I have got to go see that trombone player. I have got fantasies like you would not believe. About this man. One time I have seen him, one time, and already I am inventing our children, like some damned subdivision housewife. I am writing the Dream Babies Blues, and two lines of it circle like bright yellow Cessnas in my head, and threaten to land.

I will turn around and walk up Grand Avenue. It *is* grand, now. Oh, God, the whole street is awash in sunlight like the gleam from the trombone player's brass, the flash of it. I will go back to Phoenix Alley, where the matrons will have cleared out by now, gone off to buy T-shirts that say, "Grandma went to Riboc Harbor and all I got was this T-shirt." The Ax Murder Jazz Band will be onstage: this is their set. I will buy a jar of Korean hot pickled cabbage at the grocery store on the corner before I get there, and I will eat it while Ax Murder plays.

I will sit chewing and listening. Rapt. I will go to the trombone player afterward and talk to him about his solo on Perdido Street Blues. He will be flattered. He will like my eyes. I will tell him they came from an Oklahoma Indian, and he will have this marvelous sense of humor and great laugh. I will tell him I am legendary. We will go together to the musicians' buffet, which is lavish to take our minds off the incredibly low pay for this gig.

They will lay out salmon of two different kinds, barbecued shrimp, crab claws, smoked turkey in nuggets so oddly shaped you would think we were eating small gerbil-like animals, spinach-feta pie in diamond shapes, baby corn, little tarts filled with apples, pickled melon rind, raspberries, black olives swollen with lust, starfruit, fresh figs!! We will eat and look into each other's eyes, oh shit, we will be something out of an old musical. No jazz. Straight arrows. We will go back to The Breezes and I will undress him and sing Baker's Blues and he will be as quiet as sand blowing when he comes. I will be writing Dream Babies the whole while. The legend keeps building.